CW00406027

70000525051 3

SPIRIT WEDDINGS

BY THE SAME AUTHOR

Fiction

Someone Else
Fly Away Home
Dances of Death: Short Stories
The Traveller and His Child
The China Egg and Other Stories
The Intruder
Looking Forward
To the City
Give Them All My Love
Journey of A Lifetime and Other Stories

Non-fiction

The Born Exile: George Gissing
The Fields Beneath: The History of One London Village
City of Gold: The Biography of Bombay
Rosamond Lehmann: An Appreciation
Countries of the Mind: The Meaning of Place to Writers

GILLIAN TINDALL

SPIRIT WEDDINGS

HEREFORD AND WORCESTER
COUNTY LIBRARIES.

F

HUTCHINSON
London

© Gillian Tindall 1992

The right of Gillian Tindall to be identified as Author of this work
has been asserted by Gillian Tindall in accordance with
the Copyright, Designs and Patents Act, 1988

All rights reserved

This edition first published in 1992 by
Hutchinson

Random Century Group Ltd
20 Vauxhall Bridge Road, London SW1V 2SA

Random Century Australia (Pty) Ltd
20 Alfred Street, Milsons Point, Sydney, NSW 2061, Australia

Random Century New Zealand Ltd
PO Box 40–086, Glenfield, Auckland 10, New Zealand

Random Century South Africa (Pty) Ltd
PO Box 337, Bergvlei, 2012, South Africa

British Library Cataloguing-in-Publication Data

Tindall, Gillian
  Spirit Weddings
  I. Title
  823 [F]

  ISBN 0–09–174505–5

Set in 11/13 pt Baskerville by
Pure Tech Corporation, Pondicherry, India
Printed and bound in Great Britain by
Mackays of Chatham PLC, Chatham, Kent

PART I

. . . 'So, the magic carpet begins to descend. After a space of accelerated time which is out of time, it is coming down into the dawn. But is it yesterday's dawn again, or is it already tomorrow's?

In fantasy, we have always known about magic carpets which whisk you from one place, time and season to another. Yet it is only in the late twentieth century, the great era of rational materialism, that this fairy tale has become real. It defies all ordinary perceptions to move so fast, so far. But the pretence is that it is quite normal: the behaviour of everyone involved in the performance is almost wilfully matter of fact. No wonder the jet traveller, under-slept, overfed, bracing himself for the miracle and trauma of descending to earth into a brand-new self, feels under strain.'

Strain. I never much consider strain. I hear the word quite often in my consulting room, even employ it, I suppose, as a shorthand for something more obscure and far-reaching that I cannot gauge in another person, but I never think about it in relation to myself. From my vantage point, two thirds the way down the main cabin of a jumbo jet that has been in the air nearly fourteen hours bar one brief, hallucinatory descent into Bombay, I glance over the littered scene. Something between a refugee transit station and a hospital ward for convalescents. Determined sleepers huddle under blankets. Those awake retreat from discomfort behind earphones or the crumpled, much read newspapers of another life, or (my strategy) defend themselves from the apathy of sensory deprivation with briefcases full of paper. Others pad about in their socks, or stand patiently in line for the lavatories, or dandle weary children. Yes, we are all docile captives in limbo here, but all secretly tensing ourselves for whatever is waiting for us. My eye, restless, skips to another paragraph:

'. . . *a civilisation as alien from his own as it is possible to be, the ultimate daunting, archaic Other Place, the Great Land, the dark side of the moon, difficult of entry to the point of near impenetrability. Yet here too lies the Great City that is so easy of access, the quintessential world city that has become an archetype of late-twentieth-century urbanisation, the equal of New York, Tokyo and Hong Kong yet itself and only itself, an island that is not an island at all, a humming web of light in the dark continent, an oasis of plenty and prodigality, a conspiracy of desire and artificiality, a fulfilment of vain dreams and yet unmistakably a real place with its own remorselessness, the well-run ruthlessness that underpins the Good Life.'*

At this point in the typescript Christopher has scribbled in his decorative but hard-to-read handwriting: 'I may tone down some of this, but I want to get the sense of the place's initial impact and the sheer man-made extraordinariness of it sitting there between the sea marshes and the mountains.'

'. . . *Almost everywhere in the City, land reclamation has been so extensive and successful that the very contours of the place have been changed. The geographical bones of the original settlement − the extinct volcano in the marsh to which the founder brought his blackguardly crew upriver from the Portuguese trading post on the shore − are as irretrievable now as the bones of the early inhabitants. These, when malaria and cholera took their toll, were laid 'until Judgement Day' in the shifting, waterlogged soil of the Old Burial Ground just outside the first fortifications, a site now vanished under the Dock-Redevelopment Scheme and the City heliport.'*

Here Christopher has noted in the margin: 'including Great-Aunt Alice's bones, I rather think, poor dear'.

' *"Old hands", both local and European, who can remember the City before the secession, between the wars, when it was still part of the Great Land and the main free port for that whole area of east Asia, recall a town of tile-roofed buildings with cast-iron pillars imported from foundries in Newcastle, Clydesdale and Rotterdam. They remember too when open canals, bobbing with boats and dirt, ran in a network over much of the City − canals that are now hygienically contained in great pipes many metres down through the foundations of the airy modern skyscrapers. Returning after many years, they can recognise almost nothing, and may indeed feel that they are returning not to the present-day City but to some city of the future, so heady is much of the architecture, so breathtaking the night vistas of shining glass. Most visitors have no opportunity today to go upcountry, over the heavily guarded frontier, but the few who manage to penetrate there are startled in turn by the lack of physical change after thirty years, and feel conversely that they have now travelled back in time. Indeed the City and the Great Land, whose history is one and who were for so long intimately bound up with one another, now seem separated from each other not only physically and politically but in temporal space as well: it is as if the frontier were a time barrier, and what lies beyond it in the Great Land were the irrecoverable past. The City dwellers of today cannot revisit it, and those who inhabit it cannot venture beyond it and indeed have probably only a vague and inaccurate idea of what the Great Land has now become.'*

Against 'the irrecoverable past' Christopher has noted in the margin: 'This whole para is for you, Dad.'

For years, ever since he became interested in Asia himself, Christopher had been suggesting I should revisit the Great City. 'You'd find it so interesting, Dad, honestly,' he would say, to my feeble excuses that I've done enough travelling for one lifetime, that I'm too old to get a kick out of roaring round the world in planes and that anyway I might find the transformed City more disconcerting than anything else.

'Come on, Dad, you're not the sort of old buffer who doesn't want to go back somewhere just because it has changed. I know you – you'd be fascinated, really. And though the City's ghastly in some ways – a sort of vast temple to consumerism – you'd find it encouraging too, I'm sure. I mean, it *is* a miracle in its way. It's got no natural resources at all and hardly any hinterland, it has to import everything, and yet people live well there, they really do. For all the overcrowding, they're healthy. They're well fed, they have money to spend. The water's clean. Everyone can read. You always said they were dynamic people, a nation of go-getters and achievers when they were given half a chance. Well, now they've taken their chance. You'd like to see that, I know.'

'Yes, I should, that's true . . . I'll think about it, Christopher. I really will.'

So I did. And so, in a sense, here I am. But the present

circumstances are not quite those that I ever envisaged.

As the plane methodically loses height, I go on reading Christopher's article. He wrote it, and gave me the typescript to read, a number of years ago, in the early days of his career as a travel writer. I know it was published later, but I forget exactly where, or whether he did decide some sentences needed 'toning down a bit'. I should think he probably did: his style seems to have got sparer and more disciplined over the course of time. I can see that that is probably the way it should be but as his father, I always rather enjoyed his verbal exuberance, his imaginative flights into related lines of thought as if he could hardly find space for everything his intelligence wanted to say. It reminded me of when he was quite a little boy and used to get so excited and interested in things that he would begin to stammer. I can hear Sarah now saying in her low, rather gentle voice: 'Christopher, darling, stop. Take a deep breath. Now take another one and start that sentence again.'

. . . *'The aeroplane comes down over the vast river delta, itself the size of one of the smaller European countries, and then swoops lower in an arc over the salt marshes, patched in summer with the virulent green of paddy, before half turning again to descend into the airport proper; it is all built on reclaimed land and has been perpetually enlarged and extended from the strip laid out by the Japanese with POW labour in 1943. It looks, for a minute, as if we are headed straight for the shining high rise blocks of the northern suburbs that are actually a couple of miles off. The whole scale of the modern City is, like that of the jumbo jets themselves, so grand, so undomestic, and yet so like a model under glass, that the human eye is fooled – a literal* trompe l'oeil *– and cannot assess size or distance.'*

Even as I read on, this scene is being enacted for me beyond the plane's Perspex portholes; it is as if my eyes running down the page and the plane running down the airway were having a race and it is up to me to make sure they finish level. I think: Christopher will be amused when I tell him this. And then I suddenly think, with a shock of pleasure and true expectation that I have not felt all the journey: I may be able to tell him, very soon.

'How different, and perhaps more satisfying, was the experience of those who arrived in the steamship era, travelling at reduced speed for two whole days under pilotage up the delta and finally docking on the

broad river at the Bundar within shouting distance of the Old Customs House while smaller river craft all blew their horns to bid the liner welcome. The name 'Bundar' is a legacy of the Indian traders and indentured labourers who poured in a hundred-odd years ago. Today the people of the City tend to be a little darker in complexion than those in the rest of the Great Land but rather less uniformly Oriental in their features. Portuguese, Dutch and British blood have made a contribution to the local gene pool in this corner of the earth, as well as Indian and some input from the Levantine Middle East, Arab and Jewish and Syrian Christian. It is almost as if here the powers above had set out to evolve the Ur-human being, an all-purpose world citizen of statistically proportionate mix – '

At this point the undercarriage is let down with a slight jolt and I stop reading. The earth is coming up fast towards us, and I want to put my papers away in my briefcase and gather myself together before the landing forces other realities on me. In any case, I know about the ships and the Bundar. They are part of my own City in the mind, perhaps (as Christopher says) the only bit I will now recognise. I last saw it in 1949 when, as a young National Service officer with hepatitis, I was taken off on a hospital ship and so missed, by just a few weeks, the abrupt escalation of the Troubles which were to develop into the Civil War. These Troubles, which a British army 'peace-keeping' force was supposedly helping to contain, affected the whole country and cost thousands of lives, including those of young British soldiers, my contemporaries and friends. The eventual Civil War, after the British withdrawal, probably killed millions more and ended by cutting the City off from the rest of the Land.

I had left from the Bundar several times before. I see myself as a schoolboy in the late 1930s, waving bravely at my hatted parents on the shore through a stinging mask of tears, for in those days Going Home to School meant a separation that could stretch into years. I could not know then – nor could they – how providentially the War was going to supervene and bring them Home, too, eighteen months later. None of us was there when the Japanese came. For a family that had been involved in the Far East, in one way or another, for three generations, this was a piece of great good fortune.

I had left from that Bundar, too, much earlier in life, when the company posted Father elsewhere for a while. I cannot recall that first departure, but I know that when we returned to the City some of the houses and streets seemed to me ghostly familiar yet odd, different and a little diminished, like locations known before in a dream. The garden wall that had been too high for me to peer over, I could now run my tin cars along. Will it be like that again, this time? No, no, of course, it cannot be. I am forgetting how much time has gone by. My whole lifetime, very nearly. In any case I know that our old bungalow, along with all the others in that district, has now been replaced by tall blocks.

Each time I have returned it has been as a different person. I recall myself – myself? – as a newly adult soldier: Father was on the dock to greet me then, visibly delighted that his pals in the War Office had 'wangled' his son into a regiment scheduled for service in what, for all my family, was our true home. Obedient to colonial and expatriate principle, I had been taught always to refer to England as 'Home', but how could I, at any rate, not look on the City as my essential home? Damn it, I was born here.

Sometimes I think that even Christopher, with all his sensitivity and his intelligence, does not quite grasp what that means. My fault, probably. I've never gone on about such things.

So where, really, did this journey I am now making, with such patent hope, such covert fear, begin?

Long, long ago, perhaps, before I or Pauline or Tessa were even born. Perhaps even before my father came out as a young man before the First World War, to take up a post with the expanding company that his uncle had recommended. Uncle George and Aunt Ethel had been in the country forty years, knew everyone and had taught many of them. George's own father, another George, had been a schoolmaster before him at the mission school that became St Saviour's, but that was in the early days, before the international companies came, when the free port was still considered a hardship posting for Europeans. Putrid water, 'putrid fevers': Great-Aunt Alice's first three babies before George all died in those humid, tainted, mid-nineteenth-century summers, as if in some terrible confirmation of what she felt on her arrival as a young wife up the great brown river, and wrote in her diary: '*Oh, the horror of it all, the sights, the smells, the sheer unchristian strangeness of everything. Oh, how will I ever bear it?*'

But I see that, like Christopher, I am wanting to express too much, all at once. Great-Aunt Alice, strictly speaking Great-great, has been dead for more than a hundred years: her diaries are safe in an archive library in Cambridge; her bones are somewhere under an office block full of electronic equipment, a shopping mall with fountains or a marble-lined hotel where Australian tourists with pink knees come and go, only a little subdued by the unaccustomed splendour in which they find themselves.

Let me, instead, take the story up about nine months ago when, you might say, this actual trip began.

One day in the winter, around Christmastime it must have been, for Christopher was at home for a bit, I was attending to letters and bills at the desk in my old consulting room overlooking the gardens and the hill. (Since I retired from full-time work, the practice has moved entirely into the new health centre in the town, which is probably as it should be today, though I wouldn't find it convenient myself if I were still having to take a regular morning and evening surgery.)

I no doubt had the door ajar. It is a heavy, mahogany door, nicely balanced, that does not bang. I've always liked to write like that, not shut away from the rest of the household but vaguely conscious of other people's activities going on as I work. Of course, in the years since Sarah has been gone, and now, in another sense, Christopher too, there hasn't been the same point in having the door ajar, but I still do it. If you are alone in this house, there is still *less* point in shutting the door.

That morning, Christopher came in his usual cat-footed way. Since childhood, he's never liked wearing shoes indoors; we used to joke that he'd acquired some oriental barefoot gene from the collective family experience.

'Am I disturbing you, Dad?'

'Not really.' I laid my pen down with a show of politeness, but I was pleased he had come in.

He placed in front of me a newspaper cutting with a photograph.

'That's you,' I said at once. I was momentarily quite sure.
'Look again.'

I did – and at once realised I had been wrong. The man
had indeed a strong look of Christopher, the same deep-set
eyes (my mother had those too), the same hesitant, rather
charming smile. But the hair was different, sparser but curlier,
and the nose was shorter and, anyway, looking again, I saw
that this man was older than Christopher, maybe by ten years.
If Christopher had had an elder brother, this might well have
been him.

I had often imagined younger brothers, or sisters. Sarah
and I had wanted other children but they did not come; we
never really established why. Trust a doctor and his wife to
have a baffling, nonspecific problem for which there was no
clear treatment.

'Who is he?' I said.

Christopher's reply was so strange that for a few seconds I
could not take it in.

'He's a peasant from the Great Land, called Baht Way.'
(Christopher didn't actually say 'the Great Land', but used
the official name of the place Mayer Dhar, which means the
same thing. The traditional British name for it is a corruption
of that but I shall continue to call it the Great Land.)

'But he can't be,' I said after a few moments. I felt like
somebody presented with one of those trick-perspective draw-
ings that don't add up.

'Apparently other people have said that to him too. But he
is, all the same. Read the story.'

I did. Its details have now become so familiar to me that
I can no longer be sure which I first read in that cutting and
which were filled in subsequently when Christopher contacted
its author. But these are the facts, as we understand them.

Baht Way was working as a building labourer on a site in
the Great City where yet more glass blocks were going up.
He was dressed like all the others in the regulation hard hat,
green overalls and duck-webbed rubber boots, the City government these days being punctilious about such things. The
American newspaper correspondent – Mike Isaacs – would
have passed this man carrying loads on his head without a
second glance, except that he was something very unusual on
a building site in that part of the world: he appeared to be

a European. Not a half-and-half or any other local mixture, but a sturdy, fair-skinned man with deep-set grey eyes, light-brown hair and other unmistakably Caucasian features. Odder still, when Mike Isaacs hung about for a few minutes to watch and listen, he heard the man exchange words with two other labourers in the local language but not in the sharply accented version that you would have expected, which is traditionally called City-lingo. Baht Way had the heavy, throaty, cleft-palate intonation of upcountry. To look at he was a westerner. To hear him, he was one of those migrant workers from the rural outback of the Great Land who have sometimes, over the years of political separation, managed to slip through a remote crevice of the sealed frontier and show up in the City with manufactured identity papers or none.

Mike Isaacs, who had been familiar with this part of the world for some years and spoke the language, was sufficiently intrigued to return to the site when the shift was changing and accost Baht Way in the street. Baht Way went pale and refused at first to speak. But after reassuring explanations and some money had been proffered, he agreed to accompany Mike Isaacs to a tea-and-fish stall (I was glad to hear they still had such a traditional amenity in the modernised City) and tell the American his story. He even seemed eager to do so.

He had grown up, he said, in a remote province of the Great Land – naming a mountainous region that, I vaguely recall, was regarded as semi-inaccessible even in the days when there was no frontier between the Land and the City and people trickled steadily from the country to the town. It was a sort of area where life of subsistence farming on tiny hillside terraced patches would go on in its own way no matter what was happening in the world beyond. The old emperors of the Land never concerned themselves much with that part; the invading Japanese did not get that far. Even the overthrow of the last emperor, the Civil War and the eventual Socialist Victory must have created only limited tremors in those mountains.

In this primitive life of varied but incessant toil, Baht Way was reared by a peasant farmer whom he apparently always knew to be his stepfather – the husband of his dead mother. Baht Way could not remember his mother, and grew up as a matter of course with this stepfather's second wife and their increasing family of younger children. From early childhood he was aware that he looked different from everyone else in the village, but he had no idea why. He had never seen a westerner. If there was a question to be asked, he himself did not know what it was or how to ask it. In any case it wasn't the custom, in those rural areas, to ask questions or make personal remarks.

He married early, a girl he had known from childhood, and was a little puzzled again when the children she bore him turned out to look odd also – not as odd as he did, but still not like everyone else. Once again, no one speculated, at any rate not aloud. It was not till he was past thirty that some relatives of his wife, visiting from a town farther south, where there was a weekly film show and greater sophistication prevailed, remarked bluntly that he 'looked just like a foreigner'.

Only then did Baht Way nerve himself to question his stepfather. The old man agreed readily that Baht Way's mother had been a foreigner and described her nostalgically as 'a beautiful, tall woman with light, curling hair'. He had met her in the City, where he had been living as a migrant worker when it was caught up in the turmoil of the Troubles that preceded the Civil War. But he had apparently forgotten her proper name, which he had never, in any case, been able to pronounce, and was only able to tell her son the vernacular 'little name' by which he had called her. He had also forgotten, or did not wish to relate, the circumstances in which she had disappeared again from his life, saying at one time that she had died and at another that she had 'gone away to her own people'.

Baht Way later told Mike Isaacs that he had come to suppose that his mother 'had been unable to settle to the village way of life'. It seemed a realistic view, in its own terms. On the subject of his natural father, the old man had been able to tell Baht Way absolutely nothing; maybe he had never known anything to tell, since that still more shadowy figure probably left the scene before the native stepfather ever entered it.

'I think he must have been a European, too, though?' Baht Way said to Isaacs. 'Otherwise I would look more like the rest of my people. That's what everyone here in the City says, and when I see foreigners in the street I understand that they're right.'

On the first occasion he told Isaacs that he had made his way into the City simply to seek work and send money back to his village: times had been hard since the latest convulsion of Socialist isolationism in the Great Land. But on a later meeting he admitted that he had also begun to harbour a dream of finding out who his mother had been and even getting in touch with her.

'Not for money,' he assured Isaacs anxiously. 'I don't want her to be afraid of my bothering her in that way. She must be an old lady now. But I owe it to my children to explain to them one day why they, too, look different. Ancestors are very important with us. My children have a right to know who their ancestors were.'

For all his peasant simpleness of speech, Baht Way was, Isaacs came to realise, far from stupid. He had conceived the idea that, if his story were reported in the West, someone somewhere might be able to tell him who his real parents had been. That was why, after his initial fear of the journalist, he had been pleased to talk to him. He had already, after much hesitation, approached the British High Commission, but they had said that, in the absence of any documentation, they were unable to help him.

Isaacs questioned him about his life in the City. He earned good money, said Baht Way, and was able to remit it regularly through the International Post Office to his family in the Great Land. It is well known that the government there, though theoretically scornful and suspicious of what the free world has to offer, is in practice not averse to their citizens earning hard currency through unofficial channels. He had once managed to get back to visit, but then border controls had been tightened again. Now he had 'better' papers and a 'sort of' work permit and hoped very much that he might be able to bring his wife and elder children, at least, down here, to join him. He missed them a lot and often felt very lonely here, where people laughed at his rustic accent or stared at him curiously or both. He lived in a shared room in the manufacturing area of the City, the most crowded and old-fashioned part.

That was the sum of what Mike Isaacs had got from him,
over the course of several meetings. Apparently it had not all
come out at once in a clear sequence. The native reticence
of his adoptive family, which had made the central facts of
his existence a taboo topic long after he had become a man,
had evidently affected him as well. But there was, it seemed
to Isaacs, no mistaking his sincerity or the amount of thought
he had given to the matter. Isaacs promised to do for him
what he could.

So it was that I read a first version of Baht Way's story
sitting at my desk in Dorset looking out over a winter wind
harassing the rhododendrons in the garden and at the rainy
hillside beyond. Christopher stood silently behind me as I read
it. When I came to the end of the column and went back to
read it through again, I was aware of his sympathy and
support like a bodily warmth near me. Christopher and I were
very close when he was a little boy, and then again in a rather
different way after Sarah's death when he was sixteen. These
days, of course, he's been out in the world for years, often on
his travels so that I don't see him for months at a time, but
this house where he grew up is still essentially his home.
Roaming around as he does on one assignment or another,
he has never so far put down roots anywhere else – never got
himself a permanent flat in London or even moved in with a
girl in the way the young do now. Whenever we meet again
nothing has changed; he's always the same dear chap. And
yet there is something about Christopher that eludes people.
Even me. Do I, I have once or twice asked myself, really
know him at all?

'You can see what I'm wondering,' he said now quietly –
and on this occasion I could; I was wondering the same thing
myself. But I waited, not quite daring to voice it, willing him
to.

'Could this man,' he said carefully, 'who looks so like me
that I even noticed it myself, and who seems such an oddity
in his own country – could he *possibly* be a cousin, my first
cousin?'

I said nothing and there was quiet between us for a bit. Of
course I knew what he meant.

'It is possible, Dad. Isn't it? The dates would fit. The
Troubles, the Civil War . . . The man in this picture could be

around forty, wouldn't you say?'

'Well, he isn't *my* son,' I said after another long pause. 'And I'm sure he isn't your Aunt Pauline's. So that only seems to leave your Aunt Tessa . . .' The feebly joking tone was a useless attempt to cover pain. Poor Tessa, a troublemaker as a child and a source of terrible grief and anxiety to our parents for two years in her teens, made a predictable mess of her life afterwards: unsuitable men, exaggerated left-wing causes, debts, altercations with the law, rows with us and with Pauline, finally drink. She died years ago. Liver damage, lung problems . . . she smoked persistently, aggressively, enjoying flouting advice to cut down. Her stubs lay everywhere, the ground-out debris of her life. If I say that her premature death had long seemed inevitable and came as a relief to me, that sounds hard and unkind; but in releasing me from the Tessa that she had become, her death gave back to me the long-lost, beloved little sister, only two years younger than myself, with whom I had played in our old-fashioned colonial-style garden in the City that has now gone too.

Could this man Baht Way, this strange hybrid, be a central clue to Tessa's erratic, self-destructive behaviour, the one we had missed all along? 'Darling, it must be the *experiences* she had all that time we were out of touch with her,' our poor mother used to say each time that Tessa, by then in her twenties, perpetrated some new piece of noisy, embarrassing or merely appalling behaviour. 'Tessa's experiences' had become a family shorthand for what none of us knew about her. When I was in my final year as a medical student, she wrote to my professor to complain that I, her brother, would not take her health problems seriously so was it right to let me loose on society as a doctor? Later, when the professor had kindly seen her and told her not to be such a damn fool, she cried very much on my shoulder and apologised profusely, but I remained annoyed with her for some time. She turned up at Pauline's large, conventional wedding in a dirty shirt and jeans with a strange Yugoslav in tow. Later, she got some money from me to help her start some sort of courier business with another foreigner, Pete the Greek, who hung around her for some time. She never paid me back, of course; I hadn't really expected her to. Another time again, during her Workers Revolutionary period when she was very keen on the

Palestine Liberation Organisation, she got herself sensationally arrested in Israel; that time it was Pauline's husband Toby who bailed her out, flying there in his clergyman's collar to pacify both the Israelis and the world's press, looking doggedly sincere and worried on television news. The next time she was arrested and imprisoned was after a CND rally where she had hit a policeman (a 'peace' rally she always called it, though no one could have been more warlike than Tessa) and she was furious when I paid her hefty fine and she found herself released quicker than she expected. Then a so-called ashram in India full of Americans, and amoebic dysentery. A bedsitter in Acton and a feud with a 'fascist' landlord. And so on and so forth, in repetitive patterns over the pointless years. Waste, sad waste of a person who (it had once seemed) had so much to offer.

So, 'her experiences' became the perennial family excuse for her, at once explicit and opaque. The phrase was most often and most forbearingly on Toby's lips. Tolerance, forgiveness and loving kindness are, after all, part of his job (as my wife Sarah once said, with some asperity) and Tessa wasn't his own sister anyway. As time went on and Tessa never learnt any sense, Pauline, always the firm elder sister, became inclined to purse her lips and say that lots of people had difficult or unhappy experiences in youth and managed to live them down. But though Pauline had been closer – literally closer – to Tessa at that time than the rest of us, she could offer no suggestions either as to what 'Tessa's experiences' might have been. 'She disappeared,' she would say flatly. 'Just disappeared. I looked everywhere for her. Contacted everyone who might know. She just wasn't there.'

For my part, I gradually came to suspect that Tessa might have grown up the same way whatever 'experiences' she had or had not had in the Far East as a girl. Or, to put it the other way, I guessed that the 'experiences' might in themselves have been the result of the waywardness that was already apparent when she was a rebellious schoolgirl. So different from Pauline – and, I have maintained, from me, though Sarah used to say that Tessa and I had a few more things in common than I would admit. But Tessa always *was* different from the rest of the family, or at any rate pulling in a different direction. People are as they are. As a doctor, you learn that.

Oh yes, you are taught to think in terms of causality and results and chances and consequences, as if we were all just equal entities rattling round the surface of the globe. But what you actually learn is that, from early in their lives, people are profoundly themselves: they have their own patterns, psychological and physical, inexorably working through time. Perhaps this, after all, is what we really mean by a person's identity, though it may take a lifetime to surface.

'The question is,' I said at last to Christopher, 'what do we do about this?' And after a pause I added:

'If we do anything, that is.'

It sounds craven, but I think that, at that stage, I might have been happy to take no action, to let Baht Way's tentative call to the West remain unanswered. To respond to such a call seemed so simple and yet pregnant with so much that I could not yet face all the implications. But my selfishness was not to be allowed to prevail.

'I would like to do *something*,' Christopher said at last, in his gentle but insistent way.

Am I too quiescent and selfish, as I secretly think? Most of my friends, associates and patients would not say so, and years ago I used, on the contrary, to be privately pleased with my own efficiency and readiness to take action. It was, after all, this enterprise in me, this morally equivocal desire to 'do things' for people that led me to a career in medicine. I had completed my interrupted army service in England and was supposed to read classics at university when the conviction came to me that doctoring was where my tastes and abilities lay. Yes, I wanted to 'help' people. And I also wanted power and special status and knowledge that isn't given to every man: I wanted to be in control. Only with the coming on of age has this conviction of my own worth and efficiency begun to fail me.

When I speak circumstantially to Christopher of 'getting old', he says: 'Oh, Dad, stop playing old man! You know you only do it to confuse the gods and distract them. Look how physically tough you still are. You've got ten – fifteen – maybe twenty good years in you yet, so don't pretend.'

His words take mine at face value, but his hasty affection indicates another level of understanding. Christopher knows me, though I am not quite sure what he knows. Of course he must realise that my reluctance, these days, to visit distant places or to take on new things is unrelated to any obvious physical weakening. He knows, I think, that over the years several things – Sarah's senseless death, perhaps even Tessa's death, to which I have always avoided giving much thought – have dealt knocks to my self-esteem and sense of purpose. There are one or two other factors also about which I have never spoken but of which, being Christopher, he may be aware all the same. Jill. He never knew about Jill. But he knew that I had 'found someone' some time after his mother's death and this relationship continued for a number of years. When he noticed that it had finally come to an end – I suppose I seemed sad and withdrawn, and ceased to go on so many 'medical conferences' to obscure places – he was tactful and consoling but never asked any direct questions, for which I was grateful.

I am a traditional sort of father: I don't think I wanted my son to know that I was carrying on with another man's wife. (Not that I ever described it to myself in those terms, but that is the truth of the matter.) I am also a traditional man: I did not want anyone to know, not Christopher nor anyone else, that I had finally failed to do what I had initially been so confident of doing; I failed to detach Jill from her husband. In the end, because she was the woman she was, a woman in the same mould as Sarah, I have now come to see, she stuck to her marriage. So much for love. Yes, we loved each other, whatever that means. She used to say that I wasn't much good at expressing my emotions, and I would reply that in youth I had not been taught to and had found it hard to learn. Within marriage, there are other ways you can express attachment, but in a clandestine relationship words matter so much, since there are so many areas you cannot explore together. I realise now that Jill probably loved her fat, noisy husband too, in a way – another way from me, I like to think, but there it is ... Yes, it was a blow to me when our affair finally ended. No, in the role of adulterous interloper you can't expect anyone to be particularly sorry for you.

After it was all over, I felt too old to try to start again. These days, I avoid doing more than I have contracted to, I avoid putting myself out seeing patients at awkward hours. I am no longer so prepared to cross the world at my own expense, or even necessarily at anyone else's, in order to observe how maternal and child health care is provided in other places; even though this used to fascinate me and I have built up a speciality in it, which is regarded as unusual in a general practitioner. In the evenings now, after dinner, instead of reading papers on 'Rural Health Networks in Western Australia' or 'Maternity Clinics in Mexico City', I abandon the world's needy without another thought. I pour myself a Scotch, settle into the leather chair that was my grandfather's, listen to Beethoven and Mahler, read Trollope, and shut out the world. I go out, of course, when I'm asked; a local doctor tends to be a popular figure, or at any rate a useful dinner-party guest. But really I am secure and not unhappy in my selfish solitude.

So I did not want now, at my time of life, to take on a new member of the world's needy, especially such a strange, heart-tugging, ultimately demanding one as Baht Way might be. What real good, I asked myself, might be achieved by making ourselves known and thus entering his life, his dreams? A westerner who was no westerner, a possible nephew who could never now become one in any real sense – No, no. In spite of my awkward curiosity, my strongest initial impulse was one of dim prudence: leave everything undisturbed and Baht Way's imprecise hopes unfulfilled. Do nothing, say nothing. Tessa is dead and largely unregretted. The past is irreparable.

But – 'I would like to do something,' said Christopher. And I knew I was lost.

I have arrived at this hotel before a number of times, though it has rarely been quite as resplendent as this. When I say 'this hotel' I do not mean this actual one in the Great City, for I was last in the City forty years ago and in those days, in my childhood and young manhood, the only large hotel was the Bristol, near the steamship pier – now as vanished as the liners, or as the couples like my parents who used to dance in its ballroom on Saturday evenings to the sound of the big band. But this palatial modern hotel in the rebuilt City is nevertheless familiar to me from other cities where my interest in community health services has arbitrarily taken me: in Mexico City and São Paulo, in Karachi, Delhi and Brisbane

I have found myself booked into this hotel and once – my only Far Eastern excursion – in Jakarta. Oh yes, and one stopover in Hong Kong, a touchdown near the territory of the past, disorienting, brief. Not actually needing the marble floors, chandeliers, twenty-four-hour room service or complimentary bowls of fruit that come with the other 'conference facilities', I have found myself on such occasions yearning obscurely for old, high-ceilinged rooms instead of sealed, air-conditioned ones, and for fans blowing up a welcome breeze. I have transiently wanted a shaded, mahogany-lined bar, a garden with trailing creepers beyond the verandah, the noise of crows and cicadas, even the noise of a big band.

If I had vaguely hoped, against all probability, to find these things again in the Great City, my hopes were, of course, unfulfilled. Here, more than in any other city, the past has been physically obliterated. Christopher had warned me of this long ago, and it was he who booked me the room in this present fairy palace.

'*Since there isn't an old-style hotel here any more – the World Bank Building, a dream in blue glass, is where the Bristol used to be – you might as well stay at the most central of the new hotels. In the hot, humid weather even the most dedicated Japanese and American consumers don't much want to come here. So grand hotels are half-empty just now, and will let rooms at what are bargain prices for the likes of you and even me.*'

Thus he wrote in his last letter, I mean latest. Dated two weeks ago. I had rather hoped to hear again from him before I left home, but Christopher, though he writes splendidly long letters from time to time, has never been a frequent correspondent. He explained once that it did not seem a good idea to be constantly in touch when he goes away, because on his long expeditions he can be out of reach of mail services for some time and if I were used to hearing from him regularly I might then worry unduly. Very sensible, I dare say.

I had also thought, without letting myself realise it, that there might be a message waiting for me at the hotel. Nothing. But then I don't think I told Christopher what time I would arrive, or whether it would be today or tomorrow. I have only to wait.

In my unnecessarily carpeted, air-conditioned room, with the standard two beds (the other one waiting for Christopher? Or Jill. Or Sarah –) and the marble bathroom full of such presents as tissues, disposable razors, toothbrushes and shower caps, there was also a folder of advertisements and a map of the City. Or rather, a version of the City, simplified to a few main roads, a handful of landmarks shown as pictures to make it seem easy. Labelled 'Visitors Guide of Shopping City' in heavy quotes but minus an apostrophe, in a chunky, curly script evocative of copybook handwriting, the whole thing looked invitingly like something out of an old-fashioned comic. A chart of Treasure Island, perhaps, scaled down for a lower age group, or a map of the land of Oz. Pots of gold doubloons here, chums, for the one with the speediest spade. Follow the Yellow Brick Road for the Best Boutiques. Come into Aladdin's cave: come buy, come buy! Here be crocodile-skin handbags from the brown river, here jewels from the distant mountains, here meticulous copies of the world's consumer durables at competitive prices, as good as or better than the originals. Famous-name goods at half-price. Special discounts for guests of this hotel – show your key tag. All leading credit cards accepted.

The dislocations of jet travel play tricks with the mind, making you feel on the one hand that there are all sorts of things you might at any moment need – food, drink, sex, discounted electrical goods, new experience – and on the other that you will never really need anything again. You do not know what you are supposed to do next, let alone what you might want to do. I tried lying on one of the beds for a while, consciously relaxing, but that did not seem to be what my system required. Next, I had a shower. After that I had to put on a clean shirt, and that seemed to commit me to going out, or at any rate downstairs. So I decided to order myself a drink first, from room service, since there is little point in staying in an Eastern palace if you do not make use of the resident genie.

The genie, when I summoned him, was a teenager in a smart uniform distantly inspired by a Victorian drummer boy. He wore his black hair in a quiff that is probably the latest thing among sharp boys of the City, but his boot-button eyes had the eager innocence of those who have grown up to fear and obey. 'Opportunities for all' is today the watchword of the City authorities, but no doubt those opportunities have to be both earned and cherished in the best meritocratic traditions. He produced his set phrases of English with a desperate pride, so that I did not feel inclined to produce the City-lingo for 'Bring me' which had suddenly risen from the bottom of my memory: it might in any case be out of date. He fetched my whisky-soda with the ceremony of an acolyte assisting at a Mass. He reminded me of our houseboys of long ago whom I, a child myself, had looked on as a species of fellow child, older and wiser than myself but on my side of the great divide from adulthood. I thought how physically large, coarse, formidable and old my present self must look to this boy – and then I thought, don't be silly: he serves westerners all the time in this place, it's all in the day's work to him. He's not thinking about you at all.

I was going to tip him, but then remembered the prominent notice at the reception desk downstairs, repeated in the folder up here, to the effect that tipping had been abolished in this prosperous First World city. I remembered then the ubiquitous beggars of my early childhood, living out their lives under the arcaded houses of old streets, and realised that those must have been abolished too. By contrast, in the Great Land across the shut frontier where (as Christopher wrote) time has moved at a different rate, do beggars still line the streets and market touts clamour for backsheesh? Is that the sort of world that drove Baht Way to risk the frontier crossing and make his way here into this alien place? But no, surely, the People's Socialist Republic of Mayer Dhar could not allow any beggars or tipping either, not openly at any rate. And, like the City, they too, no doubt, would claim that there are jobs, food, health care and equal opportunities for all.

Since the end of the racking Civil War and the splitting off of the City from the Great Land, the Land has been nominally ruled by an elected senate but in practice (it would seem) by a small mafia of now aging men, several of them members of the same family. The last emperor was deposed and then apparently murdered during the Civil War once the British forces were no longer there to protect him. I say 'it would seem' and 'apparently' because even dedicated watchers such as Christopher find it hard to describe exactly what goes on there these days. With its sustained refusal to allow any foreign diplomatic missions whatsoever on its soil, and its practice of granting visas to foreign visitors only in official groups with some defined purpose and usually only for three days at a time, it has for the last thirty years been the most impenetrable of countries. Unlike such comparable fortresses as Russia, Albania, Burma and China, the Great Land has not allowed its wilful seclusion from the world to erode over the years but has, if anything, increased it. Its conviction of its own right and integrity, which contact with the rest of the world could only contaminate, does not, however, appear to be based on a coherent political faith. The Lay Balint, the vaguely communist guerrilla forces who were a feature of the Troubles ('freedom fighters') were early demoted to the status of 'bandits', and eventually 'Marxist' itself became a dirty word along with 'western' and 'Capitalist'. At least the Great Land, continuing the tradition of its ancient emperors, is evenhanded in its suspicion of all external influences.

Other countries labelled 'socialist' were initially ready to claim the Great Land as a natural ally, but she seems to have rebuffed them all. A brief honeymoon with Soviet Russia around 1960 (second-hand Russian army uniforms, sad cement boulevards ploughed through the only two towns big enough to accommodate them) ended abruptly when a Russian delegate was deemed 'patronising'. An intense but even briefer affair with China during its Cultural Revolution (a temporary change of alphabet, mass rallies to extol the Thoughts of Chairman Mao) ended when the Great Land suddenly decided the Chinese notions of family limitation were, after all, a sinister plan to dominate them genetically and destroy them. I rather think that there was little that China could have taught them about governmental control and oppression anyway.

Today, clutching its incorrigibly large families to its collective bosom (I quote Christopher), the country seems to have lapsed back into a primitive agrarianism, as self-sufficient as it is possible to be. It maintains no airline and virtually no motor vehicles except military ones; it runs its sparse and old-fashioned industries and its many steam trains on its own low-grade brownish coal. It is known to have, thanks to its numerous rivers, an adequate modern electricity supply and also a very large number of traditional wooden water wheels. It is no doubt the presence of these wheels, which tend to be featured in rare pictures of the place, that has given currency to a popular Western idea that the Great Land is ecologically pure, an *echt* Green place, Eden before the Fall. (Yes, I am quoting Christopher again.) I should think that the powers that run the place are quite happy for this image to be projected, though 'image', with its associations of tourism and marketing, is perhaps hardly the word. For whatever reasons, sound or dotty, the Great Land persistently discourages tourism of all kinds. Perhaps this is its most lovable characteristic – at least to my uninformed eye.

Apparently the citizens of the Great Land are regularly told by their government that the City of today (their 'lost' city of Mayer Teen) is riddled with unspecified Western diseases, the direct result of international commerce and tourism. Behind its ultramodern façade, they are also told, Dickensian conditions prevail – for Dickens is known in the Great Land, it seems, along with Shakespeare, Pearl S. Buck and the improving Sunday-school books left behind by Great-Aunt Alice and her kind. Yet alongside this insistent mythology of the lost City as a place of perdition, there is clearly a different underground myth in which it figures as the Promised Land. Or why should even men from remote places, men like Baht Way, risk life and health to travel here and, having done so, stay?

Some of this, Christopher wrote in his letter. He also wrote:

I am on the track of Baht Way, but there has been a slight hitch. Mike Isaacs (who seems to have various irons in the fire, but I haven't yet found out quite what) wasn't here when I arrived from Hong Kong. He'd gone upcountry for a bit, I mean up into the Great Land. It is possible to get a visa for longer than three days, depending on who you are. (As you may imagine, I'm working on it.)

He left me a friendly note, but imprecise, saying that Baht Way knows of our interest and that he, Mike, would tell me more as soon as he got back to the City. But so far no further word.

Because I am at a loose end here and had keyed myself up for the great meeting, I decided to go and have a look for Baht Way myself. I knew the part of the City he was living in – Teyn Bira, which actually means 'Valley of the Flowers', but as a description this is rather out of date. Do you remember it? It's now the great district of small manufac-

tories – radio parts, finishing work for the garment trade, handmade leather goods, outwork of all kinds. An old-fashioned, crowded sort of place; one of the last areas which have not been rebuilt.

I had the original newspaper cuttings in my pocket plus that other photo Mike sent us, and just maundered around in Teyn Bira looking for likely people to ask. I came across a gang of workmen dressed like Baht Way in the newspaper picture, off duty and eating at a cha-beyin stall, so I tried them. They couldn't help but after some initial confusion (they thought the man in the picture was me, logically enough, and couldn't understand why I was looking for myself), they sent me to an old boy in a chemist's shop nearby – I say 'chemist's' but it was full of the usual collection of frog's semen and powdered viper, plus more or less standard Western medicines, plus liquor, plus (I rather think) some more exotic substances under the counter. The old boy himself looked the soul of respectability, however, and knew where Baht Way lives – I suppose he's been rather conspicuous in this part of town.

So I went there. A room above another little shop down an alley. Whole place full of tin roofs and overhead wires and, since Teyn Bira is low-lying, a network of drainage ditches like miniature canals and smelling too: salt swamp and old cooking oil. God, so different from most parts of the City today. But I should imagine Baht Way feels more at home there than he would in more elegant surroundings.

However, he wasn't. At home, I mean. And the people downstairs didn't seem to know when he'd be back.

I thought of leaving him some sort of message asking him to contact me, but then thought: It's his business and very personal, and he may be sensitive about anyone else knowing it. So I just came away.

After that, with assurances of being in touch again when he has anything to report, expectations of seeing me here soon anyway and an affectionate scrawl, the letter ends.

The huge, chandelier-hung reception hall of this hotel has two glass lifts, one each side, which, from the third floor upwards, run clear on the outside of the building with breath-catching views over the City, as if from a balloon. I took one of the lifts, and as I rode the blue velvet night sky with lights all around and below me, I did feel for a few moments as if I were floating freely down into an Aladdin's cave of rarities and new experiences glowing somewhere there in the City's heart. Then the lift reached the lower floors and the hotel foyer closed round me once more.

As I was about to leave my key at the desk, the clerk said: 'We were just ringing your room, sir. There's a gentleman to see you. He's waiting over there.'

Filled with sudden pleasure – and also, yes, I could now admit it, relief – I looked where the clerk was indicating.

'Where? I don't see him.' Among the sprinkling of dark-suited locals and loudly dressed westerners still around in the foyer at that hour, Christopher's tall figure was nowhere to be seen.

'There, sir, by the tour desk. The gentleman in a red-and-white checked – yes, that one, sir.' For one of the westerners had now detached himself from a broody contemplation of the posters for visits to diamond workshops and crocodile farms, and was ambling towards me. Mike Isaacs. Of course.

I suppose that my disappointment showed, for once he had spoken his name and greeted me, he said a little truculently: 'I guess I'm not really the person you want to see – either of 'em. But as they're not around tonight and you were due in, I thought I'd better come along.'

I did not quite take this in for a moment. I said: 'How did you recognise me? Or did one of the clerks point me out to you?'

'I recognised you all right. You, your son Chris and Baht Way – you've all got the same face, haven't you? Variations, but the same face. I'd have known you anywhere.'

I could not say anything of the kind to him, for he struck me as a particularly anonymous-looking American: tallish, like Christopher, but some years older, regular features but without being particularly handsome, Jewish, I suppose from the name, but not noticeably so, not noticeably anything: an all-purpose late-twentieth-century Western male, travelling model.

The only distinctive characteristic I registered, as we made our way into the bar at my suggestion, was that, for a stranger who had bothered to come and greet me on my arrival, he seemed rather morose and withdrawn. Perhaps he was regretting having come. Or perhaps I was merely picking up, as one sometimes does at first sight, a fundamental aspect of a personality which, on further acquaintance, was to become overlaid by other perceptions.

After a few minutes he seemed to become more relaxed, or

perhaps just more sure of himself. I have noticed that the prospect of meeting an Englishman in the Far East, particularly of my generation, can raise all sorts of wordless expectations and defences in people of other nationalities. Perhaps I have managed to reassure him by my manner that I, too, am just a harmless traveller on the face of the earth.

It became clear, as he began to talk, that in the interval between Christopher's last letter and my arrival here the two of them had met, and on more than one occasion. This was a relief, and I listened eagerly to what Mike Isaacs had to say, though he spoke of 'Chris', a shortening we have never used and which always makes me feel it is a stranger who is being discussed. When Christopher was little we called him Kit, after a seafaring eighteenth-century ancestor of mine. A couple of his childhood friends and his cousins still call him Kit, something I always find absurdly heart-warming when I hear it. In his adult professional world he is always Christopher, and I am not aware that any of his newer friends ever call him Chris. But of course I don't know everything about his life these days.

I suppose that Mike Isaacs (firmly 'Mike', I gathered) just meant to suggest friendship all round in shortening my son's name. As he talked on – Chris said this, Chris and I did the other – I began after all to see here a personality amiable and forceful enough to have Baht Way's confidence.

Then, in the middle of a detailed monologue, delivered almost as if it were the rough draft of an article or a radio talk, about how 'Chris and I' had gone back to Teyn Bira and managed to interview Baht Way's landlady, he broke off to say:

'But see, I've something I should tell you. I said I would.'

'What?' My imagination was at once morbidly alert.

'Baht Way has gone back home. I mean, upcountry.'

'You mean – back to the Great Land?'

'I do mean that, yes.'

A second emotion – relief mainly, I think, though tinged with disappointment – went through me.

'Do you mean he's gone back there permanently?'

If he had, it would solve a lot. Even if it seemed rather an anticlimax after all this.

'He's changed his mind, then?' I added flatly.

'Well, I'm not sure. If you ask me, the guy's in two minds. Partly, he's got cold feet, I think, after all these years of dreaming. But partly he really wants for us – well, you and Chris – to go seek him out. If he makes the first move towards you, he's afraid he might get rebuffed. That's what Chris thinks, anyway.'

'You mean, seek him out in a general way?' I said. 'Make him feel we're really interested in him?'

'Yeah. Something like that.'

'But in that case we'll have to wait till he comes back to the City. I mean, we can hardly go looking for him in the Great Land. No one would let us, anyway.'

But even as I spoke I realised that this was what Christopher must have had in mind when he wrote: '*It is possible to get a visa for longer than three days, depending on who you are ... As you may imagine, I'm working on it.*' And Mike had recently been to the Great Land himself.

'Where is Christopher at this moment?' I said suddenly. 'He's not in the City at all, is he, or he'd be here now.'

'Yeah, I was just coming to that – '

'Has he gone to the frontier, up into the Great Land – to look for this damned Baht Way already? You better tell me.'

I suppose I sounded sharp, for Mike Isaacs was defensive again.

'Yeah. Like I said, I was just going to tell you. Don't blame me. I suggested he should wait till you came.'

'Why didn't he?'

The answer sounded awkward and unlikely on Mike's lips, as if he were just repeating what he had been told and didn't really believe it, but it rang true in my ears.

'He thought if he could find Baht Way quickly and talk to him, he could have him back by the time you arrived.'

'But he hasn't reappeared yet?'

'No,' said Mike Isaacs, 'he hasn't.'

He added, after a longish pause, in a subdued voice: 'I'm sorry. I tried to get him to wait. But he's very determined, your son, isn't he? Seems a quiet, laid-back type, but he goes his own way.'

And after another pause he added, quite unnecessarily, I thought: 'Don't worry about him too much. Myself, I think a lot of this stuff you hear about things that happen there is pretty much exaggerated. I mean, people who were supposed to have been murdered by the Lay Balint years ago have turned up alive and well in those mountains.'

PART II

'I would like to do something,' Christopher said – about Baht Way, when we first saw the news item, about the inconclusive sadness in which his Aunt Tessa's memory had now been filed away. Christopher is like that, these days. A young man who has so avoided taking on the traditional responsibilities that the rest of his generation are assuming, a man without a fixed job, a wife, children or even a settled home – he yet seems to feel a responsibility towards the past. Not a duty, more of a family role. 'Duty' is not, I think, a word he would ever use; that is my sister Pauline's word. She frequently speaks of her or, rather, 'one's' duty, and I have even heard her use, with only a tiny laugh of embarrassment, the phrase 'one's duty to society'. Christopher's approach is quite other: uncensorious, increasingly disinclined to take a partisan line on most subjects. 'Easy-going' I have even heard my brother-in-law Toby once call him. But those who know Christopher better, or who are simply more astute than Toby can afford to be, know that Christopher is not at all easy-going inside his head. He may be unwilling to pronounce judgements on others, but he judges situations. Unusually free of involvement on one level, at another he wants to intervene and influence people's lives. His coercion is gentle, unthreatening but secretly insistent.

I recognise the syndrome – the doctor, priest or natural-leader one – of course I recognise it. It is there in me, though I think I have always disguised it less skilfully than Christopher. For Christopher, loving, warm and supportive though he is, is a man in armour. He is also relentless.

Was he always like this? I think back to when he was very young, and see a happy but highly strung little boy who was passionately attached to his mother and was capable of frantic misery at the world's injustices and cruelties as they were haphazardly revealed to him. You could say that there was already a highly developed sense of general responsibility, but not the slight, perpetual sense of his separateness from everyone else that now seems to accompany it. Will he now, I have once or twice asked myself in something approaching panic, ever make himself vulnerable enough to marry, to beget children, those hostages to fortune? I wonder, too, if he was always going to be like this, if this was his true identity from the start, merely hidden at first in the soft bud of childhood. Or did something happen to him?

We didn't send him to board away from home at eight as a number of our friends did with their sons. Sarah was against this, and she did not have to try hard to convince me: my memories of the misery I experienced myself in a boarding prep school in England in 1939 were vivid. But when Christopher was thirteen we sent him to my old public school; I could afford it, and it seemed by then the appropriate thing to do. It wasn't as if he had a string of brothers and sisters to keep him company at home. He used to mope a bit at the end of each holiday (we did not foresee, and nor apparently did he, what an inveterate traveller-from-home he would one day become) but his letters from school were cheerful enough. He got good reports, played in teams, made friends. Then, when he was sixteen, Sarah was killed in that senseless accident.

It was fine autumn weather when I drove across England to break the news to him. I – and Sarah, and Sarah – had last seen him a month before, when he went off at the beginning of term after a successful holiday we'd had together south of Bordeaux. One of his cousins, Pauline's eldest boy, had joined us for part of the time, and we'd done a lot of swimming and sailing and beach cricket. When not in or beside the Atlantic, Christopher was reading Mauriac's novels which are set in that part of France. This was his mother's doing, of course – she read much more than I did, and took a lot of trouble finding the right material to feed Christopher's eager, bookish intelligence. One novel was actually called *The Paths to the Sea*. I still remember him bringing me a passage in it that had particularly struck him. I was lying in a deck chair, looking through a fat report on something or other. He was so stirred by the bit he had found that I felt even at the time that my own response was stodgy and inadequate.

'The life of most human beings is an old path that peters out into nothing. But some know, from their childhood, that their particular path is leading towards the unknown sea. From a long way off they sense with surprise a sharp wind, the taste of salt is on their lips – until the moment when, as they come over the last dune, the great, moving infinite washes on to them its sand and its foam. At that point they can only cast themselves upon the sea with open arms – or go back the way they have come.'

I know that was the passage because I looked it out weeks later, on that dreadful day in early October, and brought the book with me on my journey to tell him he would never see his mother again. I think I had a vague idea that I might be able to use the remembered passage to make some point about Sarah's own life, even if tragically cut off, having had its own purposeful path, not petering out into nothing. No use, of course, as I realised when I finally came face to face with him and stammered out the awful news: he was far too shocked that day for any such facile, intellectual comfort.

I can see him now, ranging the housemaster's study (in which we'd been tactfully left to ourselves), banging into furniture in an abandonment of grief, banging his head at one point against the mantelpiece, weeping, weeping. (Have I, on reflection, ever seen him cry since? I don't believe I have. He may have cried, of course, but I haven't seen it.)

I did not bring him home with me at the end of the day. I should have; I knew that, I think, even at the time. But the truth was, I just couldn't face it myself. That drive, that afternoon, had taken the last of my strength from me. If Christopher came home and raged like that at the funeral I just could not cope. I think I intimated as much, cowardly, to the housemaster, who became enormously tactful and reassuring and said: 'Of course, old chap, of course – absolutely right: I couldn't sympathise more. Funerals are morbid affairs, aren't they? Best get through it on your own. Leave

Christopher in our hands. We'll take good care of the lad, our matron's awfully good at these sad times, and he'll be better off here with his chums and his usual routine . . .'

And so on and so forth, the received unwisdom that was still current fifteen years ago. I knew, really, then that it was rubbish; that this was no way to deal with death, with pain, with irreparable loss. But, in my weakness, I let the man soothe me and made my craven escape from my son's grief.

In those days after Sarah's death when he was exiled at school and I withdrew from him, did something break in Christopher, I have sometimes wondered? And, if so, was it something that had to break sooner or later, to free him to live as a man? Or was it something that need not, should not have broken, the loss of which profoundly affected him?

Christopher walks alone. Does he, as it sometimes seems, have some driving, exalted purpose which he does not yet choose to reveal? Or is he pursuing, less rationally, some more obscure and compulsive destination?

Or are these just the amorphous, unfocused worries that come to many parents of grown children when they wake at dawn? With the accumulating years comes the knowledge of one's essential impotence, either to protect those one loves most or to affect the course of life in general. You do not get braver as you get older. Sarah used to say this, in fact, years ago, before I had begun to notice it or to know what she meant. She used to have spells of waking early, particularly once Christopher was away at school, with what she referred to in ironic shorthand as her 'sense of doom'. At first I thought she must have some specific doom in mind, and used to attempt elaborate reassurance – how I was sure Christopher was being well looked after, how basically sensible he was anyway: never accident-prone as a child, not a tearaway now he was in his teens . . . Eventually she said, almost irritably: 'Stephen, you needn't go on. I know all that. It isn't any one particular thing I worry about. Not any sort of cause-and-effect thing that one can predict and take steps against, anyway. Can't you see? I don't know what it is I worry about; it may not even have to do with Christopher at all. It's probably just generalised intimations of mortality, as suited to my time of life. If it was something more manageable it might not wake me up in this way.'

And, yes, later, when she was killed in that unpredictable and unavoidable accident – a wheel came spinning off the car ahead of her on the road to Oxford – I was tempted to believe, for a while, that she had foreseen it, had at some level known that this was what her obscure sense of doom had all been about. But the simplicities of clairvoyance have never appealed to me as a theory of life (nor to her either) and by and by some sort of glum integrity reasserted itself: the 'meaning' of Sarah's death was that there was no meaning, in that sense. It was vain, I decided, to look for one. She wouldn't have thanked me for trying to impose a dramatic perspective on an emotion of hers which she herself had diagnosed more honestly.

So now, when I find the same syndrome in myself all these years later, when I half wake at dawn with a sense of something amiss, some lurking anxiety or foreboding, and range in my mind over various possible areas in which it may be located, I try to tell myself, as Sarah did: It's nothing particular. Just everything. Life. The passing years. The system gearing itself up to confront another day. The human condition. Or may be those vague aches and pains in my aging joints which, on waking, send messages of discomfort which the sleepy brain does not at once manage to place and thus misinterprets as signals from elsewhere. That, at least, is my latest theory on the matter, and I wish I could discuss it with Sarah now.

When it began to be clear that Christopher was probably going to remain our only child, I became temporarily enthusiastic about the notion of adoption, the traditional next move. It was easier in those days; I had myself cheerfully suggested it to infertile parents from time to time as a 'solution'. I think I had a sentimental masculine fantasy about how nice it would be to have a daughter to make a fuss of me; neither my imagination nor my intellect had explored the prospect any further. But Sarah did, and did not entirely like what she found there. Her own initial warmth for the idea faded. Finally she told me, sadly but with great resolution, that adoption had come to seem to her a hazardous, arbitrary step with a strong element of make-believe in it which she distrusted.

'The two of us and Christopher – we are as we are. I don't

think we should force fate in that way. It seems sort of conceited, thinking that if you can't get what you want in one way you can get it in another. People plan too much today. It might not work out at all well.'

'Lots of adoptions work out well,' I said, no doubt sounding like the sort of proselytising professional I actually distrust.

'Maybe so, but perhaps those are people to whom it comes naturally. And it wouldn't to me. I'm sorry, Steve; I can't do it.'

At the time I was disappointed – but not deeply, which shows you how little thought I'd really given the whole thing. Only years later, after her death, did her words about not being so conceited as to think you can plan your life to circumvent fate come back to me with an altered meaning.

A few days after Christopher first showed me the newspaper story about Baht Way, we were invited for Sunday lunch with Pauline and Toby. On the drive over to Hampshire, Christopher said: 'Don't say anything, just for the present, Dad, about our mystery relative.'

'OK.'

'I want to do a bit of detective work on my own first. Otherwise, the moment I mention it – well, you know what Pauline's like.'

'She'll seize the ball and rush off with it.'

'Quite. And before we start on that, I'd like to make sure that it really *is* our ball. So to speak.'

'OK,' I said, 'but, you know, they may have seen the newspaper themselves and be bursting to tell *us*.'

'Yes, I thought of that, but I don't think so. They read the *Guardian*, don't they? They're always asking if one has seen this or that article in it, and being surprised if one hasn't. They never look at any other paper, and this story was only in *The Times* – I've checked. Pauline didn't say anything to you, did she, when you rang her last night?'

'I got Toby, actually. No, not a word about anything, but he's been seeing the rural dean again about the ordination-of-women saga. He said he's going to tell me where it's got to at lunch today and how I'll be interested to hear.'

Toby is vicar of several widespread parishes. He spends a lot of time and energy driving from one large, dilapidated

church to another but once, when I pretended to think that
the reason he supports the ordination of women is to get some
of these handsome white elephants taken off his hands, he
was not amused.

'Did you tell him not to bother because actually you won't
be at all interested?' Christopher murmured.

In the same deadpan tone, I answered: 'No. I thought of
saying that, but then I thought he just might suspect me of
being rude.'

We drove in companionable silence for a minute, and then
Christopher said:

'Actually, my guess is that what he said was that *Pauline*
said you'd be interested to hear.'

'You know, I do believe he did.'

Christopher has never much liked my elder sister. When he
was a very small boy he used to complain that she was 'noisy'.
It isn't that Pauline has a loud voice; her tones are actually
rather harmonious and low-pitched, the firm voice of a local
committee woman and seasoned campaigner for the National
Trust, Council for Rural England, Nature Conservancy, and
CND. But she is too interested in others to be able to leave
them in peace.

Perhaps it is because I have been aware, ever since childhood, of the burden my kind elder sister's keen interest and
undoubted good intentions might place on me, that I have
always made myself rather scarce. For years, when we were
first in Dorset, this was easy. Pauline and Toby and their
growing family moved round parishes in the north. Toby came
from there, and Pauline, in those days, appeared to despise
the south of England as being 'less real' than Lancashire and
even 'suburban'. Nevertheless, they eventually came south 'for
the sake of the children' and settled in a spacious, unheated
vicarage in a commuter village near Basingstoke.

Even then we did not see each other all that often, although
mutual efforts were made, with some success, to get the
children to fraternise. Toby's not a bad sort, and I believe
he's quite well liked in the Church – friendly, unpretentious,
a willing packhorse, good with old ladies, I should think – but
he and I have so few interests and tastes in common. And
Sarah and Pauline, I was always half aware, really did not
like each other very much, though they both honourably went

through the motions of family and female loyalty. If Sarah's work (she was an archaeologist) came up in conversation, Pauline tended to say things like 'Of course I know nothing about that, I'm no intellectual', 'Of course, as we were all out in the East I never got to university. Not that I really regret it . . .' For a long time I supposed that Sarah would find Pauline's defensiveness on such matters amusing and faintly touching, as I did: people's vulnerabilities make them more attractive. But once, when we were driving back from Hampshire, Sarah broke a long silence to say:

'If she goes on any more in my hearing about how important family life is and what a force for good and how she'd happily have a fifth child tomorrow if only Toby's stipend wasn't so small, I shall scream.'

For myself, I've never thought much about whether I like Pauline or what indeed I actually think about her. She's my sister, for better or worse – and there the analysis seems to stop, or at any rate to become redundant. I rather suspect that she has the same view of me. It is certainly because she is my sister, and now my only surviving one, rather than because of any deep natural affinity between us, that she has consistently made efforts about me in the years since Sarah died, inviting me to Hampshire far more frequently than I care to go. Is it because she is genuinely fond of me that she is disappointed when I don't go there 'over' Christmas for a period of days on end? Or is it because her sense of family propriety is offended by my preference for other and more varied company, and because she likes to feel she is doing her duty by her widowed brother?

Was duty born into Pauline, or bred? Perhaps, in the way traditional for the eldest girl, she grew from toddlerhood into the role of mother's little helper: she was certainly far more like Mother in character than Tess ever could have been. At any rate, duty was, I am sure, ensconced in her by the time she was sent Home to a large girls' boarding school in England. The same boat from the Bundar which bore me off to a first year of intense misery at my prep school at the age of eight carried her to a happier place. She was older than I was, and I dare say girls' schools were different: anyway she appeared to thrive at hers, and stayed there cheerfully throughout the war, eventually becoming head girl. After the war she went east again with our parents: Father was one of the first civilians to return to the City and the Great Land, sent there by the company to pick over the wreckage left by the Japanese occupation and begin putting things together again.

So it was that when at last I arrived back with my national-service regiment, and saw the Customs House and the Bristol Hotel and Father waiting on the Bundar to welcome me, Pauline was already settled in the place. She'd done the sort of minimal secretarial course that was all that was expected of pretty, slightly posh girls in those days, and had a job with the military establishment – mainly making tea for the brigadier, as far as I remember, but no doubt I underestimated it. Perhaps, on reflection, that was just the sort of brotherly misconception I pretended to hold in order to tease her. (I teased, she bossed: the traditional roles.) I know that in those unimaginably distant days – almost as socially distant from us as the Victorian era – she played a lot of tennis on the baking courts behind the old Turf Club, and was frequently escorted to dances wearing a strapless white evening dress on the boned back of which her dancing partners (she daintily complained) used to leave the marks of their 'great sweaty paws'. Many of these dancing partners were young officers, my fellows. The City was considered a pretty good posting at that time, before the Troubles began. Of course it had never actually been a British colony, but the way the free port functioned, there on the rim of the Great Land, gave a colonial feel to life, and the presence of the British army in the years after the war strengthened this illusory impression. It had been the British, along with the Australians, who had liberated the place in 1945, and a peacekeeping force were 'invited to stay on' (in the phrase of the period) by the restored emperor – who turned out, as it happened, to be the last one. In the late 1940s a self-contained world that Britain was elsewhere losing and was soon to relinquish everywhere, was for a few years artificially created under the City's bright sky.

It was while I was there with the army, dividing my time between the social life of the cantonment on the one hand and, on the other, forays upcountry pursuing rumours of communist-inspired guerrilla forces, that Tessa too appeared. Our family circle, as Father declared in one of his occasional moments of sentiment, was now complete. Tessa, too, arrived straight from school, but unlike her elder sister she had left precipitately, two terms early and 'under a cloud'. I never did discover the precise nature of the cloud: Mother and Pauline were great ones for forming a female cabal and keeping 'the chaps' in ignorance. But anyway there Tessa was, pretty and barely seventeen, as yet unable to type and loudly declaring that she *hated* dancing with stuffy young men. What was to be done with her? The matter was earnestly debated, mostly out of Tessa's hearing. She was already professing left-wing sympathies, though Pauline was crisply inclined to dismiss these as mere 'showing off'. (Pauline was not then a *Guardian* reader.) For better or worse, therefore, Tessa was hastily found unpaid work in the Displaced Persons' Advisory Bureau, a welfare outfit which had been set up to deal with the increasing number of upcountry citizens, with throaty accents and strange rural ways, now pouring into the City in a great, stealthy flood.

Months before, the emperor's regime had instituted a residence-permit system, in an attempt to stop people shifting from the mountains to the plains, from the interior to the coastal belt, from the entrenched and ageless demands of land to the melting pot of this city. But in spite of law and decrees, the people kept coming, and not just itinerant labourers but rural landowners and shopkeepers, headmen, goldsmiths and school teachers; the elite of the village societies they had left behind. And along with them came strange stories, rumours and fears: people were disappearing, the incomers said.

'Of course they seem to be disappearing,' the British High Commissioner, the military C-in-C and the municipal dignitaries testily replied. '*You* are disappearing from your villages, coming here to the City. Why don't you go back?'

'We don't want to go back. We are afraid. If you try to send us back we too will disappear. At home, people we know have disappeared – the headman's son, the apothecary, the monks from the local temple. And there are mounds of fresh earth in the next valley . . . We are afraid.'

At first there was much talk in the City of the Lay Balint, who had borrowed their name ('the witnesses of God') from a resistance force in some long-distant imperial battle, and were known to be operating now against the emperor in the mountainous regions. The upcountry British army presence was strengthened. But were the Lay Balint really the only villains? Were they, indeed, even Communist? The British assumed so in the spirit of the time, and so, officially, did the emperor's entourage of yes-men, but no one seemed to know for sure. Since the postwar restoration, the emperor's court in the old imperial capital was officially run on constitutional, democratic lines, but foreign observers there remarked that most of the time-honoured shows of autocracy and the old regard for ceremony were once again in evidence. At the same time the emperor himself was said to be 'weak'. There might, it was evasively suggested by local watchers in the City on the delta, be some additional element at work in the country. By and by other tales began to circulate. A City-based merchant who regularly sent his travelling salesmen upcountry on mules, or far upriver to the imperial capital, reported that his men were losing their nerve. One of them had returned with a story about having come upon a mountainous cave full of skulls which, when he had passed that way years before, had been inhabited by nothing but a colony of bats. Another man had returned with a more incoherent recital about ritual mutilations he would not or could not describe precisely, and refused point-blank to resume his usual tour even when threatened with the sack. Then a third salesman disappeared entirely, though of course he may simply have absconded and found somewhere else to settle. It was a huge country. People had always disappeared into it.

It was about this time that the rumours began about the bodies seen floating on the brown river far inland; some of them were said to have had their hands and genitals hacked away. No one seemed quite sure where they had come from, since the water might have borne them, bloated, some considerable distance before they finally burst, disintegrated and sank; British attempts to get accurate eye-witness reports on the business ran into all kinds of difficulties. The culture of that part of the world has always had a deep-rooted taboo on naming unpleasant facts clearly. For this reason or for another, the emperor, although professing himself delighted to have the British army protecting his citizens against dissident Communist elements, seemed to want to play down the whole matter of the bodies. It even began to be rumoured that the relationship between the emperor and the Lay Balint was not quite the simple opposition that it seemed. Whatever the truth of this, the British army took comfort in the fact that the mutilated dead were said to be 'only locals' even if they were also whispered to include women and children. If a patrol of British soldiers had been sighted floating on the river minus various appendages, it would of course have been a very different matter. Until then, there only had been isolated military deaths in small-arms interchanges with the Lay Balint in the hills.

There were also persistent stories about people found wandering at night on the swampy edges of the City, who seemed strange, distant, like men drugged or in a dream, and whose hearts turned out, on examination, not to be beating.

At this, the young officers naturally laughed in relief and said: There, it all goes to show! Hearts not beating, indeed – who examined them to find out, I wonder? Can't believe a thing these people say. All that about floating bodies a pack of lies too, I shouldn't wonder.

In the mess, I too joined in these expressions of jeering optimism. I was a very young man having a good time with others; I did not want to believe in darker things any more than they did, or in the brutal intricacy of old societies: I did not want to be made afraid. But really I knew, because my Father and the other old hands out there knew, that what we were being told in the tale of the unbeating hearts was something both less and more extensive than the literal truth. The religion professed by most of the people in the Great Land laid emphasis on the ceremonial disposal of the dead: only then could their spirits pass into the sphere where they could receive their due veneration as ancestors. The spirits of those who had not had the proper rites performed for them were believed to roam the world, unable to leave it fully. To meet, they seemed like ordinary mortals, merely somewhat distressed and distracted, but their dead hearts turned out, on investigation, to be still. Other massacres and pogroms in the Great Land's long and blood-spotted history had produced similar accounts of these night wanderers. The rumours that were circulating in the City in 1950 were not all to be taken literally, but they were a way of raising the alarm. The people were saying, in effect: 'Something is happening. Mass killings and other horrors are going on, somewhere beyond the City. We are all getting to know about it one way or another, but we are afraid to speak about it. So, we take refuge in our legends, to say the unsayable.'

I did not say it either. Even with Father, or with my one close friend on the cantonment, Tommy MacFarlane, I barely discussed it. The Land was naturally restive, disturbed by the years of the War, the Japanese occupation and its aftermath. A tiresome Communist virus (or 'bug', in the phrase of the period) seemed to be 'going round' east Asia, but one must simply stand firm against it and not let it 'get a hold'. It was hoped that, under the calming influences of the restored emperor, the British peacekeeping force and the upturn in world trade, the whole place would settle down again into political health.

Such was the time and place in which Tessa, her schoolgirl hair now frizzily curled, took her place as a voluntary worker in the small downtown office of the Displaced Persons' Advisory Bureau. She was given a filing cabinet and a telephone, and was put in the charge of a long-suffering Eurasian secretary called Myrtle. Tessa was full of excitement at the prospect of a 'real job' and at the possibility of 'helping these poor people'. Apart from a passionate attachment to one or two members of the Labour Party then in power back in England – Aneurin Bevan, I recall, she particularly loved for his Welsh accent and because he was worried about coal miners getting silicosis – her ignorance of the world was almost total. She did not even seem to have the basic awareness and feeling for life in southeast Asia that Pauline and I had acquired in childhood; probably she had been too young before the war, when she had returned Home in haste with our parents.

For about three months all went smoothly, if 'smooth' is a word to describe the constant slight ferment that Tessa created around her, like a miniature whirlpool. She took her job very seriously – 'too damn seriously', Father said in exasperation. Being sensitive and sympathetic was all very well, but girls weren't supposed to take the world's troubles to heart in that way: they were meant to have a jolly time. Tess was jolly enough, in her way, but that way consisted of becoming passionately partisan on behalf of 'her' DPs – 'the *poor* people. You should come down to the office and see them for

yourself, Daddy' – and haranguing and badgering on the
subject everyone she met from the High Commissioner down-
wards.

The official – or rather, the agreed but nonofficial – policy
was to advise the DPs to return upcountry and only to help
them with accommodation or handouts on a very limited
basis. This, Tessa decided, was 'monstrous'. The notion that
the British, as the emperor's guests, were in a delicate position
and could not be seen to act too cavalierly against his
residence-permit laws was outside her ken. She did not scruple
to say what she thought, and by and by had found an ally
who egged her on, a young journalist out from England who
was working for the *City Gazetteer*. He had a name which my
family regarded as unsuitably pretentious but which I forget,
and a North Country accent, and Father began calling him
'that bloody hack'. ('He's even tried to call at the house,'
Pauline told me, with the automatic assumption of social
superiority which she would, today, as firmly repudiate. 'What
a cheek! Daddy sent him packing, of course. Tessa's such a
baby about these things.') Then it came to light that the DPs,
when given rail passes back to their own lands, were simply
converting these into cash at a heavily discounted rate and
using the cash, such as it was, to stay on in the City. It was
suggested that Tessa had put them up to it, but this she
indignantly denied. I believed her, for her own extreme
innocence and palpable, embarrassing honesty were such that
she would hardly have been capable of suggesting a subterfuge
to anyone. It was much more likely the Bloody Hack who
suggested it, if anyone did; the desperate refugees were quite
capable of thinking it up for themselves.

Recalling all this now, so long after, I am only surprised
that Father ever let Tessa loose on such a potentially storm-
raising occupation in the first place. I can only assume that
she was meant to be a token English receptionist, just the
usual pretty girl to lend a touch of class and authority to a
modest enterprise, and that, having very little of the local
language, she would not in practice be called on to do
anything very much. Evidently Tessa succeeded in making far
more of the job than this – as Father should have expected;
but, there again, perhaps he hardly could. He had not been
exposed to Tessa for any length of time since she was about

twelve and he, Mother and Pauline had returned East at the end of the war. Tessa spent most of her holidays with our grandparents while I, as a hulking adolescent, was farmed out to school friends or to a bachelor uncle who taught me to sail. I don't think any of us really knew much about Tessa at all. That shocks me now, but it didn't then. That was, for families of our kind, the way things were. Perhaps we even believed that it was the natural way, and that everything – the free port, Father's company, the British propping up the emperor, the Lay Balint being kept in their place, the whole shaky, temporary postwar edifice of sub-imperialism – would stay that way more or less indefinitely.

Of course it could not and did not. The fact is that while Tessa was stirring up trouble from her downtown bureau, and Pauline was making tart elder-sister remarks and playing tennis, and I was swaggering pointlessly around in my military garb, and Father was in his large office talking peaceably to people around the world about rubber and phosphates, and Mother was busy at whatever harmless nonoccupations married women busied themselves with in that place and time – it was all just on the brink of its precipitous end.

It ended for me three weeks before it did for everyone else, since that was when I developed my hepatitis and was judged sufficiently ill to be shipped out of the humid heat to Australia for treatment. Subsequently this fortuitous personal event came to seem like an omen: it was as if my own metabolism had broken down as a forewarning of what was about to happen generally.

The abrupt escalation of what had been termed 'isolated incidents and rumours' into Troubles that no one could ignore – the steady seepage of refugees into the City becoming an uncontrollable rush; the undeniable corpses arriving down the river now for all to see; then the news of the ambushing, apparent torture and murder of a British officer, a sergeant and twelve other men caught out on an upcountry patrol – these events reached me in my hospital ward in Perth like blows to my stomach, yet muffled in space and air. I was out of it, I never saw it happen; I had, unintentionally, deserted them all. I was not there.

I lay in bed and fretted consciously and sincerely about my family and my army companions. Yet at some level, I am sure, there was operating within me the cut-off that saves us the worst of vicarious pain: we feel that those who suffer what we have never expected to suffer are different from ourselves. If they then rejoin us, palpably the same, we can re-adopt them as our own kind, enlarge our own experience through them. But if they do not reappear, if horror seems to have closed their heads and claimed them, then whatever our conscious distress, at the deeper level this is like a confirmation of what we have been feeling: *They are not like us. They have gone away. They are different, now, even if they were not before.*

Not till the following year, when the news reached me that Tommy MacFarlane also had disappeared upcountry with two of our Nepalese rangers, did this sense of estrangement fail to protect me. The word 'disappear' may in itself seem vague and protective: nevertheless it is from Tommy's vanishing that I date the conviction that has reappeared at intervals throughout my life: *You missed your fate once, by a fluke. Next time, you'll be for it.*

I quite soon received a cable from Singapore, whence Father and Mother had been evacuated. For the second time in ten years they had had to leave the City hurriedly, under High Commission orders, forced by events over which they had no control. And this time, as it turned out, they were never to go back: by the time the City re-established itself as a world trade centre, Father had retired. So it all ended for them, all our century-long family connection with the Great Land, in less than a week. I am glad they did not know it was all over as they landed in Singapore with one suitcase apiece, desperately worried about the daughters they had had to leave behind.

In Pauline's case the worry was tempered with the knowledge that she had only stayed on as army personnel, that she had been moved into the cantonment along with the rest of the civilian staff, and that the brigadier himself was '*keeping an eye on her. If the situation deteriorates further – which God forbid, but if,*' Father wrote to me in the letter that followed his cable, '*the Brig has assured us that all remaining civilian personnel will be shipped out at once. So, although of course we hope matters won't come to that, we are staying on here in Singapore for the moment in case Pauline may soon join us.*

'*Of Tessa, we still have no news at all. But communications are not good, so we continue to hope she may already have turned up safe and sound. As your mother says, Pauline will certainly be looking for her, and we all know how determined Pauline is and what a competent girl she is.'*

Yes, I knew about Pauline's determination and competence. But I also thought I knew how difficult Tessa could be, and how lightly attached she really was to any of us, in spite of her affectionate airs. I was also just adult enough to have an inkling of the depths of our parents' anxiety, grief and suppressed guilt on her behalf. Well might Mother take comfort in the notion that her elder daughter was so satisfactory that she would actually manage to find the younger one and rescue her from some unimaginable fate: no other pretext for comfort offered itself.

It was not till later, when Father, Mother and I were back in England, that I understood how it was that Tessa had been left behind in the first place. She was living at the bungalow with our parents, and should have been evacuated with them to Singapore. But, being Tessa, she had arranged to go with two other volunteers from the bureau on a fact-finding tour upcountry; she had not mentioned it to our parents in advance, no doubt because she knew she would not be allowed to go. The morning when she came down swinging a small travel bag and airily announced that she would be away for four days and, no, she couldn't stop to argue about it because the jeep would be waiting for her downtown, happened to be the morning the first really disturbing news was beginning to come in. Whether Tessa herself had any inkling of that at the time, or would have appreciated the significance of it if she had, was never clear.

She kissed our parents in propitiatory haste – Father, I imagine, still saying: 'Now, look here, Tessa – ', Mother saying 'Darling, you can't just *go* like that, we haven't talked about it' – and ran down to get her usual rickshaw, skipping between the jacarandas and the canna lilies and out of our garden gate to freedom and non-being.

From that hot but cloudy morning on, there descended abruptly over Tessa a great silence and space. She was not heard of again for the best part of two years. For all that time, no sighting was reported later than the first day or so, and no word was received. Many, many times over those two years our parents must have woken at dawn and thought: 'She's gone. She's dead. We'll never see her again.' But, mutually keeping courage and hope alive, they could never bring themselves to say so – not to me or Pauline, and not even, I believe, to each other.

Pauline, as it turned out, stayed on in the City for another fifteen months. Although the country was by then in the throes of what was eventually admitted to be the Civil War, the City continued to function as a well-defined separate enclave and, in doing so, began to transform itself into the independent state it eventually became. It was bursting with refugees, but since it was also the operational HQ for the British army it was well provisioned by sea and air and, after initial chaos, public services more or less functioned.

Pauline, by her own account, expended her energies and ingenuity making enquiries everywhere for Tessa in the first chaotic two or three weeks, and then abandoned the search because there seemed nothing further she could do. A couple of months later the brigadier asked her if she would like to go home and be a comfort to her parents, who were now back in England themselves.

'I said to him I'd rather hang on in the City,' she told us when she eventually came home. She looked and sounded older and more authoritative than the bouncy tennis player I had last seen: she had begun to cultivate the measured voice that is now so much part of her. 'I mean, it was fairly obvious to everyone concerned that if Tessa – that is, that she must be stuck upcountry with no way of getting a message through. But I said I'd rather hang on all the same, just on the off chance . . .

'Now, though, I feel I ought to be at home with you all, which is why I'm here. It looks as if the British army's going to be pulled out soon, which seems to me like letting a lot of people down but there it is. I can't stay on for the rest of my life in the City waiting for Tessa to walk in one fine day at the door of Divisional HQ – particularly if Divisional HQ is going to be wound up.' She added, with what I took at the time to be the same sort of morale-boosting, valiant optimism that our parents had tried to sustain:

'I have a feeling she is OK, somewhere in the Great Land, though. I just have that feeling.'

Her 'feeling' was justified, though by then I had given up
hoping that it might be. Four months later, Tessa did apparently come walking up to the gates of the cantonment, a thin,
down-at-heel figure wearing one of the dresses in local woven
cloth that were sold in the street markets. She addressed the
surprised sentries in the tones of an English boarding school.
She wanted to see her sister Pauline, or, failing that, the
brigadier would do. She had decided she wanted to go home.

So when, as we were driving to Pauline's house in Hampshire
almost forty years later, and Christopher said to me: 'Don't
say anything just for the present about our mystery relative',
that remark contained much unspoken meaning. I agreed that
nothing hasty should be done.

Pauline is a good cook and takes a lot of trouble over it,
but I could wish that, in recent years, she and Toby had not
become committed vegetarians. If she merely served her usual
array of soups and vegetable casseroles and home-made bread
without drawing attention to the absence of meat, I expect I
should eat it all with pleasure, but the foreknowledge that the
meal is likely to be accompanied by a dollop of proselytising
makes me start having perverse fantasies of juicy red meat on
the drive over. The irony is that in the consulting room I
have for decades tried to edge my patients in the direction of
good eating habits. But the possibility that I may not actually
need lectures on the subject does not seem to have occurred
to Pauline.

Toby, of course, lets Pauline have her say on the matter,
while he presides genially at the head of the trestle table over
whatever sizzling nut roast or fragrant bean cassoulet she has
put in front of him. I seem to recall him looking equally genial
years ago over the Sunday joint. The children, all now
grown-up but still coming and going in the household, seem
to have followed Toby's example in this and other ways –
except for Marcus, Christopher's contemporary, who has con-
stituted himself the family rebel in a mild, cheery way. Marcus
works in advertising (a thorn in his parents' side) and is the
only one of those children I have noticed baiting Pauline to
tease her.

This time his chosen topic was alcohol, which might seem
a little unfair since Toby and Pauline have never stinted guests

in pouring out their home-made wine, a more or less palatable concoction brewed from chicken wheat and potatoes. But as lunch progressed this time, I noticed a vague hum of watchful concern emanating from Pauline in the direction of our glasses. She is a devoted reader of popular health columns, and I recalled there had been a recent spate of articles on the demon drink. Myself, I think this sort of scaremongering does little good, but I had a feeling that Marcus should not get away with jeering at it wholesale.

'OK, *OK*,' I finally said, looking from his truculent face to Pauline's pained one. 'I know what you mean about nervous old ladies of both sexes. But if the general effect is to make people realise that alcohol is a poison and to induce an allround respect for it, that can't be a bad thing.'

'So you do basically agree that three glasses of wine a day – three *small* glasses and not every day at that – should be the limit?' said Pauline at once.

That note in her voice made me feel tired. It always does. I hadn't wanted to seem to side with naughty Marcus, but I found myself saying now: 'Look, Pauline. Anyone who drinks three small glasses of wine even every day, and believes themselves on the edge of having an alcohol problem, does have a problem, I grant you – but alcohol it is not.'

They all, except Pauline, laughed at this after a moment. Toby, who likes a drink and believes that a parson should be able to 'mix in the local over a pint', seemed to find it particularly funny. I could see him mentally storing up my clever-clever remark, or the basic model of it, for one of his sermons. It must be a considerable strain having to produce an informal moral lecture week after week, year after year. I have noticed before in Toby a certain worried preoccupation with useful quotes, good phrases and all-purpose jokes.

Pauline thought we were laughing at her and got up abruptly. She went through to the cavernous kitchen to fetch the chocolate pudding and dumped it on the table with a martyred air, which seemed a shame because she takes a pride in her puddings.

I said truthfully, intending to propitiate: 'That looks delicious.'

'Well, I'm afraid I didn't put any cooking sherry in it this time,' she said. 'You may be disappointed, but, you see, I happen to take this whole alcohol problem quite seriously.'

'Darling, we didn't mean – '

'Pauline, I've already said that I – '

'Oh, Mum, come off it! Can't you take a joke?'

We all started and stopped together. Pauline stood over her chocolate confection and stared at us all balefully out of her rather large, pale eyes. She's still quite a pretty woman, though bleached-looking these days, with a lot of little fine lines round her mouth and eyes. I don't think she looks her age, which is probably important to her since Toby is quite a few years younger. She married relatively late, had her children late: the youngest is only just out of his teens now. In any case no age-gap is obvious between her and Toby, who has been a balding, roly-poly figure for years.

With quick tact, Christopher weighed in.

'Of course you're right, Pauline. We know that really, we're just wriggling, us drunks! But I think Dad means that it may not actually be much use telling someone who really does have a drink problem to cut down to a level they're never going to achieve. They won't even feel it's worth trying.'

'Yes, that's exactly it,' I said hastily, though I know this is the sort of argument that Pauline, a great one for principle, does not much appreciate. 'And anyway,' I ploughed on, 'you just can't lay down hard and fast rules about this sort of thing. People's metabolisms vary so much.' I eyed the chocolate pudding momentarily, thinking how I dislike, these days, that stuffed feeling a three-course meal gives me, and then hastily continued: 'The trouble is, what's true for one person may not be for another one. Some people just have the constitution of an ox in a way we can't really test or codify.'

Pauline looked mollified, I was glad to see, and was listening politely to me, but I knew in wider terms I was getting nowhere with her on this subject, as I have got nowhere before. For Pauline wishes, as many people do, to believe that medicine is an exact science in which fixed laws of cause and effect operate in predictable ways. The odd time when I have tried to explain to her that this is not actually so (I believe that Tessa's death, which greatly upset her, was the last occasion), she has refused to take the information on board. If pressed, she will maintain that she *thinks* she understands, but that if, as I say, it's all so complicated . . . Well, of course, she's no intellectual, never went to university. Da-di-da.

In fact, Pauline's resistance to understanding this does not result from any lack of brains but from something else. Sarah once said – I forget exactly on what occasion but the words have remained with me:

'Pauline is afraid of things just as most people are. But she's not going to let anyone else know. I don't think she even lets herself know.'

Now Pauline said: 'But surely we should all *try* to lead a healthy life and foresee potential problems. I mean, isn't that what preventive medicine is all about?'

'Yes. Yes, that's true, but . . .' I hesitated, since the whole subject, highly fashionable in recent years, is one on which I have come to feel caution, not to say cynicism. To do her justice, I don't think Pauline knew this. It would not be like her to be provoking me on purpose. Pauline just 'likes to get to the bottom of things', as she would put it, and her tendency to argue with others merely stems from this.

'It depends,' I said at last, 'on what you mean by "preventive". Of course you know I agree with you' (let's get that in) 'about a balanced diet and exercise – that's hardly controversial. And I take my patients' blood pressure when they stray into surgery after a long gap, because it's sometimes a useful guide and can't do any harm as such. But I'm never happy about instigating procedures which can lead to trouble for everyone and rather questionable long-term benefit.'

I could see she did not know what I was talking about, so I added reluctantly, suspecting already that I was treading into another minefield: 'I mean, all this mammography and cervical testing that is being pushed so hard these days.'

'Oh, but I thought those tests were supposed to be a jolly good idea?' said Toby in frank surprise. 'I mean, isn't it absolutely right that the Health Service should be offering this to women?'

When Toby says 'women' in such a context there's a tiny note of reverence and emotion in his voice, as if women were an endangered species, which should not irritate me but does.

'*We* think they're a good idea,' said Pauline from the end of the table. She was glaring at me again.

'Yes, so did a lot of us some years ago,' I said. 'Trouble is, these tests seem to be turning out, statistically, such poor predictors.'

'Oh, statistics . . .' Toby gave a small, dismissive laugh. 'Of course Pauline and I don't know much about these things but we tend to think in terms of the individual.'

I should not have risen to this profoundly silly remark, but I did.

'I think in terms of the individual too, Toby. Statistics, you know, are made up of individuals. And it is individuals I see in my practice who've been frightened and upset and put through invasive and even damaging procedures which, statistically, are likely to have been quite unnecessary. Or useless, anyway.'

'But surely, if they save *one* woman from dying of cancer – ' That was Pauline and Toby's eldest daughter Vanessa.

'Well, you have to measure the cost. The cost in human terms, I mean,' I added quickly, seeing Pauline and Toby both bristling again, scenting a good clear-cut cause on which they 'feel strongly'. 'Leave the use-of-funds issue out of it altogether – '

'Yes, for goodness sake do,' Marcus muttered, 'or we'll never get our pud.'

'But if women want these tests it is not for you to refuse them, Stephen.' Pauline, the campaigner.

'Yes, but why do they want them? Because they really know the issues involved? I think not.' The devil was in me now, and I went on, knowing even as I did that I was behaving badly. 'I'll tell you why. It's because they've been pushed into the notion that these tests are "a woman's right" by a lot of busybodies who don't really know themselves what they are talking about. If they did, they would realise the influence in all this of the private medical schemes who see "recommended tests" and all the hocus-pocus about catching things in time as a nice little earner. Why these particular tests anyway? It's all so arbitrary. Why not mass random testing for cancer of the prostate? That's commoner than cervical cancer and kills more people. But no one goes around trying to boss men into having themselves poked up the backside at regular intervals when they've got no symptoms.'

'Catch most men letting themselves be bossed into that!' said Christopher, laughing.

Marcus, delighted at the inelegant turn the conversation had taken, added: 'Yes, they'd all be off before you could say "Drop your trousers"!'

Pauline got up from her chair and walked off into the kitchen. I was taken aback because, while I do agree that the prostate is an unsuitable topic for conversation over chocolate pudding, I've never known Pauline be particularly prudish.

In the sudden silence that followed, Vanessa, looking pink, said: 'Uncle Stephen, I think that was rather unfair to Mum.'

'Oh, come,' I said feebly.

There was another silence, in which Vanessa continued to glare at me with her mother's eyes, then Toby said awkwardly: 'Oh, actually, Vanny, I don't think Stephen knows – I mean, we haven't seen you for so long. We really ought to get together more often – keep up with the family news. No, what Vanessa means, Stephen, is that Pauline's very committed to this counselling she's taken on.'

'Council?' I said at random. 'But she's been a parish councillor for ages.'

'No, no – different spelling. You know.' Toby flushed, for some reason. 'She's recently become a counsellor at the Women's Place in Basingstoke. Women's problems. Separation. Maintenance. Domestic disputes. *You* know. And a general health-awareness programme . . . Of course I'm all for it. These centres really fulfil a great need . . .'

His remark was followed by a short silence which even Christopher, it seemed, did not feel like filling.

In every argument, it is said, it is not the argument itself we are defending but ourselves. I do sincerely believe that the current emphasis on 'catching things in time', trying to root out the seeds of mortality before they have even germinated, has become a neurotic preoccupation which should not be encouraged. Playing old doctor, as I do these days, I maintain that good doctoring is knowing what not to do, what not to set in train. Ah, but why does people's naive fantasy of being in control of fate grate on me so much? Because of what happened out of the blue to Sarah? Or for some other reason yet to be fully revealed to me or which I do not care to explore?

We got our pudding at last and, having had my destructive say, I spent the rest of the lunch working to smooth matters

over. In this I was assisted by Christopher and Marcus, and
by Toby, who hates not being on good terms with anybody
for very long, and will go through remarkable contortions in
the interests of 'seeing the other fellow's point of view', as if
this in itself were a prime virtue. ('Of course I absolutely see
what you mean, Stephen, about these tests – most interesting,
I must give it some thought. But at the same time Pauline
knows I do very much support her in what she's doing at the
Women's Place . . .')

Needless to say, Toby is the sort of modern clergyman who
both does and doesn't believe in the Resurrection of the body.
One Easter years ago I asked him about it. After all, as I said
to Sarah, I'm quite happy to have people ask me about my
own professional speciality, and so it seems reasonable to
suppose that he feels the same. I don't believe in the Resurrection myself, but then it isn't my job to, and I'm interested
to hear what people whose job it is make of it today. However,
Toby became tense when I tried to establish just what he
really thinks, finally retreating to a defensive 'Well, Christ lives
in us all, does he not?' Even Pauline, on that occasion, did
not seem to think this would really do, though she's usually
very protective of Toby. Quite right too, no doubt. It can't
be easy being a Church of England priest today.

Toby was back to his equable self over the cheese and
coffee. Their younger daughter had just got engaged: she was
not there, but Toby was expressing his unfeigned delight in
the whole prospect. I found myself envisaging him clearly, in
a way I never dare envisage myself, as a grandfather, at his
kindly best, presiding over an ever-increasing tribe. Pauline as
a grandmother I could not, for some reason, see so clearly.

I thought the varied disputes had been decently shelved.
But, as I might have guessed, Pauline returned to the fray: my
sister, as I have said, is a woman of principle. She worked the
conversation persistently back to her Women's Place – asking
me if I saw many battered wives in my practice, expressing
disbelief when I told her it did not often seem to arise.

'Well, I'm really very surprised. We see quite a lot of it
here.'

'Maybe Basingstoke is a rather different sort of area from
rural Dorset.'

'Oh, I don't really just mean in Basingstoke. People come

to us from the villages around as well. It's quite wrong, you know, to suppose that certain things don't happen in nice country districts.'

'Yes, Pauline. Thank you. I do know that. But "battering" isn't a medical term. Cases of injury wouldn't necessarily get classified under that heading.'

'But surely you'd *ask* if you had any suspicion?' said Pauline.

'Sometimes, yes. But sometimes not. It all depends – oh, on a lot of things. People need not tell me things unless they want to. I'm a doctor, not a social worker.'

She began talking to me about the counselling course she had recently taken. I always seem to be hearing about such courses these days. Marriage-guidance counselling, counselling for the single, grief counselling, counselling for those with too many children and for those with none, for those who have had abortions and those who haven't; for every grievance both real and imaginary and for every event from the irreparably tragic to the transient and commonplace – nothing, it seems, is either too horrifying or too trivial these days to escape the offer of counselling.

In the practice, and among our Health Visitors and Community Nurses, I've become something of a self-parodying music-hall turn on the subject. Now, in Pauline's living room, I launched unthinking into my usual routine.

Of course it was not well received. She heard me out and then said: 'Very clever, Stephen. But then you always were cleverer than me. Of course I don't aspire to your sort of knowledge. But I just happen to feel that what I'm doing now at the Place – helping people to talk through their problems – is a useful job within my capacities. Such as they are.'

'It may well be useful, Pauline, for some people. That, I wouldn't deny. Perhaps not for others, when it comes down to it. Their hopes may be raised unrealistically. Or they may be led to brood on things that are in any case irreparable. That's all I'm saying.'

'Well . . .' She looked somewhat mollified. 'But surely you'll agree it must help people to have the opportunity to discuss their problems – to communicate?'

'Why? Why, in every case? You can discuss something into the ground. It doesn't necessarily change anything. On the contrary.'

'Well, it helps people to have an insight into their problems. Surely?'

It was the third time she had said 'problems' in as many sentences. I should not have reacted so but I did.

'Problems, problems – I do wish people wouldn't flourish this word around and attach it to every nonspecific grief and grievance that flesh is heir to.' (I was back in my music-hall turn again.) 'The word misleads people into looking next for "a solution" and that's not usually a useful approach. Far from it.'

'Oh, I don't agree at all,' said Pauline, who had now decided to fight back. 'Why, I – we – had a case only last week, which achieved, well, some sort of resolution, anyway. Once the woman concerned had been helped by us to confront her own situation.'

'What happened?'

'Oh, she was able for the first time to really talk to her husband – to express to him all the hostility towards him she'd been building up for years.'

I burst out laughing: no doubt the nervous tension that seemed to have dogged this whole lunch was affecting me.

'That must have been a lot of use, I must say! And what next? Do the couple, having uttered appalling home truths to one another, then go on just as before? Or do they get divorced?'

'Naturally,' said Pauline, tight-lipped, 'if the woman decides in the end she wants a divorce, we will try to support her through that process.'

'I should think it might be the husband who decides he'd like a divorce, having been told what a brute he's been all these years!'

I was not, of course, being entirely serious, but I see that this in itself was probably as offensive to Pauline, in her present mood, as my words. I think it must have been, for the next thing she said to me was something extremely unpleasant about myself and Sarah.

She can know nothing about Sarah and me but what she saw of us together, and in any case she has no business to say that kind of thing, ever, to anyone.

I told her so, quietly, but in a tone that was evidently sufficiently emphatic to make others look nervously in our direction.

I went on: 'The trouble with you, Pauline, is that you want to control everyone. Husbands, children, women who come to your blasted Place, all those committees you sit on: the whole damn lot. Life, too. I sometimes get the impression you think even old age and death won't happen to you if you keep your tabs on everything enough. You think that God will recognise you as a Truly Responsible Person and make a special exception for you.'

It was a brutal thing to say and, naturally, was not well received. I'm not sure, on reflection, if Pauline in her heart of hearts believes in God. But, if she does not, then my words must have struck her all the harder.

When we left, it was Toby and Marcus who saw us off, both waving with exaggerated cheerfulness. Vanessa was indoors attending to her mother's sudden migraine.

I have described this occasion as I perceived it at the time. It is easy, now, some time after a subsequent event, to be wise. Hindsight supplies a slightly altered view of this tension-racked lunch – the last one, I think, at which Toby presided. Indeed, was my own aggressiveness and provokingness also due to the fact that I was picking something up subliminally? It is easy, now, to think so.

Coming back in the car it would have been easy, also, for Christopher and me, who feel the same in so many ways, to discuss Pauline at length. But I think we were both wary of such cosy self-justification, for where would it have got us? She is my only remaining sister, Christopher's only aunt.

After a few constrained remarks – probably we felt a little depressed, heavy with too much food and the consciousness of having been ungrateful guests – Christopher said gently:

'It's really just that neither of them seems to know anything, do they? So they both try to make up for it in rather heavy-handed ways.'

'Not know anything?' I said stupidly. I seemed to remember Pauline being a know-all to me since earliest childhood.

'No. They're innocent. For all that running around being involved with things, they both live rather on the margins of life, don't they? Not their fault. It's Toby's job, and who they are . . .'

He added after a moment, rather tensely:

'I suppose I see this in other people because, in a different way, it's one of the chronic problems that can hang over a writer. Not being part of life quite as other people are, I mean. A sort of permanent observer, an outside witness – almost a spy.'

Christopher very rarely speaks of himself as a writer or mentions his ambitions at all, at least in my company. At another moment I would have been glad to hear him talk a little more about himself, but this afternoon in the car, with the winter twilight already beginning to descend on the cold, quiet fields, did not seem the time.

Christopher was driving. I sat watching the skyline change, and remembered a snowy drive along this road when he was a little boy, with Sarah, and we'd had to stop and change a tyre. That vanished child whom this man had replaced was suddenly very clear to me, in his scarlet anorak that we'd bought him for a skiing holiday, handing me the wheel nuts one by one. I wished briefly, intensely, that I could have that dependent child at my side again.

After a few minutes, I said: 'Now I know even less how to broach the subject of our mystery relative to Pauline.'

'I know. She seems to be on a particularly interfering kick just now.'

'Quite. Perhaps we'd better just say nothing.'

'What, not ever to any of them?'

That was in fact what I meant, but I said: 'No, I see that perhaps that wouldn't work.' The apparently self-contained nature of the Baht Way situation, combined with its huge potential significance, created for me a peculiar difficulty. I felt it was like diagnosing a possibly life-threatening illness when there were no symptoms.

Christopher said: 'I've arranged to have a drink with Marcus in London early next month. Maybe I should say something to him then, but tell him to keep it to himself for the moment?'

'Yes, that would be a start. But do impress on him to keep his mouth shut till we've found out a bit more. When you mentioned Pauline interfering, I had a sudden hideous image of her getting on a plane to the Great City from Gatwick the week after next!'

Christopher smiled faintly and said: 'Yeah, taking her counselling handbook with her . . . Luckily I don't think she could afford it. They never have any money, do they? They never go anywhere.'

I thought about this for a while. Pauline, for whatever reason, has never had a job herself since marriage. She has regularly referred to their penury, which I suppose has made me perversely resistant to taking it seriously. But bringing up four children on Toby's salary must have been a struggle – or 'challenge', as she would prefer it. No wonder it has brought out some rather obsessional habits in her.

'We shouldn't forget, though,' I said, 'that Pauline does know the East and the Great City, or did once. After all, as well as being a child there, she was there for – what? Over two years as an adult. Much longer than I was.'

'It's rather difficult imagining her there now,' said Christopher. 'Of course, it was so long ago. And that City has largely disappeared. Buildings all different. No Europeans running the place any more.'

'Yes. Another life and time . . .' I was still thinking of Pauline. 'But people don't really change, do they, not in essential ways.'

'I've never been quite sure,' said Christopher. Nor, in fact, have I.

After a long, companionable silence, Christopher said: 'This Baht Way business – our mystery relative. That's about identity, isn't it?'

It was, I suppose, a writer's remark. Anyway, it took me a minute to see its scope.

'You mean, is he or isn't he connected with us?'

'Yes, but not just that. It's the Ugly Duckling story, isn't it? He grew up in that remote village knowing he looked different from everyone else but not knowing why. Or it's like one of those fairy tales in which the king's lost eldest son has been brought up as a swineherd. Or a changeling story, even.'

'Well, I just hope,' I said, 'that your changeling swineherd doesn't have too many grand daydreams about turning back in to a prince and being restored to his kingdom. It isn't as if we had a kingdom to give him.'

'Let's cross that bridge when we come to it,' said Christopher. I knew then from the way he spoke that he was plotting, but I did not then know what.

From that moment, I started to worry about the unknowable dangers that lurk in the Great Land these days. But I did not say this to Christopher. He was still pursuing his fairy tale, for after a while he said:

'I used to spend great chunks of time when I was away at school being a prince in disguise in my head. Or, if not a prince (I was getting a bit old for princes), then something else powerful and romantic – an international spy, even.'

'I never knew you did that.'

'I never told you, or anyone else. No one guessing was all part of it.'

Except for that one time after Sarah's death, whenever I saw him in his school setting he always seemed cheerful, extrovert even. Sarah and I were grateful that he had adjusted so well to being away from home and surrounded by other boys day and night. But perhaps this successful schoolboy persona was in itself part of a more elaborate game. Even then, he was quite a private person.

'You must have enjoyed that fantasy,' I said at last. 'I suppose it was an extension of those terrific pretend games you used to play on your own as a little boy, rushing about the garden talking to yourself?'

'Oh, those! Yes, I remember, but I used to try to get other, visiting kids to join in and some would, particularly the docile ones who didn't mind letting me do most of the inventing. But I could never get Marcus to understand what it was all about. I used to say "I'll be Captain Hook and you be Starkie" or whatever, and he'd say "But what for?" and keep wondering how we scored and how we'd know who was winning. And when it was a battle game he'd say things like "Now there's a free fire to me."'

'Typical! He'll go far, that young man – in his own line.'

'Mm, not sure, he's a bit lazy,' said Christopher at once. Adding, while I was still thinking about this: 'Just as well, really. It makes him a nicer person. Yes, I suppose my disguised-hero act at school was a follow-on from all those pretend games but by the time you're in your teens you're too self-conscious to try to draw anyone else into them. And I didn't so much do it for fun: it was more of a refuge, I think. A way of giving myself a rest by slipping out of my surroundings.'

'I've never had that sort of imagination myself; that comes from your mother's side. I wish I had had it, as a child anyway. I was eight when I went to boarding school, as you know, and quite unprepared for it after the very jolly, sheltered family life we'd led in the East. A pretend game or two might have been some sort of help. A place inside my head to hide.'

'Hide?'

'Oh, just from the usual school bullies.'

'What, you, Dad? I can hardly imagine it,' said my tough son, suddenly sounding young and vulnerable himself.

I grinned. But, like a gate opening in my mind, I saw again rather than recalling distantly the jeering faces of the Lower School gang in a ring round me. I smelt their spit, like the smell of my own fear which haunted me all that first dark endless English winter, heard their voices chanting, chanting – about me, my torn-up family photos, my purloined Meccano set, my destroyed model plane – heard, too, the voice of the largest one on the stairs behind me; *I'll get you, Mason, you sneak, you Matron's-boy, Matron's little bed-wetter – you're going to die, Mason'* – and felt his hand coming down on my neck. The gate banged shut again.

Now I heard myself say hastily: 'Oh, well, at least an experience like that early in life means that nothing again will ever be quite as bad. Public school, the army, being so damned ill with hepatitis, the Tessa business, starting medical training later than most of my contemporaries, never getting enough sleep in my first house jobs – I sailed through all that. Compared with prep school, it was all quite manageable and bearable.' Everything except Sarah's death. Yes.

'Yes, I've heard other people use the argument,' said Christopher, back to his usual self-possession, 'but it never, you know, Dad, seems to me to stand up. In the first place, by that same logic, one might as well do the most arbitrary and appalling things to a small child just as a sort of inoculation – stick pins in them, roast them at the electric fire – or suddenly tell them their mother's deserted them, or something . . . And, in the second place, it doesn't strengthen people to put them through things they can't really bear. It weakens them, in a radical way. I've seen it.'

I knew, really, that he was right, but I wondered how he

had learnt it. After a few minutes, he began to tell me.

'Do you remember I was back in the Great City last year on my way to Malaysia? It was the third time I've been there, and I was beginning to know it quite well.'

'Yes. I remember you telling me you'd managed to get inside that extraordinary tenement block somewhere near the old docks that the police leave alone because they know it's full of refugees from the Great Land and they don't want to interfere.'

'That's right. Ak Teem – "the Forbidden Place" – that's what the people living round about call it. It's where the old jail was once, either the same building or one on the same foundations. I looked it up on the nineteenth-century map. So the name may go all the way back. But it's a very odd name, because that phrase is used in ordinary speech to mean what it says but it is also used as one of the euphemisms for death, heaven, the afterlife or whatever.'

'How odd . . . Though I seem to remember that their language goes in for the same word having more than one meaning?'

'Yes. Well, anyway, I got myself taken into the Forbidden Place, and I met, as you say, a number of people who'd escaped from the Great Land. None of them wanted to say too much, you won't be surprised to hear, but through the person who was acting as my interpreter I got a general picture of the Great Land as repressive, sinister, corrupt – really just as bad as it was in the days of the emperors.'

'That's no surprise.'

'Quite. So much for those optimistic newspaper articles a few years back about the place having evolved an ecologically pure alternative life style. I remember, now, you and I talked about this after I'd been to Ak Teem. But what I think I didn't tell you then, and I'm not sure why but perhaps it was because I was shocked by it and wanted to think about it for a bit – what I didn't tell you was that I gradually realised that each of the men I spoke to seemed to have been tortured in . . . in a rather horrible way which they could hardly bring themselves to describe.'

'I see.' I felt he knew I didn't much want him to describe it now, but braced myself in case he did.

'But the point I am getting round to is that these men were

not in any way strengthened or helped by having survived such an experience, and come through it. I crassly thought there might be, at least, a pride and defiance in having escaped and being there, in the Great City, in freedom of a kind. But it wasn't like that at all. It was more as if they had had to draw on reserves of strength they just didn't have and couldn't have, and so they were completely knackered. They didn't even see their escape as any sort of victory over the system. It was more a final defeat confirming their own unworthiness.

'It was as if "the Forbidden Place" *was* the land of the dead, for them. You know what they reminded me of, when I thought about it afterwards? That story you told me yourself about the bands of people whose hearts weren't beating who were said to be roaming around in the Great City and outside it at the time of the Civil War. And that's an old myth, of course; it crops up regularly in their history. Well, these men I met, so depressed and disoriented – it was almost as if their hearts weren't beating any more. They'd had their identity destroyed by what they had suffered.'

After a while, when I too had thought a bit, I said:

'You don't think that Baht Way – ?'

He said at once, almost too quickly: 'Oh no, I shouldn't think so, really not. After all, he's been working more or less openly in the City, not apparently afraid to make himself noticed. Or to have hopes and plans and dreams. And it's known that there are quite a few of these itinerant workers, so called, in the City, whose presence is tolerated. No, I get the feeling, don't you, that Baht Way's heart must still be beating?'

The dark had come while we were talking. Off the main road now, on country ones, Christopher drove on full beam, once picking up in the frosted hedgerow the eyes of a hunting cat, nervously transfixed for the moment of our passage. Another wandering creature. Did its heart still beat, in hope and love and fear? I should be glad to get home tonight – to remove the extra jersey necessary in Pauline's rattling house. To shut the door and pour myself a Scotch and pick up my current Trollope or the *Lancet*, while Christopher typed mysteriously and used the phone in the front study that was Sarah's and which still has all her books in it. Much later, he would make bulging sandwiches, and we would watch the news together.

'What you told me,' I said, with a small laugh to cover the constraint I was feeling on the subject, 'seems to have taken us a long way from my prep school.'

'Has it?' he said. 'Has it? I don't think it has. My guess would be that what you suffered – what kids do suffer, when they are too young and weak to defend themselves or to understand what's going on – may be as awful to them in its way as oppression and torture are to an older person?'

'Well, yes, I think that must be right. In fact I got a bit of a shock, twelve years ago or whenever it was that your granny died, and I was going through her things. There was my first group school photograph – it must have been sent out to them in the East and she'd kept it with her personal things for the rest of her life – with myself looking minute and lost and rather scruffy in the front row. But what was so odd was there my tormentors were, whom I remember as all-powerful psychopaths – and they were all chubby, vulnerable children, too! And I thought, what a little mutt! How could I have been so terrorised by them? And yet, you know, recognising their horrible faces – I could name them all – I was still terrified.'

'I'm not at all surprised,' said Christopher firmly. He continued with that fluency of his that can sound almost flippant but is not: 'You'd been sent away from home to a cold, strange place, shut up in a prison of a school – Dad, it doesn't bear thinking about. Let's not think any more.' We were nearly home.

But I went on thinking, not then but afterwards, when Christopher had returned to his elusive life in London and my life had settled into its low-key winter pattern. I thought about what Christopher had told me regarding the shaken and depleted escapees from the Great Land. I thought quite a lot about Baht Way, and sometimes he appeared to me as a potentially dangerous cuckoo in the nest and sometimes, indeed, as the Ugly Duckling that at last fulfils himself in discovering that he is a swan. Twice, in these bird shapes, I dreamed at night of him, or someone who seemed to be him.

And I also found myself thinking of my first school, and of the time when I was very young and very much alone, far, far more alone than I am now when people wonder if I am 'lonely' on my own. Perhaps these thoughts came simply because Christopher had made me recall my prep school. But perhaps it was also because, at my time of life, you begin to know that eventually, if not just yet, another event will transform that fluid, continuing life into a completed destiny. For Tommy MacFarlane, for Sarah, for a handful of remembered and regretted patients, it came abruptly; for me, perhaps, slowly and mundanely after all – but it will still come. As if to be ready for that ultimate experience that none of us can fully undergo or fathom, however much technical knowledge of the process we possess, I have started tentatively connecting the remote, forgotten beginnings with middle years and the possibilities still to come.

PART III

'*That stretch of the waterfront which George tells me is called the Bundar is very lively, with many steam ships at anchor and smaller country craft sailing around among them – much coming and going too between the harbour and the shore. Half-naked coolies with headloads, and others carrying a kind of sedan chair just as I have seen in Mr Burford's pictures. I had plenty of opportunity to observe this scene of animation this morning from my bedroom window. We are staying for these few days with Mr Nicholls, the Deputy Customs Officer, who is kindly putting us up till our new quarters at the Mission School – which is just outside the town in a place called, in the local tongue, "Valley of the Flowers" – shall be ready for us. Both George and Mr Nicholls (who is a bachelor) say that, in spite of the business of the Port – which increases yearly – there is still no respectable Hotel in the City at which a European lady would quite like to stay. But then, of course, there are not a great many European ladies here as yet, certainly, I am told, few British ones. I do wish that one of my dear sisters could have accompanied me here: Cissie, in particular, I miss dreadfully.*

'*From the window, I enjoyed the view, but by the time I had bathed and dressed and breakfasted and the carriage had been brought round to take us on a tour of the City, the day had become so oppressively Hot that my head was aching and I was feeling quite out of sorts. Mr Nicholls put himself to a great deal of trouble to show us interesting things, and he and George talked most animatedly of native customs (some of which sound terribly unchristian in the general sense as well as the particular), but I did Not enjoy the excursion. The streets were so noisy with strange, throaty cries, and, though colourful with the bright signs and the people's blue and yellow clothing, so full of dreadful sights that I hardly knew where to look – beggars, some of them without limbs, thrusting themselves forward, little naked children Doing Things in the gutters, a mother selling red pimentos from a great basket and suckling her babe openly at the same time, and some men dicing before the door of what was surely a low tavern. George remarked to me that it was not unlike visiting Whitechapel, and a great deal better than the slums of Edinburgh where the Demon Drink reigns supreme. I am sure that is true, but then I am not accustomed to the slums of Whitechapel or Edinboro', and in England at any rate people are more or less respectably clad. He also said that at least most of the people here, even the beggers, look quite well nourished and Not Unhappy but, while this struck me also, it gave me little satisfaction: surely their apparent equanimity is that of heathen ignorance steeped in sin which does not recognise its own plight? I have read that Terrible Things are sometimes perpetrated in this Land in the name of their own benighted Faith, and human suffering is set at naught. The missionaries have great difficulty in tackling the matter directly because, of course, those in charge of the Free Port regard it as a Political one and do not wish to be drawn in to it. Trade, it seems, is everything, and these people's Immortal Souls nothing . . .*

'*Tuesday. Today George and Mr Nicholls took me to see the Mission School. They did not want to take me there before our new quarters (four rooms on the upper floor) were, as George so amusingly put it, free of sawdust and pails of whitewash and fit to become a palace.*

'*I feel I could face sawdust and whitewash with calm cheerfulness if only it were not for this Dreadful Heat, which is so unlike the pleasant summer heat we are used to at Home – more like sitting in a steam bath, and so Debilitating.*

'*What I find hard to face (and for dear George's sake I try to put on a brave face but it is not always easy) are the incessant strange noises here – the cawing of crows and other birds, the creaking of buffalo cart wheels, and water wheels, the crying of babies in hovels, the clanging of a great bell in a heathen pagoda – all sounds plainly audible, I fear, in the Mission School, which is an unpretentious building situated on land near the river where the main road north leaves the City.*

'*I also find it hard to bear the unceasing dreadful smell, both in the City and without, which I feel is not only constantly in my nostrils but gets into my hair and clothes and contaminates all food. George says this miasma is indeed partly the odour of the barbarous local cooking (oh, how I Long already for a plain roast beef and English greens) and partly the stagnant water that collects in the canals which have been cut in the outlying areas of the City for drainage. He says that all countries that have a hot season tend to be thus afflicted, and that we shall get used to it. Mr Nicholls, who has lived for some years in the country, seems indeed not even to notice it, but then I have come to realise that he has been much coarsened by the life he has been constrained to lead . . .*

'*Thursday. We shall be moving to our new home on Saturday. How I dread what lies ahead of me.*

'*George, who, poor man, found me weeping foolishly over my photographic likeness of Cissie, Clarrie and dear Mamma taken in the garden at Steyning, says that my Extreme Dejection is no doubt due to my probable Condition, and that, in a few months, if not before, I shall feel much more cheerful. I do pray he may be right. But, to me, it is almost as if I am dreading what I already foresee all too clearly . . . it presents itself to me like a remembered bad dream, but it is as if the memory lies not in the past but in the Future . . . Oh, how can I bring forth a child in this country? How can I dare hope that the babe I fear I am carrying will survive the rigours and the uncleanliness, spiritual and physical, of such a Place?*

'*Oh, the horror of it all – the sights, the smells, the sheer unchristian strangeness of everything! How will I ever bear it?*'

Poor Great-Aunt Alice. Her foreboding was well founded. That child died, and she lost two more before she managed to keep and bring up my great-uncle. I thought very much about her as I ambled around in Teyn Bira three days after my arrival in the City. I had exhausted the hygienic modern delights of the central districts by then and was beginning to trace the older, hidden City beneath, like studying an X-ray plate. In my nostrils was that pervasive old City taint which overwhelmingly recalled my childhood but which I had not tracked down again, except in isolated whiffs, till that morning. Like Mr Nicholls a hundred and thirty years before, Christopher has accurately diagnosed it as 'salt swamp water and old cooking oil'. To me, it was a breath of childhood and innocence and long-lost things, with only a hint of obsolete menace at its heart. But then the message of a smell is wordless; it belongs to another, older area of the brain, and this one made me feel illogically happy.

I knew, really, that this was not an excursion to a country that was safe because it lay in my past. It was a place which, despite appearances, had forgotten nothing, and that which is not forgotten goes on being a potent force. When, years ago, I had first read Aunt Alice's journal, I had patronisingly judged her perceptions to be all of a piece with the delicate, swimming, brownish copperplate in which they were penned. Now, at a recent rereading in transcript, they had come to me with greater meaning. Perhaps, through the shell of her mid-Victorian prejudices, Aunt Alice was sensing something more timelessly threatening and intransigent in this place, some genuine horror at its heart. She was no fool; and contrary to the impression given by those early journal pages, she was a survivor. After the death of her third baby (the second had expired soon after birth but this one, like the first, flourished for an agonisingly deceptive few months), she wrote no more for nearly three years. When she took up her pen again, 'Georgie' was already a robust toddler in the care of 'an excellent Amah', and she herself had become a brisk mission-school teacher fluent in the local tongue. The remaining volumes of the journal are filled with unalarming day-to-day matters, and seem to have been kept as an *aide-memoire* rather than a release for the anguished heart. She bore another child (my grandmother) and appears to have had at least two miscarriages – *'Our recent hopes were disappointed early last Sunday morning. I am on the mend, and should be myself again soon. No doubt it is God's Will and perhaps, as George says, really for the best in our modest circumstances'* – but the pain surfaces no more. Nor, if tales of Terrible Things taking place upcountry from time to time still reached her, did she see fit to mention that fact in her journal. Whatever endemic horror Aunt Alice had glimpsed in her early, vulnerable days in the country, she had buried and would not disinter.

I only realised once I was in the City that the crowded industrial district where Christopher had recently gone in fruitless search of Baht Way was the same Valley of the Flowers where the mission school once stood almost in open country. I wondered if he'd registered the connection himself. I also wondered whereabouts Baht Way's lodging was and whether he might have returned there. I had no means of finding out just then: I was not due to meet Mike Isaacs till later in the day. Although I'd recalled the name Teyn Bira from my youth, I don't believe I ever went there either as a child or as a young officer. The place must have been squalid then. Today it has benefited from the general transformation of the City, and no doubt the opaque green water running in the drainage channels is acceptably free of mosquito larvae; but it still has the air of a poor district, claustrophobic with its repetitive vistas down lanes where the houses have tin roofs and are festooned with television aerials. There were not many people about at that morning hour. From prefabricated sheds and older brick warehouses came the clatter and clang of metalworking and the massed whirr of sewing machines.

I knew, from a prewar map I have, where the late-nine-teenth-century mission schools had stood. But these, I also knew, were a replacement for the first 'unpretentious building situated on land near the river' where Aunt Alice spent much of her married life. Not a trace left of that: the river itself has been partly sectioned into a canal at this point; the grid-pattern lanes and their attendant ditches must be on reclaimed land. The very notion of 'place' as retaining some essence of permanence loses itself here. I had half hoped to find the later schools still standing, but they too have gone as I should have expected: their site must have become valuable. I did, how-ever, locate almost by chance, as I was walking away down a side street, what seemed to be the rump of a Gothic building with a new, bare end wall abutting on to the yard of a petrol station. It was marked by a neon sign 'St Saviour's Anglican Chapel', so I knew then that I had found one enduring trace of my Great-Aunt and Uncle's life work.

Locked, of course. The times of services, alternately in English and the local tongue, were painted on a fading board. I made a mental note of them, thinking to come back then to get a look at the inside and maybe find a family memorial plaque. By then, Christopher might be able to come with me.

Beneath the neon sign, at the other end from the garage, was a stone cross and, below it, what looked like a crude altar made from a packing case. On it stood two half-burnt candles in jam jars, a sealed bottle of the ubiquitous palm cooking oil, rice cakes at which the crows had been pecking, and several pieces of fruit, still fresh.

Poor Great-Aunt Alice, how dead she is now, down beneath the central office blocks! How outraged at this perversion of the true faith she would have been! Or would she – once she had lived in the country for many years?

As I stood looking at the food and trying to summon up what little I had ever read about the obscure, Manichean religion of good and evil still current in the City and the Great Land, I noticed that a cat beneath the wooden altar was gnawing with delicate precision at a piece of dried fish. It was a small, scruffy, whitish cat, as they always are in the East. Having demolished the fish, she stretched on her hind legs to inspect what else might lie on the altar – then caught sight of me watching her and vanished, snakelike, round the corner of a Gothic buttress. Down the street on tip-tapping high heels came two girls in the elegant little silk shifts of assistants in a central department store. As they passed by me, they paused a moment in their birdlike chatter and slid in my direction curious, slightly resentful glances. Had I come to their emporium to buy expensive presents for the folks back home, they would have been orientally solicitous of my every need, proffering the much-advertised Shopping City Welcome, but I was out of place here. Presumably Europeans are not seen much at St Saviour's any more. Does the Saviour himself ever visit, I wondered?

I was meeting Mike Isaacs for lunch at my hotel; I thought I might as well get back there early. I could sit for a while in the roof-terrace bar, gazing out from the eighteenth floor across the City in the dazzling brightness at the near yet inaccessible hills of the Great Land.

I had decided that I probably took against Mike that first evening because of my own jet lag, my disappointment that he was not Christopher and my unease when he told me that Christopher had managed to get himself through the frontier and into the Great Land. I had had three days now to get used to this news, and I determined this time to be pleasant to Mike at least. He, I suspected, had made similar resolutions about me, and as a result our lunch passed off in a warmer atmosphere than I had dared to hope.

He had had no further news of 'Chris' – nor had I – but then neither of us really expected to till he reappeared. There are no local mails these days between the City and the Great Land. Letters via the International Post Office take weeks, and anyway if Christopher had managed to bypass the attentions usually paid in the Land to the rare foreigner, he would hardly want to draw attention to himself by trying to communicate with us. Or so I had worked out.

Mike said that since Christopher was bound for Baht Way's distant home territory, he would have to reckon on two to three days' travel by train, with a number of changes, and then probably a whole day's haul up a mountain road by a local bus. 'Say, four days to get there, at least two to see Baht Way and turn round, and then four back. That's a minimum of ten days, but I guess we should allow more – say fourteen. And he only left on the Tuesday before you arrived – I told him he was cutting it too fine. So we shouldn't really start to think about seeing him again and hearing all the news of Baht Way till this time next week.'

I thought he might now be overestimating the time Christopher would need, in an attempt to appease my anxiety, but of course I was glad to be appeased. He spoke authoritatively, seeming to know a remarkable amount about the railways on the other side of the frontier – what meandering routes they took, how fast they went (or rather, how slow) and even what their varying gauges were. Presently I remembered that the Great Land was said to be an Eldorado for steam-train addicts: I realised that, in Mike, I was encountering such an addict. Encouraged by even my rather mild interest, he launched into an expert discourse as he ate his way steadily through the hotel's overwrought version of Danish smorgasbord and fish soup, Marseilles-style. I decided at this moment that he was both more eccentric and simpler than he had at first seemed.

Eventually I said: 'It's notoriously difficult to get permission to cross the frontier on your own and stay there for more than three days. I'm rather surprised that the authorities there will let you do it just to look at trains.'

'On the contrary, that's the sort of dopey reason they will accept,' he said at once. 'They think trains are kosher – harmless, I mean. Trains, or Nature. They've got a lot of great butterflies and birds and game up there as well. I put Chris on to that one, as he said that Nature meant more to him than locos. You have to produce a specialist club-membership card and a written introduction on the letter paper of an academic institution. Well, I fixed all that up for Chris, you see.'

'Very efficient of you,' I said, with mixed feelings – and then at once began to wonder what else this odd young man could fix.

As if he could hear what I was thinking, he said after a while: 'Understand – I love steam locos right enough. Have ever since I was a kid. They were just on their way out then, but a sort of uncle of mine, who'd spent his working life in the engine sheds at Pittsburgh, he used to take me to see them. It was like going to see a race of elephants that was threatened with extinction. But the fantastic old turn-of-the-century elephants they've got still on some of those lines in the Great Land aren't the only reason I frequent the place, I'll admit to you.'

I suppose I looked suitably enquiring but docile, for presently, after a few more hedging remarks and a story about a friend's father who'd been a prisoner for years in Korea, he began to talk about MIAs. He'd worked his way diligently through a great fishy tureen and most of the wine; he leaned towards me across the table on his muscular elbows and talked low but steadily, close to my face. To an outsider, our conversation must have looked intimate, but I sensed that his intimate communion was not really with me: I felt like a member of an audience at a lecture. Not liking to interrupt the intensity of his thought, it took me a few minutes to realise that 'MIA' must signify 'missing in action', and that Mike was not talking about the Korean War (as I had at first distractedly assumed) nor of course about the Vietnamese conflict of ten to fifteen years later, but about the Civil War here in the Great Land – or, more exactly, about the Troubles that preceded it. Some of the UN peacekeeping force involved in that had, he claimed, disappeared as the fighting upcountry spread, and were still unaccounted for.

'Still? But it's the best part of forty years.'

'So?' he said sharply.

I adjusted my reaction. 'I just mean, if they are still alive, as no doubt they could be – ' for he was staring fiercely into my eyes as a patient sometimes does when he does not want you to evoke even the possibility of death – 'then they must be getting on by now. My age, anyway.'

'So? You look pretty much alive and well to me. And what's age got to do with it anyway? Why, the other year a couple of old Japanese came out of the Malayan jungle and gave themselves up, and they were well into their seventies. They'd been there since World War II. Didn't even know about Hiroshima.'

'Yes, quite. But all I meant was that if there are indeed men still in the Great Land who were taken prisoner by the Lay Balint in the early 1950s, then they've lived out the greater part of their lives there. I – forgive me if I'm being slow, but I don't quite see what purpose looking for them would now serve?'

'Is it ever too late to liberate people?' he asked rhetorically.

'Well, in theory, no. But, in practice, I can't help thinking that men who've been there for decades, and presumably settled down to some sort of local existence, will have come so far from their original identities that it might simply be too late. For them to return now to New York or Sydney or Indianapolis or wherever. Particularly if they've never shown any sign of trying to contact outside and Western powers in all this time.'

'And if they've been prevented from making any sign to the outside world? If they've been banged up in camps in the northeast mountains all these years – would you still say "Don't bother with them"?'

'Of course,' I said, 'if you put it like that I have to agree with you.' His one-track view put me in a dilemma. The fact is, I did not really believe that those missing conscripts, boys for the most part barely out of their teens, were even now aging, hollowed men shuffling round barbed-wire enclosures in infinitely remote upland fastnesses, quarrelling over ladles of watery rice stew, gazing dawn after dawn, year after year, at the cold, alien sun. I thought that their young bodies had long since finished rotting in the stony earth of the ravines where they had been lined up and shot. My friend Tommy MacFarlane's body among them. That, at any rate, had been the generally received view: there were no survivors among those captured by the Lay Balint, or by any of the several splinter groups and secret forces by that time working in their various nasty ways in the dark centre of the Great Land.

On the other hand, you cannot prove a negative. I could not tell Mike that his appalling archipelago of hidden prison camps, more cut off even from the world than those of China, does not exist just because no one has ever reported seeing them. On the contrary, if it is even theoretically possible that some soldiers have survived as perpetual prisoners, and are without any chance of reprieve because no one believes they exist, then that adds the final touch of horror to their fate.

In addition, the very notion of such camps opens the further possibility – no, the likelihood – that newer prisoners are occasionally added to them. People were 'disappearing' in the Great Land during the Troubles; untold numbers of the indigenous population are thought, by outside sources, to have continued to 'disappear' over the intervening years. A few westerners are known to have disappeared in the literal sense in that they have entered the Great Land and never been heard of again. The word 'disappear' has usually been accepted as a euphemism for death – but what if it actually means the living death of being thought to be dead? *Are* you alive, in any real sense, if your heart still beats but your confinement is for ever and your spirit is completely broken?

I thought of the wandering spirits of those who had suffered in the Great Land and were said to be without a heartbeat – which is perhaps a mirror image of the same thing. I thought about the escapees from torture whom Christopher had encountered in Ak Teem, the Forbidden Place, and whose very identities seemed to have been damaged by what they had suffered.

I thought, with foreboding, of a number of things, all of them quite unpleasant.

But Mike was talking again, another persuasive monologue. It wasn't necessarily just a matter of prison camps, he said. Of course such camps existed – he'd had reports of them from reliable sources that he could not disclose. But, in addition, there were rumours of people of Western appearance glimpsed in remote provincial towns. One or two had even made signs to visiting foreigners, but had been hustled away by local people before contact could be established. One had managed to brush past an official group of train spotters who were on a station with their guide, and thrust a note in to a man's pocket. He made off, but the note had proved to be an appeal, in English, for money 'or any other help' addressed to an American living in Chicago.

'And when the note was transmitted, did the Chicago

resident recognise the signature, or the writing?'

'Ah, that I can't tell you. I'm a foreign correspondent, as you know. My work is all at this end.'

I did not say very much. The story suggested various possible explanations, not merely the missing-in-action one on which Mike Isaacs seemed fixed. I realised that I was beginning to feel exhausted by his insistent manner, at once communicative and secretive. I felt at that moment that he was a mythomane whose perceptions and advice were not to be trusted at all. My own unvoiced foreboding increased.

I decided to get him back to the subject of Baht Way – another man of Western appearance mysteriously living in the Great Land. Of course he could only have been an infant at the time of the Troubles. It occurred to me to ask Mike if he had any idea who Baht Way's natural father might have been.

'Baht Way hasn't,' he said promptly. 'And nor did his stepfather in the village, apparently. I told you that before, I guess. But I have a notion, yes.'

'Well?'

'It's not much of a notion. I mean, I don't have any one individual in mind – yet. But it's significant that the guy doesn't know where his name comes from. See, Baht's clear enough, that's his family name. His stepfather's family, I mean. They put their given names last in this part of the world.'

'Yes. Actually I did know that.'

'Well, Way isn't an ordinary name. Baht Way says he's never met anyone else called that. And it has occurred to me to wonder whether that was his real father's name – Wayne. You know, they have difficulty with "m" and "n" endings.'

'I suppose it's possible,' I said doubtfully. 'But Wayne used to be such an uncommon name itself in England that I think in that case his real father would have had to be an American. And if Baht Way's right in what he told you about the circumstances and time of his birth, that was surely before the UN forces arrived in the Great Land?'

Mike reluctantly conceded this, but said: 'He could have been an Australian, though. Wayne's been a common name there. And there were some Australians there early, along with the British.'

I pondered for a while. Christopher and I had accepted readily, from Baht Way's appearance, that he must be a close relative, and my sister Tessa seemed the only possible candidate as a parent. But we had, as yet, no direct proof at all, and now, probably in reaction against Mike's relentless theory-building and fantasising, I found my mind ranging over other possibilities, each more conjectural than the last. Could Father possibly . . . with some other European such as a secretary at the British High Commission . . . ? No, no, preposterous, for anyone who knew my parents and the nature of the life they led. But they say no man is a father except in so far as a woman tells him that he is: could I myself, as a young soldier, inadvertently, without even knowing . . . ?

Oh, don't be so absurd! The first woman you actually slept with, as you well know, was that kind, pretty nursing assistant in the convalescent home outside Perth where you were sent after your hepatitis to wait for a passage home. Get a grip on yourself.

That only left Tessa. And Pauline, of course. Pauline herself.

I decided to think about that later. Various things to do with Pauline had happened recently. Indeed, when I had left England, it had been with a nagging knowledge that I was abandoning an earthquake zone where my succour might be needed, though I did not yet know how strong further tremors would be.

Back to Tessa. 'If you don't mind,' I said, 'I'd like to get clear in my own mind what our hypothesis is about Baht Way and my younger sister. I'll run through it, if that's all right by you, and you can correct me on any point where you feel I've gone astray?'

'OK by me.'

'We know – or we think we know – that my sister Tessa, who was working for a voluntary organisation in the City when the Troubles came to a head in 1950, got caught upcountry where she was then with a small team on a fact-finding trip.' I paused at that point, suddenly wondering why none of us had ever thought to make enquiries at the time about the other members of the team. Or perhaps enquiries had been made and they had been fruitless? That was much more likely. There was a lot, I was coming to realise, that I didn't know. I decided to think about that, too, later, and went on:

'Anyway, she disappeared. And as, within a few days, the

roads going north and the river crossing at Jedu Sumna were all blocked, if she was still in what is now the Great Land itself she would have had no way of getting back.'

'Sounds likely to me – for a while. But the roads didn't stay completely blocked, and she did come back to the City quite a time before that reappearance of hers at the British army barracks that Chris has told me about.'

'But how do you know she came to the City before that?' His voice was level and easy; I tried to make mine sound casual as well.

He lent forward, eyes bright, and I realised then that he had something new and real to impart after all and, for whatever complex reason to do with himself, he had been waiting all lunch to produce it.

'Because it turns out that Baht Way wasn't born in the Great Land, as he thought and told me and I told Chris. He was born right here in the City in a charity hospital – St Saviour's, it was called. I think it was in Teyn Bira, in fact, not far from where he's living now, though the place itself has been pulled down.'

'How do you know he was born there?'

'Because it's on his registration of birth.'

'You've actually seen a birth certificate for him?'

'I've seen an entry in a register.' Triumphant tone.

After a pause to digest this, I said:

'I have been supposing all along that my sister – if it *was* her – gave birth to Baht Way in the stepfather's village where the boy grew up. I had rather assumed that, if Baht Way was registered at all, it would have been as a local under his stepfather's name.'

'So did I, and so evidently did Baht Way, but we were all short on lateral thinking. It struck me recently that there's no hard evidence that your sister ever went to the village at all. If she had, someone there would have remembered her and would have filled Baht Way in on her a little more. He told me: "I don't blame my mother at all for abandoning me. She gave me my stepfather, knowing that he would care for me. Otherwise, I would have died." That doesn't sound to me like she ever went back to the stepfather's home place herself.'

I saw now that Mike could sift and judge facts very well when his particular obsession was not involved.

'Well, the other day I did what I guess I should have done before. Baht Way himself tried, in fact, before I ever met him, but he got nowhere because he didn't have any name to go on, and, thanks to you and Chris, I did. "Work from the other end," I said to myself. "Make an informed guess and track it back." I was at the High Commission anyway, checking on one or two other bits of business of my own. I quite often go there. So I asked the guy I know there if he could look up the register of births for around 1951, which is when Baht Way has always said he was born. The guy obligingly did it and he was there.'

'You mean, Baht Way's birth was there? Just like that, all the time?'

'Hang about. Not just like that, no. There was nothing under that name. But there was – is – an entry for May 1951, that a Teresa Elizabeth Mason gave birth to a boy at St Saviour's Hospital in Teyn Bira. That would be your sister, wouldn't it?'

'Indeed it looks very much like it. Must have been. Well! There we are. Thanks, Mike.'

I wanted to say more. But I couldn't, for the moment. The proof, so casually delivered, of what for months past I had guessed, even begun to take for granted, was still deeply disconcerting.

At length Mike said: 'Of course, the entry doesn't actually prove any connection between that baby and Baht Way. For legal purposes, I mean.'

'No. I realise that. I was just working that out.'

'For that, you still have to rely on the remarkable similarity of looks.'

'Quite . . . You didn't get a copy of this certificate, by any chance?'

'No, it was just an entry in the records, and they can't issue duplicate certificates here – for that you'd have to apply in London, I guess. I've met that problem before. But now I've checked that there is an entry there, why don't you approach the High Commission yourself and take a look? It's your right, really, as you're the family.'

'Yes, I will. In fact, I was going to contact someone there anyway, for other reasons – a man I know who used to be the cultural attaché at the Embassy in Mexico City . . . Thank you very much, Mike, anyway. I'm most grateful.'

We both sat and ruminated.

'My guess,' said Mike, 'is that the guy who was responsible
for Baht Way abandoned your sister a while before the baby
was born, and the stepfather came to the rescue. You know
he met her in the City? He was working here.'

'Yes. Your original article said that. I'd forgotten. It all fits.'
The idea that this three-part drama, which had until now
been impenetrably cloudy, might all have been happening for
months only a couple of miles away in Teyn Bira, while
Pauline, oblivious, waited on the brigadier in Divisional HQ
up at the cantonment, shed a different light on the whole
story. I should have to think about this – ask Pauline a few
more questions about her search for our sister.

Pauline had definitely not arrived back in England till
autumn 1951: I was certain of that from my general knowledge of my parents' movements and my own at that period.
While I believed that Tessa might have given birth during
that year far from the City in some mountain fastness, any
time lapse between this and Pauline leaving the City herself
had not seemed significant. Now, it did. Why, if they were in
the same place, had Tessa not contacted Pauline? Fear? And
a shame almost impossible to experience today? Not really
very likely, that, from what I had known of Tessa in all the
years afterwards. Childish inability, then, even after all that
she must have been through, to grasp how desperately she
was missed? Desire to prevent any of us, even her sister,
knowing of the child's existence? Perhaps she had thought if
no one ever knew, and she quickly abandoned it, then in some
sense it would never really have happened. Like a young cat
or bitch too immature to nurture the litter she has inadvertently produced . . .

'I do wish,' I said, grimly busy with these thoughts, 'that
Baht Way's stepfather and Baht Way himself had managed to
overcome their inhibitions and discuss things just a little more.
It's going to be so damned difficult to discover the truth of
anything now.'

'These people are like that. Oh, they communicate all right,
but they wrap things up. They don't believe in speaking out.
Or embarrassing each other by asking direct questions. It just
isn't done.'

I had a sudden, wry image of Pauline, at the other end of
the world and the other end of time from our youth here in
the City, strenuously advocating talk, 'insight' and 'confronting
problems' as the key to human relationships. But then it had
not seemed recently as if this recipe was going to work any
more for Pauline.

'Why do you look like that?' asked Mike edgily.

'I didn't know I was . . . I was just thinking about my sister.
My older sister, I mean, the one who's still alive. Incidentally,
she doesn't know about any of this yet.'

Mike, an intriguer by nature, nodded, but made no other
comment. By and by he said: 'They say it's what their spirits
communicate that really matters.'

'They?' Distracted by another recent picture of Pauline,
angrily kneading dough as she listened to the radio in her
Hampshire rectory, I had no idea whom he meant.

'The local people in this part of the world. Baht Way
believes that he and his stepfather have always had good spirit
communication even though they were not father and son by
nature. They didn't need to explain things to each other. They
just understood. I guess that's one reason Baht Way's different
appearance didn't seem important to either of them. Baht
Way told me how really fortunate he feels he has been in his
life to have had a stepfather whose spirit so much matched
his own.'

'What about the stepmother?'

'He doesn't say much about her. She's dead now. I think
she was a decent enough woman. Rather ordinary – and she
had a lot of other kids to care for by and by. But he does
believe about his real mother that her spirit kind of matched
his stepfather's too, and that that was why life brought
them together against all probability and she gave him her
child . . . Hey, you know what he said to me after I'd first
heard about your family, and was able to tell him that the
person who was probably his real mother was dead? He said
that his stepfather will die soon, and that when this happens
he means to hold a spirit wedding for the pair of them because
he suspects that they never had a wedding in life.'

'A spirit wedding?'

'Yeah. It's quite an old part of the religion in this area of
the world. Spirit weddings are officially banned in the City

now as a "primitive superstition". There's a tradition of them at some old tombs just the other side of the border, beyond Jedu Sumna, and City people sometimes sneak over there because ceremonies conducted there are supposed to be extra potent. A bit of the marriage ceremony is read, I think, and there are clay dolls dressed in silk to represent the dead couple. They're melted afterwards in water, and food and money is left out for their wedding journey in the other world. So then all concerned know they've done the best they can for the dead, for eternity, and they can at last feel good about them and go home happy . . .

'You know,' he added, after a pause during which we both, I imagine, thought our own thoughts, 'I really do find these deep-seated beliefs speak to me. In myself, I mean.' To my surprise, there was the brightness of tears in his rather dull, dark eyes.

I came away from that lunch thinking long, speculative thoughts not only about Tessa but also about Pauline.

In fact, Pauline had been inescapably in my mind for other reasons. In retrospect, trouble should have perhaps been apparent to me at that lunch party in December. However, my first awareness of it dated from a visit from Toby in the late winter. I had been filling in for an absent colleague at morning surgery, had had a bite of lunch, and then returned home planning to finish off a paper I was writing. Suddenly Toby was there, on the gravel drive in front of my house, getting out of that battered little Renault of his. Toby is a poor driver, not so much dangerous as inconsequential: his car always carries dents and rusting scratches where he has misjudged width or parking spaces.

I made welcoming sounds which were the warmer for my curiosity about what had brought him. I never recall either him or Pauline turning up before unannounced in all the years I've been in Dorset. He embarked on an overcircumstantial tale about how he had just happened to be passing the end of my lane. I offered him some coffee.

' – You have had lunch, I suppose?'

'What? Oh yes, thank you, Stephen. Coffee would be delicious.'

I saw that he was not really focusing on either coffee or lunch. I made two mugs and sat down at the kitchen table.

He prowled around wondering aloud if I found my oil-fired Aga satisfactory. They had always had a solid-fuel one: more trouble of course, but 'since I work from home myself, stoking the Aga's always been one of my jobs, you see'.

I was wondering if he was in need of a loan to do up his kitchen, and was framing a tactful enquiry in my mind, when he said:

'What I've come to tell you, Stephen, is that Pauline and I are thinking, ah, of a trial separation.'

I won't pretend that I wasn't taken by surprise. Indeed silenced, for a moment. But like all general practitioners, I have been the recipient of this sort of confidence too often not to have developed a set reaction to it. So I said after a long silence, during which Toby continued to pace:

'I'm very sorry to hear that. Do you mean that she wants to leave you, or that you want to leave her?'

In my experience, that euphemistic phrase 'trial separation' nearly always covers one or the other truth. Toby stood still and flushed.

'Well, actually, yes, since you put it that way, I am thinking of, ah, making certain changes. But not out of the blue, Stephen, I wouldn't want you to think that – '

'No, I'm sure not, Toby. There's always a history to these things. Why don't you sit down and tell me, now you're here?'

I don't feel myself that his wife's brother is the best confidant for a husband preparing to leave, but I didn't think Toby would see it in that light. Toby, so committed to understanding the other fellow's point of view, expects a similar service from others.

Out it all came, or a version of it at any rate. Toby had clearly been practising in the car: the rehearsed phrases were launched on the air where they bobbed and floated rather than coming to rest as meaning: 'Been in a bit of a trough for some years ... Feel now I've come to a crossroads in my life ... Crisis ... Perhaps both of us have travelled as far as we can in one direction. Personally I'd be happy for us to take a new direction – a new lease of life, you might say ... Another dimension ... a different form of understanding – not necessarily less deep, merely wider. But. There it is. But.'

'But what?' I said obediently.

'But, well, Pauline doesn't want to change. Doesn't want even to talk about the idea.'

I bet she doesn't. 'I thought you two believed in talking things through?'

'Well, I'm quite prepared to – I want to.' An injured expression settled on Toby's aging cherub face. 'But she just gets angry at what I suggest, and then there isn't anything to talk about.'

'You mean, she won't agree to what you want?'

'It isn't as simple as that,' he said crossly. He looked away. After a silence, I said: 'Toby. Who is she?'

'Pauline – ?'

'I don't mean Pauline.'

Another thing I have learnt in a lifetime of family doctoring is that there nearly always is another relationship on hand when one partner in a long-term marriage develops an abrupt and untypical urge for what is usually referred to as 'freedom', 'space' or even 'being on my own for a bit'.

Toby flushed, and said after a moment: 'That's not really the point.'

'Men usually say that. Look, Toby, I'm not much of a one for counselling or insights or all the rest of the neo-Freudian stuff.' (I couldn't resist that dig in the circumstances.) 'I'm never quite sure what all these deep insights are supposed to be for, in an imperfect world with people subject to all sorts of other, outside pressures besides their own hang-ups. But I offer you, for what it's worth, my experience. Which is that, in the sort of situation in which you find yourself now, men often say that the third party is only an incidental factor. I don't think that's necessarily true, but they say it. I think men feel foolish admitting that they are in the grip of a passion strong enough to override other considerations. Women, on the other hand, are more likely to justify wanting to break up their marriage by saying that they've met the love of their life. Again, I'm not sure that's true, in every case, but that's how they see it.'

I think this difference is interesting, but it was rather a lot to expect Toby, in his state of mental turmoil, to be interested in this way. He looked most unhappy, his double chins tucked in, his lower lip almost trembling. He had hoped to spread his floating canopy of words such as 'crossroads', 'change of direction', and 'not necessarily less deep but wider' over the abyss that had formed beneath himself and Pauline. The attempt had not worked; the abyss was there. I could see it, and so could he, and he was distressed and frightened. Could it really be that Toby Baird, nice chap, good servant of God and the Church, good family man, loyal husband and partner on life's long road, was going to have to revise his view of himself – and, worse, see other people revise their view of him also? He sat down at the table and put his head in his hands.

After a bit, to get him started again, I said:

'By the way, what's her name?'

'Helena. Helena Davis.' I could hear in his voice the emotional resonance surrounding it. He added after a moment, with transparent pride: 'She's a deputy headmistress. Near Poole – yes, down this way. An awfully good sort of person. She hasn't had an easy life. She was involved for years with someone who let her down – an absolute bastard. If you'll forgive the word.'

'Toby, I'm not one of your parishioners. I'm not likely to be shocked by anything you say. Tell me whatever you want to.'

'It's just that life has been so damnably unfair to her.' He lifted one hand and rubbed it across his forehead and eyes. I could see that, at this moment, he was really suffering.

'I do feel most strongly,' he said after a pause, 'that she should have her chance to fulfil herself properly in this world.'

'Can't she do that without you?'

There was another silence, during which I felt slightly ashamed of the last remark. Then he said passionately, as if debating with someone other than me:

'I mean, why should *she* miss out on her chance of family life, of parenthood? Why should her happiness be sacrificed to – other things? Helena would make a wonderful mother, too, I just know she would. And something as positive as that cannot be bad. Stephen, I keep trying to explain that to Pauline. I keep telling her that, with good will on all sides, we can surely work something out. She just doesn't want to know.'

'You mean some sort of sharing arrangement?' I said.

He balked at that word, trying belatedly to re-erect his

canopy. 'I just mean some arrangement that might meet everyone's needs. Or most of them. Taking these various needs into account. With give and take on both sides. There'd have to be compromises, of course, I accept that. I'm prepared to compromise – do whatever I can . . . Helena's prepared to compromise.'

'But I suppose Pauline isn't?'

'No.' He looked hunted. 'She won't. Even though I've explained that this isn't a desertion – that we'd still go on. In many ways, that is. I mean, I'd still be there most Sundays and often at other times too. She'd still have my love and support – '

'Rubbish.'

'What?' His head jerked up, and he stared at me out of his fearful blue eyes.

'You've no right to say that,' he said angrily after a minute. 'I care for my wife. I always will.'

'No, you don't. I'm not blaming you for that, Toby. We can't necessarily rule our emotions. But the fact is that, at the moment, you neither love Pauline nor care for her.'

'Well, I'm trying to do my best for her – for all of us – in very difficult circumstances,' he snapped back. I preferred him more openly angry.

'No, you aren't. I'm not saying that I or any man would do any better in your position, but doing the best for Pauline you are not. You are trying to manipulate her and push her into allowing herself to be relegated to a sort of retired-senior-wife role. You'd go on pretending to be married to her and turning up when it suited you and for the sake of appearances, and all the time you'd be living the most significant part of your life elsewhere. That's your plan, isn't it? Or something like that.'

He was silent.

I went on: 'But Pauline – if I know my sister – is the last person to let herself be relegated. If she had been, neither I nor anyone else need have been told about it, or not for some time anyway. But she won't play, will she? So you're now thinking of leaving her.'

Head in hands again, he moaned: 'I don't want to leave her.'

'What about your profession, if you do?'

'That's just it! At least – ' He had the grace to look a little embarrassed at what he had said, and added quickly:

'Of course, that's not the only reason I don't want to take the drastic step of leaving. Far from it. But I'm afraid it's also true that, even today, a minister of the Church of England can't . . . that is, it isn't usually possible . . .'

'You mean, if you leave Pauline in any public way, you'll get the sack?'

'Well, not absolutely certainly, of course, but in practice . . . That's why I did hope – perhaps it was foolish of me, but I want to do the best for everyone, I really do, Stephen. I did hope that somehow with discretion and good will on all sides . . .'

'Suppose Pauline herself decides she wants a divorce after all this? That would leave you free to marry Whatsit – '

'Helena.'

'Yes, Helena, sorry. But then you'd definitely be out of a job, wouldn't you?'

'Oh God, Stephen!' he said vehemently. 'It seems so bloody unfair! So hard on Helena – apart from everything else. These days, if I were anything but a clergyman – a doctor, say, like you, or a lawyer, or a headmaster even – a divorce wouldn't destroy my career. But in my case I could actually face a sort of court charge – in Church Court: "Conduct unbecoming to a Clerk in Holy Orders." The Church is so damned reactionary and old-fashioned still. I've been saying that for years.'

'Well, but Toby, it seems to me that the Church is entirely consistent, within its own terms – which are also the terms of your contract, so to speak. If priests, of all people, don't keep their promises made before God, and the Church is to condone this, how would that make the Church look? You might argue a case for an unfortunate vicar whose wife had left him and he'd done his utmost to get the woman back before looking elsewhere, but that would hardly apply in your circumstances. You made promises to Pauline in church, Toby. "For better, for worse, till death do us part." I was there, and I'm sure you remember the occasion quite well too.'

Looking very black, Toby said after a while:

'Of course I regret it, Stephen. And feel guilty. Of course I do. But "for better, for worse" – that's really just an ideal, you know. Naturally clergymen try to live up to their ideals, but we can't always manage it any more than the rest of you can.'

'Oh, really?' I said. 'I would have thought an ideal was just what "for better, for worse" was not. I would say it was, on the contrary, a good practical recipe for hanging on through a bad patch. I always found it so, anyway.'

I had said to Toby that nothing he recounted was likely to shock me. I did, however, find myself shocked by the view he had just expressed. I have never expected much of Toby, but I did not expect, either, to see him in the guise of a dishonest broker murmuring that business is business and that's just the way of the world, you know . . .

He must have sensed my withdrawal from him. His face seemed on the point of disintegration.

'Oh, Stephen,' he moaned. 'The Church has been my job all my life – my livelihood. I just don't know what to do. I'm fifty-five. I don't know how to do anything else but be a vicar. And it isn't just my daily bread. There's Pauline to consider, from that point of view also. I'm at my wits' end.'

I believed him, and liked him better again. I saw how much he must have keyed himself up to this encounter, hoping desperately and against all likelihood to find in me an ally who would tell him: Yes, Pauline must see reason about this – things must go on, on the surface, as they always have. My refusal to play had broken his fragile nerve.

'You do have a problem,' I said heavily. I was already envisaging awful family conferences.

'I know I'm pretty much a fool, Stephen,' he said abruptly, raising his head from his hands. 'I do know that – I always have. I'm nothing like as intelligent as you. Or Pauline, come to that. I never did particularly well at school. But I always wanted to be a clergyman, ever since I was a kid. It seemed a fine thing to be; the vicar was an important man in the little place where I grew up. My family made sacrifices so that I could stay on at school, and I really worked so hard to get into the college. I have tried, all my life, Stephen. Perhaps not always in the right way, but I have tried. Made the best of myself. Or so I thought. And now I can't even do what I want for Helena. I'm letting everyone down . . . Oh God, I'm sorry to blub like this . . .'

'Don't worry. In a doctor's surgery people often cry.' It must have sounded rather stony, but it is the plain truth. I pushed the roll of paper towel towards him and, as an afterthought, made some more coffee.

When he had blown his nose, I said: 'Just let me get one thing clear, though. You said something a few minutes ago about how Helena should have her chance of parenthood too, and how she'd make a good mother. Excuse me asking, but is there actually a baby on the way now? Is that what's precipitated all this?'

'Oh no, not yet,' he said distractedly. 'But I can't deny her this indefinitely. She's thirty-seven – thirty-eight soon. It's her *right* to have a child.'

'There isn't any "right" to have a child,' I said. I have had to say it to different people many times before. It always makes me feel sad.

' – But my dear old lad, if you're really set on giving this person a child, how on earth did you think you were going to keep everything else running smoothly? Suppose your bishop got to hear about the baby?'

'I know it probably sounds very stupid. Just a dream . . .'

There was another silence between us, during which I reflected, but did not say to Toby that, without dreams, very few heartfelt projects, including marriage and child-rearing, would survive. I could hardly risk encouraging him in his visionary folly.

He said: 'Can I ask you something, Stephen? Did you ever fall in love with anyone other than Sarah?'

I was about to say yes, when I realised that he meant 'while you were married to her'. It was a relief; I did not want to speak of Jill to him.

'Not seriously in love with anyone else, no.'

'You had your difficulties, though, didn't you? I don't mean to pry, Stephen. But Pauline did tell me . . . And she mentioned it again recently . . .'

I waited, and presently he went on:

'Pauline ran into Sarah in Oxford, didn't she, accompanied by someone? She thought it her duty to tell you.'

Why should he speak of this now? It didn't add any weight to his own case. Rather, the contrary. But I knew why, even if he did not really know himself. He was trying to get his own back on me for the suffering of the last half-hour.

Against my conscious thoughts about the things to which Toby referred – so long ago, survived and over if never quite eradicated – I felt my heartbeat accelerate. Anger stiffened my neck and shoulders.

'Pauline and her "duty",' I said. 'What business was it of hers? How Sarah and I conducted our lives was our affair and no one else's. At times, Toby – as I possibly don't need to tell *you* – my sister can be a spiteful troublemaker.'

'I've thought that myself,' said Toby. 'Just once or twice. Some time ago now. And then again recently.'

He looked at me, his face aghast and still at the heresy he had just uttered. Then he collected himself, and spent the rest of the afternoon, till I managed to send him on his way, telling me what a good wife Pauline had always been (had); and how much he owed to her, which was no doubt true. I let him tell me.

It is easy, in retrospect, to rewrite the history of a marriage, as if the seeds of its destruction were there from the start. Easy, and usually false. It has always seemed to me that no marriage, including the best and most lasting, can be without its endemic strains. It doesn't 'take two to break up a marriage' in the facile wisdom of today. It takes one person with an obsession. Before, Pauline had been the one with the obsessions, but they had always been of the kind that tend to keep a marriage going: her use of what Christopher called 'the marital We' even when referring to actions or thoughts that were simply her own.

I said this to Christopher when he came down shortly afterwards for the weekend. I added that it was a fine irony, among others, that Toby, who had always seemed to cooperate enthusiastically with Pauline's PR for family life, should now have changed tack so drastically.

'But has he changed?' said Christopher. 'Perhaps he hasn't, and that's just the trouble. My guess is, he's enjoyed being father-of-a-family so much he wants to go on doing it. His kids are all grown up now, so he has an urge to push off and found another family while there's still time. Like he says, it's something positive working in him, in a way. He's a seed planter. And poor old Pauline's a used-up field.'

Christopher spoke with dispassionate interest, like one

observing the habits of an alien tribe.

In any case, Christopher was rather less interested in Pauline and Toby at this point than he was in the remote events that the newspaper report on Baht Way had revealed. By this time, he was in contact with Mike Isaacs, had received more details than had been in the original story, and had had at least one long-distance telephone conversation with Mike. Mike sent us a copy of a small photograph Baht Way had entrusted to him. This had apparently been taken some twenty-five years before when a travelling photographer had visited the family region, and showed a teenage version of Baht Way flanked by stepfather on one side and two step-brothers on the other. The stepfather may not then have been an old man in years, but he seemed worn by time and labour. His face was weathered, his mouth fallen in over gums from which most of the teeth had gone. Baht Way, his hair cropped like that of his two young stepbrothers and clad, like them, in a high-collared jacket and three-quarter-length cotton drawers, was a head taller than any of them. He did not look as much like Christopher as he was to as an adult. Instead, he bore a disconcerting, hallucinatory resemblance to a cabinet photograph of my mother's brother at a similar age in the uniform of a Dartmouth cadet. (That boy went down in the Battle of Jutland in 1915.)

All in all, our conviction that Baht Way must be my nephew and Christopher's first cousin strengthened and solidified during this spring, so that, when we spoke of it to one another, we no longer bothered to qualify our remarks with 'if' and 'possibly'. There also solidified then, I now see, my own false mental picture of the entire drama of Baht Way's conception and birth taking place in some remote mountain fastness in a Great Land racked by civil war across which Tessa had no chance to return to the world from which she had come. No doubt I preferred to believe that was how things had been. In fact I came to see Tessa in my mind as something of a Persephone figure, renouncing her former identity, born away to an Underworld of the heart and mind from which she could make her eventual escape only by a second renunciation and loss. This romantic version of events may seem inappropriate to the untidy, noisy, unhappy woman that Tessa in later years became. But no doubt I also preferred to remember

Tessa as the glowingly innocent girl she had once been. And
indeed I put her chronic unhappiness down to her return to
everyday Western life for which her sojourn in the Other Place
had for ever unfitted her.

Meanwhile, Christopher and I still had not revealed Baht
Way's existence to Pauline. It would be too much, we said to
each other, to load her with this information at the present
time. She was entirely preoccupied with whatever Toby might
now be planning or doing, and this was hardly surprising.
Long telephone calls from her punctuated my musings on
Tessa's past. It was rather as if the Tessa–Baht Way story were
some complex piece of music, in a minor key, which was
coming in snatches from a distance and which I could only
imperfectly hear. Then Pauline's voice would break in, loud
and close to my ear, with a wholly irrelevant major theme –
which, however, as I listened, seemed tantalisingly to have
chords or fleeting pieces of phrasing in common with the
distant, other melody.

Presently it came to me that this was probably because
Pauline was now adopting the same scathing, exasperated tone
about Toby that she had used for years about Tessa. Toby,
'obviously' had 'gone slightly off his head'. If only he could
be 'got to a psychiatrist', this treatment might lead him to see
the error of his ways.

'But Pauline, psychiatry isn't some sort of emergency-inter-
vention technique. Anyway, I can't refer Toby to a psychiatrist
if he doesn't want to see one. Which he tells me he doesn't.'

'But look how he's behaving! Stephen, you can see he's sick.
It's self-evident. Quite frankly, I think he's become quite irrational. I've been wondering if it could be a food allergy . . .'

I listened while she told me about this interesting article
she'd read on people whose personalities disintegrated when
they ate the wrong sort of bread. Listening was easier than
trying to explain to my sister that if her husband wanted to
leave her that was not in itself a sign of insanity.

I felt for her, since Toby's behaviour seemed infuriating, but
not in any way out of character, as I had always known him.
Although he had announced to her that he 'might have to
leave to be fair to everyone', he was, she told me, around the
house more, if anything, than usual, and was busying himself
with putting up extra shelves in the vicarage's dilapidated

pantries and scullery. He said they would 'come in useful for Pauline' and that he 'didn't want her to feel neglected'.

There was an excusable fury in Pauline's tone when she recounted this on the phone to me. Then her voice cracked and I thought that, for once, she was going to cry, but instead she hurried on:

'Of course, he won't actually leave, Stephen. That's obvious.'

I made an interrogatory noise, my standard noncommittal one.

She said impatiently: 'Of course he won't. Don't these shelves and things make it clear? He's just playing little schoolboy games and is really terrified that I might take him seriously. He hasn't got the guts to go. Not him. He's always been a coward.'

I was inclined to take the same view. The contempt in her voice was so great that I did wonder, in passing, whether to ask if she was sure she wanted to retain a husband she apparently despised so much. (All right, I know really that marital attachment does not function upon such rational lines. I did not ask.)

But we were both mistaken about Toby. A week or so later he appeared at my door. He seemed shaken and did not stay long, but 'thought I ought to know' that he had left home – 'just for the moment' he added, typically. There was a fresh dent on the mudguard of his car and the back seat was piled with heterogeneous belongings – loose clothes, books, some framed photos, a pot plant that had spilled its earth among a lot of ecclesiastical grey socks. I wondered whether he or Pauline had dumped this lot in the car and in what circumstances, but did not like to ask. I did not ask, either, if he had let anyone else know what he was up to, but very much hoped he had not – particularly not his seniors in the Church. Least said, soonest mended. Pauline might still be right, it might just be a silly game, though I did not think so. It must have taken a remarkable degree of resolution, in his position and with his personality, to go at all.

I offered lunch, but he said, looking hunted, that he could not stop – that he was 'already late the other end' – and drove jerkily off, presumably in the direction of Poole.

I tried several times later that day and the next to ring

Pauline, but the number was unobtainable. I guessed that she had left the phone off till she had rearranged her ideas and the expression of them.

I tried to ring Christopher to impart the latest development to him. But then and for the next few days I got only his answerphone. When he eventually rang back he just said he had 'been out of London', but followed this up with a promise to come down to Dorset again very soon. I have known Christopher like this at intervals over the years: unforthcoming in a way that is not typical of him, solicitous but a little remote. I have always assumed, without speculating much – none of my business – that such behaviour is a sign that he is busy with a girl. Or a woman, I suppose I might say these days.

Before Christopher did appear the following Sunday, the feeling that Pauline might want me to visit got the better of me: I drove over to the Hampshire village to see if she was in fact at home. The weather had become suddenly mild; the birds were singing passionately, green haze was thickening on the bare hedgerows. On such a day it was difficult not to feel light-hearted. When I stopped at a pub, I was able to take my bread and cheese to a table outside. The buds were big and sticky on some horse-chestnut trees across the road; I cut some short branches to take to Pauline. At one time I did this each spring for Jill; she used to put them in water, where the buds would gradually unfold into delicate, feathery leaves, as confident of their right to exist – at least for a week or two – as if they had still been attached to a tree. They used to make me think of our rare, snatched, hidden holidays together. Living in London, Jill loved these country offerings. I don't know where she told her husband they came from. Regents Park, maybe. Or maybe he never asked.

At least, I thought, I have never been party to the destruction of a marriage. Neither my own nor, years later, Jill's. That's an achievement, of a sort, to set against the losses. That morning, driving to Pauline's and remembering the bitter tone in which she had last spoken to me of her husband, my thought comforted me.

Pauline was at home. 'Oh, it's you,' she said in a kind of exasperated relief, as if she had been expecting me for some time. She led the way straight back into the kitchen, where she had apparently been listening to the radio as she stood at the table kneading dough. I say 'listening', but when I asked her if she minded my turning it off she snapped: 'No, of course I don't mind. I wasn't paying attention to it anyway.' She returned at once to her kneading. There was a 'Give Peace a Chance' poster on the wall behind her which, to my knowledge, has been there for several years, and a vase of primroses by the radio were withered brown and dry. For something to say, I asked her what she was making with such concentration.

'A batch of decent loaves with stone-ground flour. I really can't stand that poisonous stuff from the baker's any longer.'

'Are the children coming for the weekend?' I was wondering who was going to eat this substantial quantity of bread.

'Vanessa said she was. And Plod, of course.' Plod is at the polytechnic in Southampton. I have an impression of Pauline making frequent journeys there, bearing cakes and blankets and bringing back washing.

It still looked a lot of bread, even if Plod was to take a consignment back with him. I remembered Pauline's recent preoccupation with food allergies, and had a sudden image of her wrapping up loaves and sending them over to Toby in Poole. He wouldn't be able to resist eating them and thus, like a magic potion, Pauline's home baking would triumph over the poison of sliced wrapped bread that has perverted his heart and mind, and he would return to her.

This fairy-story notion was reinforced a few minutes later, when I realised that the venom with which I had last heard her speak of Toby had now been transferred to Helena Davis. Toby – 'poor lamb, I feel for him so' – was no longer a despicable coward playing silly games but the almost innocent victim not only of poisonous food but also of a poisonous person. If Pauline, determinedly thumping and slapping her dough, was forced to become a white witch, that was because the unknown Helena was a black witch – 'a nasty, cold, scheming person who's obviously taken cynical advantage of him'.

'Have you met her, then?' Apart from curiosity, I had a more specific reason for asking this. Pauline paused only fractionally before answering:

'Not actually met, myself, no. You can't imagine, surely,

Stephen, that I would want to meet her? But I have a friend at the Women's Place who used to live in Poole and whose children went to that school she is supposed to teach in. She – my friend – remembers This Person quite clearly, and says she knows how to ingratiate herself with people and do showy things like putting on the Christmas play, which makes the parents say: "Isn't Miss Davis wonderful?" ' (Vicious mimicry.) 'An obsession with being centre-stage herself, I gather. She's never been married, apparently. According to what my poor old Toby's let slip about her, I suspect she's one of those frustrated, childless creatures who take out their resentment on wives and mothers. But she must be clever, you know, Stephen. Very clever.'

'Actually,' I said, 'I rather think I've met her. Several years ago now.' I had only realised this thinking about it in the car on the way over.

'No – *really?*' The large, pale eyes set below the seamed forehead stared into mine, avid yet afraid. *Tell me. No, don't tell me. I don't want to hear. I have to know.* Patients are thus, when they come to hear the dreaded result of a test. 'Where did you meet her?'

'At a Health Authority subcommittee I was on. She only came a couple of times, I think – some issue to do with the school psychological service, it must have been.' Weakly, in the face of Pauline's furious stare toning down whatever I might have said, I went on: 'She didn't actually make much of an impression on me, which is no doubt why I didn't at first connect the name or the job when Toby told me about her – '

'Oh, Toby told you first, did he?' Pauline didn't like that. What other betraying things might Toby have said to me? Pauline has always resented the idea of others talking in her absence about anything that concerns her, even something trivial.

'Yes. I asked him, so he did ... Yes, Helena Davis: all I recall is that she seemed quite ordinary – in a neat, pleasant, primary-school teacherish way. Not unpretty, but nothing special. Certainly not brilliant or anything.' I had thought to cheer Pauline up with this tepid and true portrait of her usurping rival, but as soon as I had spoken I realised that this was not what Pauline wanted to hear.

'She's a career woman, of course,' she said darkly. 'She pushed her way up and now she thinks she's entitled to have her cake and eat it. All that – *and* someone else's husband. The worst sort of modern materialist grabber. This beastly world is full of them.'

Struggling mentally with an image of Toby as a cake, I murmured something placatory about it being fairly usual for a woman to have both marriage and career these days. That wasn't the right thing to say either, but Pauline let it pass. She set the dough on the Aga to rise, and went to wash her hands at the sink. As I stood there, trying unsuccessfully to recall anything else I had ever heard about Helena Davis, it occurred to me that she was not unlike Pauline herself. Less strident (but I had only seen her in a professional setting); earnest, a little bossy, devoted to 'her children'. Yes, I thought wearily, she would suit Toby just as well as Pauline and more so. If she had been the flamboyant manhunter of Pauline's imagining, then the affair would hardly last. As it was . . .

'What I can't forgive him,' Pauline said with her back to me, in a different, wretched tone, 'is the way he went and did this behind my back. All that lying – telling me he was going to the dentist again in Southampton when he was really going to see *her*.'

'But my dear old thing, if he was going to commit adultery – or even if he was only going to hold hands in a teashop,' I amended quickly, seeing Pauline's face as she turned round on this remark, 'he was bound to do it behind your back. I mean, he could hardly do it in front of your face, could he?'

'He lied to me, Stephen.'

'Well, of course he did. In these circumstances people don't have much choice but to lie. If they want to keep everything in its place, that is, including their marriage. Couldn't you look at it differently and give him credit for that, at least?'

As if she had scarcely heard me, Pauline went on in the same hypnotic tone: 'And he'd have gone on and on lying, living a lie . . . if I hadn't found him out.'

This was news to me. I had assumed, from Toby's account, that he had been the one to reveal all to a previously unsuspecting Pauline.

'How did you find out? If that's not an impertinent question.'

'I was suspicious. Things didn't add up. It was strange that, if he was in Southampton, Toby didn't bother to see Plod, and once when I tried to send an eiderdown over with him he made such feeble excuses . . . So I rang the dentist's receptionist to check whether Toby had had any recent appointments. He hadn't since before Christmas.' This said with a note of triumph.

'Perhaps it might have been better if you had not found out.'

'*What?*'

'Oh, never mind,' I said hastily, 'I expect some sort of crisis was coming between you anyway. That's what Toby said.'

'It's not true. She's made him believe it but it's completely untrue. We were fine. Until *she* came along . . . Stephen, I want you to go and see her.'

'Oh, Pauline, I can't possibly. Surely you can see that.'

'Why not? No, I don't see.'

'Because, why, because they've both been grown-up for twenty or thirty years. So have you and so have I – longer, in fact. I can't possibly play the role of Dutch uncle or outraged brother-in-law at our collective time of life. It wouldn't serve the slightest purpose. What exactly would I be supposed to say to her, anyway? "Leave Toby alone, I won't have my sister upset"? "You're a bad woman and I shall tell the Local Education Authority"? "Damn it, madam, if you were not a member of the female sex I would give you a good hiding"? For heaven's sake – '

We wrangled about this for a while. Accusations of cynicism, lack of moral sense and other things, to which I tried not to listen, were flung at my head. Eventually Pauline burst into tears and wept for a long time. As I stroked and patted her, I reflected that at least my useless, cynical presence (yes, yes, I agreed with that) had provided the opportunity for her to give way to grief. Which I suppose was really what I had come for.

By and by I managed to steer the conversation on to the most worrying and practical aspect of Toby's situation: his job in the future, if his behaviour were to continue and become generally known.

Suddenly, in the middle of my tentative enquiries about her rights in Toby's pension and the possibility of expeditious early retirement, Pauline said:

'He needn't think he can get away with it, you know – not with anyone. All our friends will side with me.'

'I expect they will.'

'And of course I shan't let him see the children. Ever.'

'But . . . How would you not let him?'

'I shall tell him I won't stand for it.'

'Pauline. These children are all grown-up too. Marcus is Christopher's age. Even Plod is – what – nineteen or twenty?'

'They're still my children.'

'They're Toby's too. And if they want to see him from time to time, or even regularly – as I should hope they might – then how on earth would you stop them?'

'Well, I shall certainly try.' Pauline the fighter. She doesn't give up on things. I should know that by now.

'Maybe you will try,' I said. 'But could you possibly, in the end, succeed? With all of them? I think not. Pauline, believe me, I know you're having a rotten deal from Toby at the moment. I really do think that. I'm not "on his side", as you put it. But what you are talking of now . . . It won't work,' I ended lamely.

Months before, when all this had been nothing but tremors and a hum below the surface of life, inaudible to my conscious senses, I had already said to Pauline what I wanted to say now. '*You want to control everyone. You think that God will recognise you as a Truly Responsible Person and make a special exception for you.*'

Well, I was not going to say it again. But since there was nothing much else left to say, I went soon afterwards.

I realised, too late, that I had forgotten to give her the chestnut buds.

It must have been not that weekend, but a later one in May when he came down for his birthday, that Christopher told me he'd had an odd call at some point from Pauline.

I listened reluctantly. He and I were now planning our journeys to the Far East. He was to leave in early July, travelling via India and Malaysia, where he had things to do, and I was to follow him, flying straight to the City in August, and combining this with a visit to two Maternal Health Care accomplices who were fortuitously going to be in Singapore at that time. I had got secretly rather excited now, and I knew that Christopher was, at the idea of actually meeting Baht Way. I wanted to think about that, and about long-ago things, including Great-Aunt Alice's journal. Of course I was seeing Pauline regularly, and Toby intermittently, and had listened for hours to the various views of their children. I had heard enough of the Baird marriage.

'She asked me,' Christopher said, 'if I knew of an agency that supplied bodyguards. I suppose she thinks of me as the sort of man who moves in such circles! She indicated that she did – stuff about how I "knock around the world" and so on.'

'But why did she want one? Did you know an agency, by the way?'

'Oh, I put her on to someone else, a rather beat-up old journalist from the PA who I thought might know. Yes, I wondered why, but hardly liked to ask. Eventually she told me of her own accord.'

'And?'

'Well, it seems that Toby's been threatening her. I thought she might have said something about it to you?'

'Not a word, no. Threatening her – with violence, you mean?'

'So she implied.'

'How odd.'

'Doesn't sound much like poor old Toby to me either,' said Christopher cheerfully. 'Never thought he could punch his way out of a paper bag.'

'No. But then we never thought he'd leave Pauline, did we? It could be true. But why should he? I wonder if *she's* been threatening to tell tales to his bishop, blast her.' I had begged her not to, for the time being, for her own sake, since any possibility of Toby's penitent return to respectability might then be compromised.

'Could it by any chance be some sort of fantasy of Pauline's?' Christopher asked after a minute.

'I suppose it *could*.'

We left it at that.

Later, I made cautious enquiry of Marcus, who called to see me. Unlike his younger brother and sisters, he seemed to be trying to stay outside his parents' quarrel, and for that was getting no thanks from either of them.

He looked blank at the word 'violence' but after a while volunteered: 'Mum did say that Dad tried to drive into her the other week. In Basingstoke.'

'Good heavens! Have you asked him about this?'

'Yes, but he didn't seem to know what I was talking about. He was rather upset at the suggestion.'

'Genuinely?'

'Oh, I think so. He may have driven at her, but I shouldn't think he even saw her. You know Dad. Never has his mind on things when he's behind the wheel.'

After he left, this cheerful, easy-going young man who was their first-born, I felt particularly sad about the whole business. It was too easy, and had been for many years, not to take either Toby or Pauline seriously: indeed, long ago I had suggested this to Sarah as the best approach. Pointless, I said, to let yourself be irritated by them. Better just lie back and enjoy them. They're good-hearted, after all.

Now this view seemed entirely inadequate. At the moment, neither Toby nor Pauline was good-hearted, not to each other and perhaps not in other directions either. And whatever canopy of ready-made phrases and attitudes each was separately trying to erect over the ruin of their marriage, the fact remained: they had been together for thirty years and now had broken apart.

What they had built up together in that great slab of time, the heart of two lifetimes, must have been something more deep-rooted and incommunicable than the PR game of Happy Families at which I had lightly jeered. The destruction of this something was, too, a cause for more unassuageable regret than any self-justifying tirade on the subject from either of them could convey. I found that, after all, I grieved about this marriage breaking up, for both their sakes, for their children's, for Toby's parishioners and, yes, even in some way for myself. Perhaps I had needed them to stick together – needed them, silly, comforting and undemanding in the background of my life; my only real family now, apart from Christopher. They were there, reliably, for thirty years, even as our parents were there till their death and have gone on existing in memory as a permanent, immutable union – even as Great-Uncle George is there, and Great-Aunt Alice and all our other forebears: a safe setting. Even as Sarah and I are now safe, in memory.

But, abruptly, Pauline and Toby were not there any longer. Their dissolution seemed to call an awful lot else into question, including much of the past; far more than I would have expected.

It was from this time that fear began to grow. It sounds ridiculous, doesn't it? Christopher and I were planning our journeys and our meeting in the City, but he was still in England at this point. In any case, he is a grown man, an experienced traveller, been at it for years – so whence my morbid conviction that there was no security anywhere just now, that this whole Baht Way enterprise was fraught with unknown dangers?

There seemed to be too many intense, conflicting preoccupations, private worlds all crowding clandestinely that summer over the same narrow space of days: Pauline's, Toby's, mine. And Christopher's too; for in spite of our shared interest in Baht Way, which if anything was more acute in him than in me, I sensed, as often before, that there was another world as well going on in him which I could not share. This new girl, whoever she might be? Or something else entirely?

None of this provided much rational ground for fear. But also I was reading about the Great Land, its history and culture, more than I ever had before. What I read made me profoundly uneasy. Things had gone on in that place, and were no doubt still going on, which had been beyond the powers of the old-style administrators and traders and missionaries such as my family to encompass intellectually. They equally seemed to be beyond the scope of modern commentators to expose. Faced with the Great Land, and with such manifestations of its monstrosity as reached the West, a Conradian incoherence descended on those trying to explain it. '*Oh the horror of it*' wrote poor Aunt Alice long ago: '*How can I dare hope that the babe I fear I am carrying will survive the rigours and the uncleanliness?*'

Did her great-great-niece Tessa feel the same?

'*I have read that Terrible Things are sometimes perpetrated in this Land*', Aunt Alice wrote: '*. . . human suffering is set at naught.*' Even her great-great-great-nephew, he who is making his career from looking clear-eyed into the heart of strangeness, sounded baffled and fearful when he said to me: 'What I didn't tell you was that I gradually realised that each of the men I spoke to seemed to have been tortured in ... in a rather horrible way which they could hardly bring themselves to describe.'

That was in Ak Teem. The Forbidden Place.

In July, a night or two after Christopher had left for the East, I had a dream in which I was approaching the City in the way one did years ago, up the estuary to dock near the Bundar. Across the vast brown water and the paddy fields the silhouette of the City stood in the distance and grew larger. Yet, as we got very near, and from the deck I could see the jetties and the Customs House and the big hotel and the Chamber of Commerce building, it began to dawn on me that they weren't really jetties and buildings at all, but natural rock formations. They were the outcrops of an impenetrable range of mountains, whose crags and passes reared up like towers, range upon range, but were in reality infinitely larger than any mundane forms and far more distant: uninhabited and uninhabitable.

PART IV

The day after my lunch with Mike Isaacs, I rang up the cultural attaché at the High Commission. I had last seen him four years ago in Mexico City, where he had, with the professional kindness and good grace of his kind, devoted a Sunday to accompanying me in a jeep up the mountainous track to the pass where Cortez is supposed to have stood and viewed his Eldorado and seen another ocean beyond. I had enjoyed the cultural attaché's well-informed company, and had hoped to lure him out on a similar expedition here – perhaps even into the Great Land itself, for which, in his position, he must be able to procure passes? Now, I had a more immediate and specific favour to ask from him. I wanted to check the entry Mike Isaacs claimed to have seen in the register of births to British nationals.

After expressions of pleasure at hearing from me again, this archetypal Etonian went on to ask what year I was interested in. 'We have more or less complete records going back to the Trading Charter year – to 1834, that is. But a section of the 1850s got soaked in a flood at one point, which hasn't improved their legibility, and white ants had a munch at quite a few isolated years before the steel filing boxes were organised.'

'I'm after something relatively recent, actually: 1951, I think.'

'Oh, that should be easy. If you give me such details as you know, I'll check it through for you. No, no trouble at all. There aren't many in any one year, and certainly not by the 1950s, when the British presence was running right down. We can't actually hand out duplicate certificates here any more – '

'So I understand.'

'But I'll see what I can do.'

'It's very kind of you, Colin.'

'All part of the job. I like those old registers, anyway. But you'll have to tell me the names you're after.'

'Oh yes, of course.' I felt abruptly self-conscious. 'Well, it's the same surname as me, Mason.'

'That would be the child's father?'

'Er, no, mother, actually. Teresa Elizabeth Mason. She – she's a vague relative of mine. Was, I should say.'

I was afraid he was about to ask if I had a name for the father, but of course he did not: he must at once have comprehended my slight embarrassment.

'I'll get you all the particulars we've got,' he said soothingly. Then he went on to invite me to a party at the High Commission three nights hence: 'Just one of the usual bashes. The British architect who's responsible for that new object like a giant Louis Quinze wardrobe at the end of the Bundar, is back in town. The wardrobe's being unveiled, or whatever one might do to wardrobes, and we're giving a little party for the man, separate from the municipal junketings. I'll send an official invite round to your hotel. Hope you can come?'

'I'd like to. I think . . . Yes, I expect I will. If I seem to be hesitating, it's because Christopher, my son, should be back in the City soon, but maybe not for some days. Well, rather than kicking my heels waiting for him, I was thinking of flying down to Singapore right away. I've got some Maternal and Child Health Care people to see there. And I've been very much in two minds, because I'm rather hoping Christopher may show up here quite soon anyway, and I've got plenty of paperwork still to do . . . I think, actually, you've decided me to stay on here. Thanks.'

'Christopher,' said Colin in a tone of preoccupied concentration as if mentally scanning a reference book. 'Ah, Christopher Mason. The travel writer, by any chance?'

'Yes, actually.' I felt quite disproportionate pleasure that his name should be thus recognised.

'I read that series of articles he did for the *Sunday Times*.

And wasn't there a book on Malacca and Macao and the Portuguese in this part of the world? Jolly good, I thought. Oh, well, if he does by any chance turn up by Saturday, do bring him along too.'

'Thank you very much, Colin. I don't really expect him back as soon as that. But thanks all the same.'

'Where's he gone – back to Malaysia?'

'No. Up into the Great Land, actually.'

Did I imagine the two seconds of hesitation or the reticence in what followed?

'Has he just? Still, an experienced Far East man like him . . . I'm sure he knows what he's doing.'

'I hope you're right.'

'As I say, I'd love to meet him, and I'm sure H.E. would too. I seem to remember that Mrs H.E.'s a fan of his already.'

'Thank you. That's nice to hear. I'll see you myself on Saturday, anyway.'

After I rang off I remained, for a while, vestigially cheered by Colin's image of Christopher so solidly there, apt to reappear at any moment.

I found, as soon as I arrived on Saturday at the British High Commission in the warm dark, that I remembered the place. The address, in a street now named after the army commander who negotiated the City's secession from the Great Land at the end of the 1950s, meant nothing to me, but I recognised at once the low, white Palladian house, with its pretty iron gates and Anglo-Indian style verandahs: it was, like Teyn Bira, one of those oases in the new City where memory still survived. I had even been to the occasional party there as a young officer, and now, at the other end of time, I stood again on the same lawn, surrounded by the same rhododendrons and wellingtonias, with a drink in my hand and the same large, low stars above.

Colin, who was probably not born last time I was in that garden, came quickly to my side.

'Very nice to see you again, Stephen. I'm a bit tied up just now with our wardrobe constructor and his entourage – I'll introduce you to him in a minute, and to H.E. – but don't make off again this evening without our having a good old chat. Meanwhile, before I forget, this is what you wanted, I think.' He slipped a folded piece of paper into my breast pocket and was off across the lawn to greet another arrival.

Perhaps he had tactfully intended that I might leave the paper alone till after the party. However, I could not resist taking a look at it. On High Commission paper, in a decorative, forward-sloping hand, it was headed: *Transcript from Birth Registers, Entry no. 3847, series 2, 24 May 1951.* I saw the word 'son', Tessa's name, her own birth dates, and one or two other particulars which, even as my eye ran in dread over them, I found I did not want to study or think about there and then.

As if I myself had been guilty of something grave, and this, at last, were the betraying evidence of it, I stuffed the sheet of paper back in my pocket. Hoping no one had been observing me, I hastened to join the group waiting to greet the High Commissioner.

The wardrobe constructor, a famous architect whose name, I realised belatedly, was familiar to me though it is not my subject, looked to my eyes like a young boxer. The High Commissioner's wife – who was, as I had been promised, enthusiastic about Christopher's last book – was a pretty, eager-to-please woman young enough to be my daughter. Absurdly, I had expected a formidable matron: evidently the young man who I had once been in that place had risen from the grass and slipped temporarily into my skin. I know that some people of my age dislike the feeling that the proper representatives of power and authority have faded away and that in their place are a cast of unconvincing juveniles, but I rather like it. I suppose that, logically, it ought to make me feel old myself, but in fact it makes me feel without age, freed into a limbo where nothing particular is expected of me and where, therefore, I might be capable of something unprecedented. I know that that evening I felt on the verge of something, though the feeling was quite imprecise. I suppose that my nerves were stretched taut – by the days of waiting for Christopher or for some further message from him, by the immediate presence of that birth-register entry sitting like a wafer of domestic Semtex in my pocket, and also by the long-term tension of interest and anxiety that had begun as soon as I had heard of Baht Way's existence. But I also know that, in that crowd of decorously cheerful people, fanned out on dark grass beneath paper lanterns hung from trees in the traditional style of the country, I felt conscious happiness and peace: a luminous interlude.

I was still talking to the High Commissioner's wife – we had moved by degrees from Christopher to her own small daughters and to the problems of education in general – when Colin reappeared and detached me. The poor woman was, as I should have realised, needed elsewhere.

'There's someone else I want you to meet,' he said diplomatically to me. 'I can't see her just at this moment, but as soon as I do . . . She's a nurse; she was here for a couple of years at the American hospital, and now she's come back again as a sister at the big government hospital down near the docks. The local nurses aren't bad, but they're obsessed with status – well, so are the doctors, come to that – and need chasing. I should think Julie's just the girl to do that; persistent but tactful. A really nice person. Oh, and she knows Mike Isaacs, by the way.'

I was momentarily disconcerted, forgetting that Colin too would very likely have encountered Mike. I wondered if Colin knew all about my family investigation and had been too polite to say so. 'Is this nurse American too?' I asked, to cover my confusion.

'Julie? Oh no, British.' Of course, that was why she had been invited, as I had, to this heterogeneous celebration of British talent far from home. Not Mike.

'Forgive me asking,' I said, 'but how has Mike Isaacs crossed your path?' I really meant, 'How do you know he has crossed mine?'

Colin looked amused but reticent.

'Oh, Mike's a mildly well-known character round here, though he does tend to behave as if he thought no one knew his name. Professionally poker-faced, you know. He comes here sometimes to chat to the press officer, and lately he's been looking the odd thing up in the registers – we've got the army lists here for the postwar period, till our lot all pulled out in the Civil War, that means, and that's what mainly interests Mike. He's got an obsession that some soldiers who went missing in action during the Troubles are still alive.'

'I've noticed that he has. Though I've only met him a couple of times.'

'Even so, you could hardly miss it, could you? He doesn't

hide his obsession, does Mike, for all his supposedly secret comings and goings. He mentioned to me that he'd met you (that's why it wasn't a total surprise when you telephoned me the other day). I assume your meeting with him relates in some way to his preoccupation?'

'In some way,' I said gratefully. 'Actually I thought it was American MIAs that he was particularly concerned with. But you say it's British soldiers too?'

'Yes, and Australian. Well, let's say he'd like to pursue the topic of British soldiers, but he doesn't get very far because his theories aren't greeted with much belief in this department. Wishful thinking, we reckon. I gather that the Australians over in Garden Road are slightly more prepared to listen, but the only ones who take his ideas seriously are his own lot. Or used to. However, their ambassador's changed recently, and the present incumbent doesn't rate Mike's stories any more than we do. Or so I hear.'

'Discouraging for him,' I said, adopting Colin's sardonic tone, which I found a relief.

'Oh, I don't know,' said that steely young man with a deceptive gentleness which reminded me of Christopher. 'I think, you know, that a mission of that nature is sometimes actually fed by disbelief. The fact that no one much believes him becomes further proof, in his mind, that there's been some sort of cover-up.'

'I'm familiar with the syndrome. I've had one or two patients like that: "You haven't so much as mentioned cancer, doctor, what are you hiding from me?" But actually I thought that MIAs weren't Mike's only obsession?'

'You mean his steam trains? Mm, I've wondered about them. Aren't they really just a cover for his MIA interests?'

'Well, I don't know. He did say to me that they came in useful for that – but he also told me a circumstantial detail about being taken round the engine sheds in Pittsburgh when he was a child. By an uncle, he said.'

'Oh, really?' said Colin, suddenly attentive, although he had been looking round, presumably for the elusive nurse. 'An uncle, you say?'

'I think he said "a sort of uncle" actually, but why?'

'Oh, well, I wouldn't like to speculate too much about that. I think the "uncle" may have been some sort of befriender, social worker or such. Mike was brought up in an orphanage, that I can tell you.'

'Was he now? That would explain some things about him.'

'Doesn't it? According to him, he never knew any of his family on either side, though he has some of their names. And although that might sound like another of his stories, I do in this instance believe him. You see, all this MIA stuff – it's actually his own father he's looking for. He's admitted as much to me. And so, even if that's all a daydream, it seems to me unlikely that he's falsified his own situation, since that's the reason behind the daydream, the motive.'

I was fascinated and not entirely surprised. I had sensed some emotion working in Mike that went beyond what he told me. So often, as a doctor, have I seen persuasive rational arguments, such as Mike's about the missing soldiers, covering a conviction that is both deeper and less logical. Often, come to that, doctors themselves employ such arguments in which to clothe the corpus of prejudices, assumptions, hopes and fears they, as much as anyone else, carry around with them.

'Mind you,' said Colin, 'there may well be other levels also. He's certainly very attached to his MIA fantasies but I'm never quite sure how much he actually believes them himself.' He added quickly: 'I mean, there may be occasions on which he finds them, like the steam trains, a convenient cover for yet other things ... Ah, here's Julie. Julie, may I introduce Stephen Mason, who is a doctor and an expert on maternal and child health, if I've got it right? Stephen, this is Julie Barron, who is here to organise the City's nurses.'

While both the girl and I struggled in momentary British self-consciousness with the neat sketches Colin had drawn, I registered that I had probably just received a covert warning. Colin had been indicating to me that Mike was in Intelligence.

At first sight Julie Barron seemed as ordinary as her name: a small girl who must, from the position she had reached, be in her late twenties, but looking younger, with large glasses and a faint Midlands accent. Only after I had been talking to her for a few minutes did I realise she was not only warm and intelligent, she was almost beautiful. She had a delicate nose and mouth, a pale skin and, behind the giant glasses, which made her look as if she were a dressed-up child, large, myopic, dark-lashed eyes.

'It's not quite true,' she said, after a while, 'that I'm a Sister Tutor. It's very kind of Colin to build me up like that but actually I'm just an ordinary ward sister. I do some teaching – well, all the time, really, you know how it is – but it's mostly informal. The administrator of the hospital is keen to get British nurses to "set an example". Such an old-fashioned phrase, isn't it? Makes me feel like a sort of Florence Nightingale.'

'It's probably true, though?'

'Well, in a way . . . They've got some marvellous equipment in that place, as good as you'd find anywhere, but the nurses . . . well, technically they're all right. I mean, they don't muddle up the doses or anything, or no more than happens anywhere else, and they're good on hygiene. Scrupulous, actually, once they've got the routine. But – oh dear, it seems an awful thing to say, but a lot of them don't seem to care about the patients. Not really.'

'I think I can imagine. Caring about other individuals doesn't figure large in their traditional culture.'

'No, I know that. It's not their fault. It's this city, too: it's such a materialistic place and they see such tempting wealth all round them, but they aren't that well paid, so each one is very jealous of her particular position in the hierarchy. They won't muck in. The local Sisters are too grand to do anything, any difficult dressing or such, that might dirty their overalls. And they despise the poorer patients, sometimes quite openly.'

'I can imagine.'

'I wouldn't get so irritated by it, though, if they didn't *talk* so much about "caring". And "compassion" and "patient-oriented". They've got all the jargon. But.'

'They've imported the jargon,' I suggested. 'Or it's been imported for them, along with the scanners and the foetal monitors and the linear accelerators and so forth?'

'Yes. That's exactly it. Oh, dear. Sometimes I think: What the hell am I doing here, among all these expensive toys and these doll-like little nurses in their new fancy uniforms saying "Yes, Sister, oh yes. Very right, Sister" and thinking about their nails? I wonder if I ought rather to be in some primitive hospital up in the Great Land itself, teaching basic procedures. I might do more real good up there.'

'Surely you wouldn't be allowed to work up there?'

'No, I don't think I would. It's just a dream of mine. I don't think they employ any foreign nationals up there, do they?'

'I'm sure not. And, even if they did, I think you might find there some of the attitudes you dislike here. Callousness and so on.'

'Yes. I do know that, really. I mean that I know it isn't just Western materialism that's got at these girls: it's that on top of something else. There's a sort of refusal to reason at the heart of things. Probably, as you say, I'd find that in the Great Land too, and more so. Oh, dear. To think I used to imagine it must be such a lovely place! Not like our society, I used to think. Different. Therefore better. What an idiot!'

'A lot of people used to imagine that. Some probably still do.'

'I know. But I should have known better.'

I found this remark, with its very slight emphasis on the 'I', touching but slightly surprising. It is, I must admit, the way I have always tended to think myself. So, I have observed, does Christopher, that tenacious discoverer. But Christopher and I are both the inheritors of a privileged class, an extensive education, whereas I had the feeling that this girl had had to work out everything for herself.

She began to tell me about the neonatal ward in her hospital, and its misapplication of elaborate equipment and procedures to hopelessly immature infants.

'Isn't this one of the things you're here to advise on?' I said. 'Have you tried pointing out to the team that their enthusiasm may be misplaced?'

'They know it. Yes, really, I discovered, talking to the doctor in charge, that he knows very well what the risks are – further brain damage from ventilators and so on. They had one baby girl there only last week, all wired and tubed, a miserable little skinned rabbit, weighing under six hundred grammes. When I asked the doctor about this, he just said: "Oh yes, poor prognosis, poor prognosis." So complacent. He didn't care a bit what the child's condition and prospects may be if she does by some chance survive to leave the hospital. If they manage to discharge her alive, that will go down as "success". I mean, it's just so illogical. Particularly when you think what they traditionally do quite often to baby girls, even perfectly healthy ones. Even here in the City, in the poorer quarters. In the big, new high-rise estates. And in older places like Teyn

Bira that foreigners don't normally see.' She looked momentarily wretched.

'I don't know,' I said gently, 'but I think I can imagine. Infanticide? I know that's always been one of their less charming traditions.'

'Worse than that, really. I mean, that would at least be honest. They starve a lot of the baby girls deliberately. They don't admit it, but they just don't feed them. Even here, in this rich city. It shows up clearly on the statistics for survival at one year.'

'Christ,' I said in disgust. 'They shouldn't need to, these days. I mean, they've got a welfare programme. And I've never seen a city with more contraceptive slot machines.'

'Oh, I know!' She cheered up. 'It isn't just in the gents'. Every ladies' loo has one too. And hairdressers and make-up departments, and even places selling tights and underclothes. You begin to feel sort of haunted by the things.'

'I think it's government policy, isn't it? To keep the population at its present level. One can see why.'

'Yes, I'm sure it is. But it doesn't make you think "population problem", does it? It makes you feel surrounded by other people's sex lives in a way that's a bit – well, off-putting.' She laughed at herself and coloured, looking very pretty.

'Yes, my son said something like that to me, too,' I said, struck by the coincidence. 'He's been here recently.'

'I know,' she said.

'You know Christopher?' I asked, completely taken aback. 'But I thought it was Mike Isaacs you knew?' I was beginning to think that, in this place, where I had at first felt so anonymous, I could meet no one who was not part of a network.

'I know them both,' she admitted. She added, as if trying to excuse some fault on her part, 'That's why I wanted so much to meet you tonight. I asked Colin Darcy to introduce us, though I asked him not to say I knew Kit – Chris . . . I was going to tell you, but it seemed rude to bounce in and tell you right away.'

Kit. Chris. 'Wait a moment,' I said. 'You call him Kit?'

'Yes. I know you call him Chris – '

'No, I don't,' I said irritably. 'That's what Mike Isaacs calls him. I call him Christopher. Hardly anyone calls him Kit now,

I thought, except people who knew him when he was a small boy.'

'He asked me to,' she said nervously. She added, in propitiatory explanation: 'Not at first, of course. It was after we'd got to know each other.'

'But – I don't want to pry, of course, but Christopher only came out here recently.'

'Yes. But I met him first when I was here the other year. He was staying in the City for a little while then, and we saw each other again when I came back to London last January.'

'Oh. I see.'

Various things began to fall into place. Realising that I had, without meaning to, intimidated her, I made an effort to smile. She smiled back, looking much happier but still scared.

'You see,' she said, 'I was here – oh, for nearly two years, at the American hospital. That's how I met Mike; he used to come in for treatment for a smashed leg which caused some problems in mending. A railway accident, it was. He was a bit lonely, and sort of got into the habit of talking to me. He was a good friend to me, too. He encouraged me to go to proper classes in the local language, and he used to help with the homework and my accent. If I hadn't done that, I could never have taken on the job I'm in now. A lot of our patients don't speak any English, you see. After I went back to London last autumn, on a course, he wrote to me sometimes. Around Christmas he wrote about Baht Way, and then, when he'd heard from Kit – Chris – he wrote and asked me to get in touch with him. He didn't realise we'd already met in the City that other time when Kit was here for several weeks. I was really pleased, because I hadn't had a proper address in England for Kit and now Mike gave it to me. I think he reckoned I might be able to help Kit in some way, particularly as by that time, I'd decided to come back here. Though actually, of course,' she added softly, 'Kit's so knowledgeable that it's been he who's been helping me. Oh – with all sorts of things.'

I recognised that tone. So, was this the girl whose unmentioned presence I had sensed months before? If so, I was not displeased: on the contrary, I told myself quickly.

But I did feel rather disconcerted. Christopher's previous girls, in so far as they became visible at all to me, have tended

to be slightly grand: an actress, a well-known novelist –
women with money and assurance, and without regional
accents. Women who wouldn't admit guilelessly to their pleasure at being put in touch with Christopher again.

'So you know all about Baht Way?' I said. I felt a sense of
exposure.

'Oh, not all, I'm sure,' she said tactfully. 'Kit only tells me
what he means to tell, doesn't he? I mean, he's like that in
everything.'

I thought, from this, that she probably did know it all –
about my sister Tessa, I mean, and maybe, now, other things
about our family too. But at least this made her some kind
of messenger from Christopher: she, like Mike Isaacs, must
have seen him more recently than I had seen him, and I
trusted her views more than I trusted Mike's.

On the spur of the moment, I invited her to have dinner
with me the following evening. She accepted and seemed
pleased, if still rather intimidated by me. As 'Kit's father' I
must, I dimly realised, seem to her old and powerful. Well,
she could hardly guess, young as she was, that I was yearning
for her to comfort and advise me.

It wasn't till I had found a taxi lurking near the High
Commission gates, and was in it and on my way back
downtown, that I unfolded again that sheet of paper from my
pocket. Of course I had not exactly forgotten it, far from it.
But while I had been talking to people in the garden I had
consigned it to the bottom of my mind.

Now I took it out and deciphered it by the weak light inside
the cab. Sure enough it recorded the birth of a son (unnamed)
to Tessa, in St Saviour's Hospital, Hospital Road, Teyn Bira,
as Mike Isaacs had said. The date of birth and that of the
entry in the register were within three days of each other.
And they were many months – the best part of a year – before
Tessa's supposed reappearance out of nowhere at the military
headquarters early in 1952.

No father was named in the entry. Well, I had not really
expected one. Nevertheless, the confirmation of that absence
came like a tiny shock of pain. I suppose that even today I
have more of the vestigial prejudices of my upbringing and
generation than I would care to admit.

There was, however, one other person mentioned. Under

'*Informant*' was written '*Pauline Sylvia Mason, sister.*'

I had planned to give Julie Barron dinner at the restaurant on the top floor of the hotel from which, by day, you can see the forbidden hills of the Great Land and, by night, the feast of lights which is the City. I had crassly felt that she would enjoy this: it is quite an expensive restaurant. I suppose I wanted her to feel, as I had wanted Mike Isaacs to feel, that I was grateful for support and interest but at the same time well in charge of things myself.

However, when she finally arrived, late, full of apologies, having had to work a double shift, I realised that she was not happy in this hotel. Its anonymous, international opulence seemed to unnerve her, in a way that the old-fashioned grandeur of the High Commission had not. She apologised for not having had time to go back from the hospital to her own flat and 'dress properly'. To my eyes, she looked both nicely and suitably clad, in a pale-yellow cotton dress that reminded me of one Jill used to wear one particularly hot summer, but I could tell that Julie felt extinguished by the marble and chandeliers in the lobby, like a moth in a tropical flower garden. She also, I presently realised, looked very tired. When she took her glasses off, under her eyes were blue smudges like bruises.

I bought her a drink and suggested, on the spur of the moment, that we go somewhere that she might know but that I would not; perhaps somewhere quiet, near the Bundar, where the main crowds left at the end of the day? For a moment, as she looked at a loss, I was afraid that this idea too was a mistake – that she would now feel a weight of responsibility for wherever we went. However, after a moment's thought, she brightened and said:

'We could go out near to Jedu Sumna, perhaps.'

'You mean, where the causeway is, the river frontier with the Great Land?'

'Yes. Not quite that far, but just downriver from there. There's a string of little places on the water, quite nice and homely really, or I think so. I go sometimes because I live not far from there. The only thing is, it's the other side of town from here.'

'But if you live out there you'd have to get back there

tonight anyway, wouldn't you? I must apologise for getting you to come here; I didn't realise I was landing you with such a journey.'

She admitted this was so: 'But I could get a taxi.'

'Well, we can get a taxi now. That way, later tonight, you won't have far to go.'

The City taxis are air-conditioned Mercedes: so different from the battered Morris Oxfords and tricycle rickshaws that I remember from when I was young. From the cool interior of a taxi, therefore, the messages of the other senses fool the eye too. Not feeling the heavy, sticky heat or hearing the distinctive squawk of the night birds or picking up whiffs of fish and oil as the cab passed through the older quarters, it was easy to believe that we were finally arriving at a temperate shoreline under a night sky with a chilly breeze. Here, the embankment of the river, leaving the docks behind, peters out into a wide, pebbled strand, a windbreak of low trees and, along the shelter of the trees, a scatter of small restaurants. Even though these are built out on wooden piles to protect them against the vagaries of typhoon tides, the impression to me at that moment was of some old-fashioned beach resort on the far side of the world. Then we got out of the taxi into clammy, enveloping warmth, and smelt salt-swamp water and tainted mud and spices. Greece, the south of France, the Dorset coastline, abruptly disappeared.

'We don't have to have local food,' Julie said as if I might have been about to object to it. 'That place over there is run by Levantines and does Mediterranean dishes. It's quite nice.'

In the City, people of any kind of apparent Middle Eastern descent are always known as 'Levantines'. The term has no perjorative overtones now, but presumably it is an artless survival from the last century, when a heterogeneous selection of the world's adventurers, known collectively and disparagingly to the British as 'Levantine traders', came here to seek their fortunes.

So we settled at a small table with a red-checked cloth, a candle in a Chianti bottle, a menu in French, and an assiduous waiter whose identification label (obligatory throughout the City's shops, restaurants and bars) showed him to be called Cyrus de Cunha.

Once we had ordered and Julie could see I was happy with

the place, she relaxed a little, but she seemed to have something she wanted to dispose of.

'I've been worrying that I sounded rather racist yesterday – you know, when we were talking about the hospital and I was complaining about people's attitudes?'

I indicated that it hadn't occurred to me to think that. Her informed opinion on her nurses was obviously worth having. 'And anyway, among friends, colleagues or whatever, one must speak as one finds. One shouldn't avoid telling the truth just because someone hearing might think one was being racist or class-conscious or whatever.'

It passed through my mind as I spoke that one of Pauline's many affectations (known to her as 'principles') is a refusal to have the term 'working class' used in front of her. Pauline! God. She had of course been on my mind almost constantly in the twenty-four hours since I had seen her name clear as a message on that registration entry. '*Informant – Pauline Sylvia Mason, sister.*' Pauline herself informed on, after all these years. Because logic suggested that there was absolutely nothing I could do about this sensational piece of information while I was here in the City, I had made an effort to drive my inevitable speculation, and its conclusions, down to the bottom of my mind. But it was there like a pain, sending its messages round my system: shock, disgust, apprehension of the inevitable confrontation to come – remorse at my own earlier lack of perception; forty years of imperception. We should never, any of us, have trusted Pauline. I, at least, should have known better.

I hoped to escape from these thoughts for a few hours in Julie's gentle company. But of course she knew, from Christopher, about Baht Way, and knew he was the reason I was here in the City. I foresaw that, unless I made up my mind now not to, I was going to find myself drawn into telling this girl just what hidden part Christopher's aunt now seemed to have played in the whole tragic business.

But Julie, naturally, was still pursuing her own theme. 'I wouldn't like you to get the impression that I don't like the people here. I do, or I wouldn't have come back here. Some of the nurses are sweet, and hard-working; a lot of the doctors are as skilled as you would find anywhere in the world. Well, a lot of them have trained in the UK or in America or

Canada, of course. It's just that I sometimes have this feeling of another world going on underneath. Another value system that just doesn't mesh with ours. The City is so Western and well run and clean and all the rest of it – '

'Free education for all. Green campaigns to recycle waste. Etcetera, etcetera.'

'Exactly. All the latest ideas. And yet you hear things – oh, sometimes terrifying . . .'

'I do know what you mean,' I said. But, prey to my own preoccupation, I added: 'Though of course one sometimes senses the presence of something terrifying going on underneath even within one's own world.' The remark was rash, it could only lead me straight back to Pauline. But then anything and everything was leading there.

In a fruitless attempt to distract myself, I began asking Julie about her life. She chatted cheerfully about her training at Guy's, about deciding in her mid-twenties to use her qualifications to see something of the world, about her growing interest in what could be done for patients at a basic level without high technology: I marked her down mentally as someone after my own heart, who might be useful to the international organisation to which I was currently linked. But, while she talked of her hopes and plans, I was conscious, as one often is at such times, of what was not being said also. For an apparently affectionate, unpretentious person, she spoke very little of her childhood. I was not really surprised to hear after a while that it had left her with a memory of unhappiness.

'Aston,' she said, in answer to a direct question. 'You wouldn't know it, I don't suppose. It's part of Birmingham. A sort of nothing place – oh, except for its football team. My brothers used to be keen on Aston Villa. I expect they still are.

'. . . Two of them. But they're much younger than me. Half-brothers, actually. My father married again when I was nine.

'. . . No, she died. A hospital mistake. A GA that went wrong – just one of those things. There wasn't a court case or anything. People didn't sue hospitals much twenty years ago, did they? My father's always been bitter about it. He didn't even want me to become a nurse.

'. . . Well, I suppose I do have a vocation for it, though it always sounds rather conceited to say that. I do love it. But, honestly, when I was eighteen I'd have gone into nursing anyway just to get away from home. There just didn't seem anything there for me any more.

'. . . Yes, my stepmother. There's really nothing I can say about her, so I'd sooner not. It just is a difficult relationship, I suppose, and perhaps you shouldn't ask too much of people. I don't like to sound resentful or as if I'm brooding about it because honestly, these days, I hardly think about my stepmother at all. I mean, I don't need to. I have such a nice life of my own now.'

The food and wine had relaxed her: her cheeks were pinker, the smudges were no longer so noticeable under her eyes. But I guessed I had touched the cause of the vulnerability, lying under the brisk persona of Sister-in-charge, which I had picked up in her from the first without being fully aware I was doing so.

'When I was about eleven,' she said, 'I used to long to go to boarding school. I'd read these silly stories, a lot of Enid Blyton and Angela Brazil books that were in the house and that had belonged to my own mother – we didn't have other books much – and I thought girls' boarding schools sounded so lovely! I was very naive.'

'Well, you might have enjoyed a good school, actually, Some girls do.' (My sister Pauline did . . . Oh, shut up.)

'The funny thing was, I thought my stepmother would be pleased to have me out of the house, so I kept suggesting it. But she just got annoyed and said I didn't appreciate home and was ungrateful. Eventually it dawned on me that of course she didn't want my dad to spend all that money on me. But you don't think of that when you're eleven, do you? Or I didn't. What a baby.'

'I can't imagine you ever having been babyish.'

She ignored this, as perhaps it deserved, but went on: 'I was puzzled at first that Kit – that Christopher, sorry – was sent away to boarding school. He doesn't seem to have liked it terribly, and his own home sounds so lovely. All your books and the fun the three of you had together and everything. Those holidays abroad he's told me about . . . I don't see why you had to send him away?'

Staggering mentally from this mixture of compliment and criticism contained in her remarks, I asked after a pause in which I felt an obscure pain:

'What does Christopher himself say?'

'Oh, he just laughs and says he's a natural loner. You know how he is about that? He says that public school was probably good for him and that he learnt things there. But I think that nearly everything he knows he's learnt from you or his mother or on his own. He does know a lot, doesn't he? I've learnt – oh, all sorts of things from him.'

Floored again by this daunting image of my son as a relentless educator, I asked: 'What sort of things in particular?'

'Oh, all sorts of lovely, interesting things. But also, well – not to be taken in by things. Politics, really, and religion. Not to think there are simple solutions to problems or to try to divide places – societies, you know – into good and bad, as if everything worked to a pattern. For instance, I remember him saying that the main reason westerners imagine the Great Land to be a basically nice place, with the right ideas, is that the people there go round on bicycles and in carts and steam trains. Kit says this reminds us nostalgically of our own countries about eighty years ago. So we get the message wrong, and go all sentimental about the simple life.'

It was a strange sensation having a version of Christopher's own words, well known to me already, played back to me by this eager girl. I wasn't sure if I liked it or not.

'Actually,' I said, 'they have no cars because they have almost no oil resources.'

'Yes, I know that now. But till Kit put it like that I just didn't think: I imagined the ruler of the Great Land had taken some sort of Green decision. I ask you!'

Even if I kept off Pauline, evidently I could not here with Julie avoid the other central topic occupying my mind. Something like it occupied Julie's too. I said:

'Christopher – forgive me, but that's what I call him – has the measure of the Great Land. He knows it is a sinister place where God alone knows what happens and the outside world does not necessarily get to hear about it at all. He told you, perhaps, about the refugees he met who seemed to have been tortured?'

'In Ak Teem? Yes.' I felt her flinch. After a moment she

added: 'I was with him, actually. He needed an interpreter, you see, and so . . .'

Of course. Of course she was with him.

'Fine,' I said quickly. 'Well, you know about it. But you also know, I imagine, that in spite of that he's gone up into the Great Land in search of Baht Way?'

She nodded and said nothing, playing with the salt cellar.

'I'm very worried about him,' I said at last. 'And as each day passes I worry more.'

The words, finally spoken, fell between us like small stones. 'I know,' she said at last, 'I know.'

I was too distraught to decide whether she meant 'I know you feel desperate', or whether she really meant 'I know, I feel the same'. After a long moment, she said: 'Mike organised the trip for him. Credentials from some bird-watchers' club. Mike's been up in the Great Land himself lots of times. He knows what he's about.'

'Does he?'

'I think so. And he said not to expect Kit – Christopher – back till some time this coming week, didn't he? At least, he said that to me. I imagine he did to you?'

'Yes. He did. But what worries me is, Christopher knew when I was due here, he himself must have expected to be back sooner. I keep thinking something has gone horribly wrong. And Mike isn't exactly reassuring, come to that, with his stories of secret prison camps into which people disappear for ever. Maybe he was just trying to cheer me up. And now you're doing the same.'

'I'm not, honestly I'm not,' she said in distress. 'I want Kit safe back as much as you do. Oh no, that's a silly thing to say, isn't it? After all, you're his dad. But I do want him back very much.' She added after a moment:

'You may say that means I'm just trying to encourage myself' (that was indeed what I was thinking) 'but I do actually think that he's probably OK.'

'Do you?'

'He's such a traveller, isn't he?' she said, with what seemed to me a touch of sadness unrelated to the present anxiety. 'Always having to go farther – beyond the next mountain range, or over the river or into the next territory where no one has been before, as if there was such a place. He calls it "wanting to see over the horizon".'

'Yes, that's just the trouble. I'm afraid it's the path to the sea.'

'To the sea?' she said, puzzled. In the Great Land, Christopher was journeying away from the sea.

'Oh, it's a phrase he and I have sometimes used. It's from a novel that impressed him when he was a boy. Mauriac. I've no idea, actually, if he would admire it today. Maybe not. Anyway, the path to the unknown sea is the one you feel you have to take and it may lead to great things . . . but of course you may drown, as well.'

'Of course,' she said soberly.

Perhaps I had drunk much more than my share of the bottle of wine. It seemed to be empty although we were not halfway through our meal. A moment later I heard myself say:

'I have a dread that this time he is going to his death.'

'I know,' she said in the same opaque way as before. 'I know.'

In the silence between us, the waiter came and took away our fish plates. Was everything all right? he enquired ritualistically. 'Yes, yes,' I assured him with a vacant grin, and then added to Julie, feeling I was being a rotten host: 'It's very good, actually, for such a little place out here.'

'Yes. I brought Kit here. He liked it a lot, too.'

Oh, God.

'Tell me I'm wrong about him,' I pleaded cravenly when the waiter had served the next course with ceremony and retreated. My hand was on her arm. She looked surprised, but took my hand in her dry, warm one.

'I can't tell you you're wrong. You know what you feel. Kit was quite sort of brisk and confident when he left – for what that's worth . . . Could it possibly be that it's more you who are worried about dying, and that makes you extra afraid now for him . . . ?

' – Of course, I know nothing about your life,' she added shyly when I did not reply. 'But I do just wonder.'

My own death. It had simply not occurred to me to make the connection. Yet I saw what she meant.

Something that, for years and years, seemed to have been working under the surface of my life, some grief, some constraint, something not acknowledged, did seem to be surfacing.

But how? As a grand gesture? A piece of suicidal folly? A violent break with the past? An illness which had yet to manifest itself openly? I had no idea. .

The unknown sea.

'Perhaps,' I said, trying to concentrate, 'I think it should have been me, not Christopher, going in search of Baht Way. As a sort of reparation.'

'You shouldn't feel guilty about Baht Way, though,' she said, understanding.

'I do and I should. In a minute, I'll tell you why.'

'I don't think that helping him and making up to him for the past is the only reason Kit has gone to look for Baht Way,' she said after a pause.

'You mean, he hasn't been able to resist the Great Land itself, just because it's there. Seeing over the horizon.'

'Yes, but something else he told me as well. Something like, he thought that meeting Baht Way might be like meeting himself, in a distorting glass. Or himself in another life.'

'A sort of *Doppelgänger*?' I suggested, but she did not know the word.

'It's as if,' she said tentatively, 'he thinks there are alternative lives for each of us, and it's a matter of chance which one we get routed on to. Oh, I don't mean he really believes that, but . . .'

'It's a way of thinking for him? Like looking over the horizon, come to that.'

'Perhaps,' she said, not really happy in these realms of metaphysics.

We sat in glum and companionable silence contemplating the person who linked us so intimately together. The waiter brought a lot of vegetables and fussed around. There were fireflies, glowing green spots, on the bushes behind the terrace where we sat. Out on the dark river, which smelt of mud and other things, a country cargo boat, gaff-rigged, hung with lanterns, was making its way slowly upstream. At Jedu Sumna causeway it would have to wait hours for its turn to be processed through the lock system that today separates the waters of the delta from those of the Great Land. On such boats, refugees and itinerant workers like Baht Way, in the temporary guise of deck hands, are said to come and go.

I found myself inexorably wanting now to tell Julie about

Pauline's apparent role in the Baht Way business, and so I did. She listened attentively. It took some time.

'Oh dear, oh dear,' she said at the end. Her soft tone made me realise how full of passion and resentment my own voice must have been. Hatred can be fuelled by a sense of moral outrage, yet hatred itself ends up being an ugly thing. I did not exactly want to hate my sister. Yet not to do so now seemed in itself a failure, a cowardly compromise disguised as Christian virtue of the kind peddled by Toby. I struggled to explain this, but probably I did not succeed very well. Julie was so many years younger than I am. It seemed to me right that she should not yet know that some griefs and angers are irreparable. I was wrong about her, in this respect. But I only found that out later.

'Do you think,' she suggested tactfully after a bit, 'that your sister sort of *meant well* by everything she did, even if it now all looks awful? I mean, in those days, particularly for a family like yours, an illegitimate child was just impossible, wasn't it? I can imagine that Pauline might have felt she was doing the best thing for everyone in helping Tessa to conceal the whole thing.'

'Yes, I've been thinking that too. All last night and today I've tried thinking it. But it doesn't work. Don't you see? Pauline knew where Tessa was and saw her the best part of a year before Tessa "reappeared" supposedly from nowhere. Pauline *knew* she was alive and, in essential terms, all right. And yet she let our mother and father go on suffering and suffering not knowing if Tessa was alive or dead and losing hope of ever seeing her again. Christ, how would I feel towards someone, a niece or someone, who did that to me? If – if Christopher had disappeared. It doesn't bear thinking of. That's what I can't forgive Pauline for, that calculated, stupid cruelty. Whatever her convoluted reason for it.'

'I'm a bit surprised, actually,' said Julie with care (evidently my voice had risen again), 'that the High Commission didn't send a message to your family about that registration of birth. You'd think they would have, if she was listed as missing.'

'That puzzled me too. Or did last week when Mike first told me the registration was there. But now it's clear. As it was Pauline who went to register the birth, she must have led the High Commission to think that everything was OK now.

Tessa was found. Pauline was family, after all, the representative for the rest of us in the City. She had a good job with the army, was a respectable and respected person. Why should the High Commission think to contact anyone else in the family besides her? They had a lot else on their hands at that time. I expect they just closed whatever file they had on Tessa with relief.

'I suppose so. It's so hard to imagine. Do you think Pauline actually told Tessa to go away again for a while?'

'God knows. I suppose she must have.'

'I wonder if Pauline ever met – you know? I don't know his name. Baht something, of course. The man who became Baht Way's stepfather.'

'I wonder that, too. God knows what she said to him. Or to Tessa. But I certainly have a feeling, from whatever I have ever known of Tessa, that Pauline somehow *made* her give that baby up. Only I can't think quite how. Since Tessa must have already been through so much, and the baby was what she had to show for it.'

'Perhaps Tessa herself thought that giving the baby up to someone prepared to care for him would be the best thing she could do for him.'

'Yes, that's what Baht Way himself was apparently told. But a local itinerant worker? A European baby? It doesn't really make any sense, even though Tessa was a bit dotty. In fact, because she was so self-willed it would have been much more like her to reappear openly with the baby under her arm. "Defying bourgeois convention", you know. Poor old Tess . . . At first, when we heard about Baht Way, I thought perhaps it was just as well she's dead. Now I can't help wishing she was still alive.'

'You may never know what really happened.'

'I may not, but I'm bloody well going to try. I'm going to have this whole thing out with Pauline the moment I get home . . . Christ, Julie, I've just remembered: I gave off at Pauline only a few months ago about how she was a pain trying to control everyone else's life for them. What I said wasn't well received, you can imagine, but that's by the by. What simply didn't occur to me then was that she might actually have succeeded in controlling poor Tessa's life.'

Julie said: 'I can't help getting rather interested in Pauline.

Kit's never said anything to me about her in connection with Tessa and Baht Way. But then, of course he wouldn't have known there was a connection.'

'Has he said anything much else to you about her these past months?' I was rather curious to know how much Christopher does, as I suspect, keep different parts of his life in separate compartments.'

'No, I don't think so. Why?'

'Never mind,' I said at once. 'She and her husband are having problems – you may not be entirely surprised to hear – but don't get me started on that.' I did not trust myself on the subject. Elements of the Pauline–Toby problem seemed to be tumbling about now like building blocks inside my tired brain.

'Let's have some pudding,' I said.

By the time we had finished our coffee it was so late that the patient waiters had begun to stack the chairs inside.

'I feel guilty,' I said. 'You looked so tired earlier. I should have thought.'

'It's all right. Really. My shift doesn't start till noon tomorrow. Anyway, it's all been so interesting, I can't tell you. Kit – Christopher – has often spoken about you, and when he said you were coming here I was longing to meet you, but I never thought we'd get together to talk like this.'

We had to walk to Jedu Sumna to find a taxi. There was a rank there near the military-police and customs posts. The causeway itself was brightly illuminated with arc lamps, but the other side seemed a dark void.

'This is the main way visitors get over into the Great Land, isn't it?' I said. When I was a child going on picnics we had passed freely back and forth across the causeway, since it was all one country.

'Yes, usually. If you can get it authorised beforehand, you can pick up the railway on the other side. Of course the line doesn't come down into the City any more. Or people can get passes to cross over here on foot just for an afternoon, but you're supposed to be in a group to do that. Mike and I did it once: we attached ourselves to a church outing. They didn't seem to mind.'

'What's it like on the other side?'

'Oh, scruffy. Poor-looking. A great contrast to the City side.

A lot of ruins near the causeway, even after all these years. Unmade roads. Kids with no shoes following you about wanting biros or sweets or City cents, then running away when they see the military guard. Sort of pretty, though. A lot of flowers, some old shrines, Mike said, up on the hill. But we didn't have time to go that far, and groups aren't supposed to leave the road anyway.'

I didn't pursue the matter any further then. I meant to ring Mike anyway, soon. I did not much want to, yet I yearned for any further scrap of information or encouragement he might be able to give me.

'What an odd young man that is,' I said tentatively.

'He really does want to help you,' said Julie, with a touch of reproach to her voice. 'Or, I should say, he really does want to help Baht Way find his original family. He's like that, he gets passionate about things.'

'He's an orphan himself, isn't he?' I said. 'Colin Darcy mentioned that with all this MIA stuff Mike is really looking for his own father. Literally so, if I've got it right?'

'Yes. He knows his father's name, and thinks he was drafted here in the early 1950s. Around the time he – Mike, I mean – was born.'

'No wonder he empathises with Baht Way.' The pattern here had only just struck me. I thought about it, and the poignancy of it came home to me, though it did not make me trust Mike's judgement any the more.

When we got a taxi I dropped Julie off at the anonymous block in a new development on reclaimed land where she had what she referred to as 'a luxurious rabbit hutch'. We exchanged promises to get in touch with each other as soon as either received news. I did not know whether she would think it appropriate for me to kiss her cheek, so I did not, and then regretted it when she was gone. There had been a faint hint of returning sadness and fear in her as she bade me goodnight. Now she was gone I missed having her at my side. You can get very accustomed to someone you like in four hours.

In the bright, unsleeping hall of my hotel, the luggage of yet another tour group was piled. The desk clerk fished two bits of paper out along with my key.

'A gentleman called twice, sir. From the UK.'

For a moment I interpreted this as meaning that an Englishman – Christopher? – had come to the hotel in person, and my heart leapt. But of course, in Americo-hotel English, 'called' just means telephoned. I looked crossly at the two identical messages.

Marcus.

'He said he would call back at midnight, sir.'

'It's well past that now.'

'Yes, sir. He called back and you weren't here again, so he will call back at oh one hundred hours, sir.'

'Oh one hundred . . . One am. Oh, damn! I want to go to bed.'

'Yes, sir. We'll put the call through to your room, sir.'

I went upstairs and, craving sleep now, tried to stay awake. At home, I have always been good at that, but it is not easy in a hotel room, where everything is organised so that there is nothing to busy yourself with.

At half past one I rang down to the switchboard and told them not to put any call through now till eight am. If Mr Baird from the UK called back again, they were to give him that message.

I fell asleep at once. Shortly after three the phone woke me. My nephew.

'Damn you, Marcus, what's the matter with you? We're eight hours ahead of you here. Can't you work out time sums?'

He apologised in the tone of one already braced for such an attack:

' – I couldn't get back to this phone before, and I couldn't phone you on the other side of the world from a public call box, which was all they'd let me use at the police station.'

'Police station? Marcus, where are you – in London?'

'No, I'm at home in Hampshire. I was in Poole. It's taken me ages to get back. The traffic's bad this evening and it's pissing with rain. Uncle Stephen, it's Mummy – '

Marcus, a self-possessed young man, would never these days call me 'Uncle' or refer to Pauline as 'Mummy' unless he were really upset.

'What on earth has happened?'

Already, with the instantaneousness of conjecture, I saw Pauline dead: doubtless one of those suicides committed to injure others, a final exercise of power – '*Now you'll all be sorry.*'

'She's been charged with conspiracy and with incitement to

murder,' said her son. He enunciated the charges carefully, as if fearing – rightly – that otherwise I would not understand what he was saying.

For a moment, I held the telephone to my ear without saying anything. On the table by the phone lay my room key and small change, the bill from tonight's meal with Julie, and my wallet lying open. I could see the snapshot I've carried for years in it in the slot meant for an ID photo: Sarah, an inch and a half square, with Christopher as a young boy in her arms. The two of them seemed far away from me tonight, in their safe past, but no farther than Pauline's son, in the rainy south of England at the ending of another working day.

'Uncle Stephen, are you still there?'

'I'm still here,' I said at last. 'Still here. Just tell me: this about murder – is anyone dead?'

It would be Toby, I thought. Poor, silly, beleaguered Toby. What more logical than that Pauline, who had never had any scruples about anything, should have wreaked vengeance on the man who had finally found the courage to walk out on her?

'No, no,' said Marcus hastily. 'Nothing actually happened. I'm sure it's all some awful misunderstanding. But the police – well, they say that my mother tried to get Helena Davis murdered.'

'Helena? I see. Good God!' Clearly my logic had been at fault. Too logical, no doubt, to assume that Toby would be the target. Too simply male.

'How on earth could she do that?'

'According to the police she contacted a – a hired gun. Through some advertisement . . .'

Then I remembered Pauline's bizarre question to Christopher about an agency supplying bodyguards.

'Only unfortunately,' said Marcus slowly and clearly, as if wary of what my reaction might be – disbelief? Wild laughter? – 'the person she contacted turned out to be an undercover detective. And when she went to meet him somewhere, he taped the interview with a hidden tape recorder.

'I see . . . I see.'

In my further silence, Marcus said again:

'I'm sure there must be a mistake. Mummy's been in a state, as you know. She couldn't really have understood how what she said would be interpreted. But, you see, it doesn't look good.'

'No. That I do see. What does your mother say about it all?'

'They haven't let me talk to her.'

'Where is she, for God's sake?'

'In the police station in Poole. In custody.' This evidently seemed to Marcus, as also to me, more improbable and alarming at this moment than anything else. 'They said she could only see a lawyer. By the time I got there she'd already sent for old Whatshisname – you know, Burnley, that Basingstoke solicitor who made their Wills for them a few years ago. But I think he's pretty much out of his depth.'

'I would imagine he would be.'

'To tell you the truth, I'm a bit desperate,' said Marcus, his voice suddenly breaking so that he sounded as he used to when he was a portly, soft-natured small boy. 'That's why I'm phoning you. They don't seem to want to give her bail. They keep talking about the "seriousness of the charge".'

'They seem to me to have a point there.'

'Stephen – Uncle Stephen, you aren't by any chance coming home soon, are you? I mean, you're so well known in this part of Dorset. And it may be a question of putting up money, too, which none of us . . . But really I just feel they'd be more impressed by you than they seem to be by me. And Dad's away at the diocesan conference and I can't get hold of him, and anyway he wouldn't . . . I mean, the police probably wouldn't . . .'

'In the circumstances,' I said, 'I think your father might quite possibly agree with the police that your mother should not have bail. All right, Marcus. All right. I see the picture. If I can get a seat on a plane in the morning, I will come home. Even if I never do anything else for your mother again.'

Marcus chose to ignore the last remark, which no doubt baffled him. He settled for thanking me copiously, and promising to reimburse me eventually for the extra journey back and forth across the globe. As I rang off, I recalled a green pottery piggy bank he had when he was about eight, from which he was always jiggling money with a butter knife, to his mother's irritation. Marcus has never been able to save. Vanessa's mauve pig, on the other hand, grew smugly heavier.

Bloody Vanessa, why wasn't she there holding her mother's
hand? That was someone else I could manage very well
without ever seeing again. When she was a small girl I wanted
to love her like the daughter Sarah and I had not succeeded
in having, but it did not work out like that.

I rang down to the desk and got them to contact the airport.
Within ten minutes they had a seat for me on a plane due
to leave soon after eight: I rang Marcus back to tell him.

I had a shower, shaved, dressed again and packed my bags.
I wrote several messages to leave at the front desk: for
Christopher, for Mike, for my Singapore colleagues, for Julie.
Then I lay down for what I knew could be no more than a
couple of hours' sleep. I thought I might doze fitfully, turning
what had happened over and over in my head, jerking awake
at intervals in the expectation of the call to tell me my taxi
to the airport was waiting. But it was as if my subconscious
refused, as yet, to process the news I had just received from
another life. Instead, I dropped into a refreshing sleep in
which Sarah and I were together in Dorset, inhabiting some
indeterminate period of the past, and found, with only mild
surprise but great pleasure, that we had a daughter after all.
She wasn't there with us at the moment, but was due to come
in at any time, with big glasses and a yellow dress.

Let no one tell me the subconscious does not have its own
sentimentality, its own delicacies and hopes and dreams,
beyond the crudities of psychoanalysis.

PART V

Marcus met me at Heathrow. 'It's so good of you to come home like this,' he said fervently. I did not disagree with him. I had been on the plane, bar an enforced break in Bombay, for about sixteen hours, many of them awake and thinking. Over there, in the other life, where Baht Way and Christopher both existed somewhere, it was already past midnight, the glowing City streets emptying of their nocturnal crowds. Twenty-four hours ago I had stood with Julie Barron in the warm night by the river at Jedu Sumna and had seen the great dark on the other side. Here, I seemed to have come down into a no-time, a no-season: a low, damp, whitish sky. It did not feel like home. It did not feel like anywhere.

'What time of day is it?' I asked Marcus, with only a mild curiosity. 'Local time' had been announced on the plane, but I hadn't listened.

'Getting on for five.'

'In the afternoon?'

'Yes, of course,' said Marcus, giving me a nervous glance. He might have pointed out that when we had last spoken I had berated him for being unable to do time sums, but he simply said:

'You got through Baggage-Reclaim jolly quick. Oh, I suppose you didn't check that bag?'

'No. I left a larger case at my hotel in the City. I'll be going back there almost at once − I trust.'

Marcus did not comment. In a minute he started a conversation about the rush-hour traffic building up and whether we would or would not be well advised to make for the M25 ring road. Perhaps he knew I was regretting having come. Once we were beyond the boundaries of the airport, the deadening familiarity of the red-brick houses in the suburban gardens, the repetitious roundabouts, the known names on the road signs, filled me with an obscure anguish. It was not nostalgia but its opposite: a sickening reluctance to return to people I had known for too long, too well – and yet, it appeared, not well at all.

I did not want to be dragged back into the confines of their lives, made to hear their various sides of the story, made to pity and perhaps even to understand. Yet here I was. Habit and self-image had prevailed. The concept of family evidently has a meaning for me beyond the individuals which compose it. Baht Way and I have other things in common besides a general physical likeness. I thought of what Baht Way had said to Mike Isaacs about wanting his own children to know who their ancestors were. Also that he and his father-of-adoption had always been close in spirit.

'Dad's reappeared from his conference,' said Marcus. 'He's in an awful state. Says it's all his fault – what Mum's done now, I mean.'

'Well, I might reproach your father for various things, but not for that. He could hardly have foreseen that because your mother was angry with him she would turn to murder. At least, I don't imagine she'd ever made an overt threat?'

'Oh, heavens, no, I don't think so,' said Marcus, as if the thought of this was in itself alarming enough. 'I feel it was just a sudden impulse on her part,' he added lamely. He didn't, this time, claim that there must be some mistake. 'I don't think she'd really worked it out . . . if you see what I mean.'

I wouldn't be too sure about that, I thought. But I said:

'Yes, it doesn't make much sense, does it? I mean, did she really think that if she only managed to have Helena Davis killed your father would return to her?'

'I suppose she must have.'

'And then life was going to go on just as it did before? With her going to church with him each Sunday and supporting him in the parish and setting a good example of Christian marriage all round, with no one, including him, ever having a clue that she was a murderess? Did she really suppose that so long as no one discovered what she'd-done then it somehow wasn't real and didn't count?'

Of course I had my own reason for posing these brutal rhetorical questions. But Marcus could not know that: it was unfair of me to go on at him. He said unhappily:

'I don't know quite what she thought. Vanessa thinks perhaps she didn't really mean that man who turned out to be a detective actually to shoot this Helena Davis person. That she just wanted her to be given a good fright. Though I realise that doesn't itself look awfully good.'

'It looks more calculating, if anything.'

'Yes. I suppose it does. But you know Mum. It sounds stupid to say this now, but she does have a great sense of – well – right and wrong. In her way. And once she's decided she has right on her side . . .'

'She'll go to literally any lengths to make sure things go that way.'

'I suppose that's what I mean. Vanessa's a bit like that, too. Of course I don't mean that Vanessa knew anything at all about this latest awful business. But she's pretty vitriolic about Helena Davis herself. She's been refusing even to see Dad – well, I think I told you that before?'

'Yes. You did. Well, I know you and Vanessa have never particularly got on with one another.'

A crisis of these dimensions calls so much in question within a family, breaking open things better left unexamined. Did I, in my low, time-disoriented state, hope that Marcus (who has always been my favourite among those children) would now express an unequivocal condemnation of his own mother and dislike of his sister? If so, I had no business to hope that.

After a few minutes I asked where we were going. I had unthinkingly assumed it would be the house in Hampshire. But of course Pauline was not there; she was in a police-station cell in Poole, that was why I had crossed the world.

'We're going to Basingstoke first,' said Marcus. 'Burnley's waiting for us at his own house. We thought that was better than the solicitor's office, in case your plane was late. Then we're going to drive on down to Poole – in two cars, I suppose, I haven't really thought about it. You'd better go in

Burnley's car, I should think? He said he'd need to discuss
the bail question with you before talking to the police about
it, and it would save time to do it like that.'

'Quite. Well, I'll do my best to impress him with my solid
citizenhood.'

I had something else in mind as well for that conversation.
During the long plane journey I had decided various things.
But I also decided not to burden Pauline's unfortunate son
with this information just now.

In a sudden access of pity for this young man, stopping and
starting in miles of traffic trailing out of London, driving with
someone angry to whom he was now helplessly indebted – I
laid my hand momentarily on his arm.

'You'd better fill me in on the details of this business,' I
said.

But there was little he could tell that I had not heard
already. Pauline's plan seemed to have been one of remarkable
simplicity. She had somehow contacted a man advertising
'surveillance work'. Either this advertisement was itself placed
by a police detective doing a little work on the side, or the
nature of her first approach to the advertiser made him
contact the police right off. As Marcus said, Pauline's conviction of her own moral right might well have made her blind
to the way her plan would look to others.

It was arranged that Pauline should go to a particular pub
in Portsmouth where a man came to meet her. There, she
and he reached what must have seemed to her an understanding. She was to meet him again a few days hence in
Poole, to indicate Helena Davis's house to him in order that
there should be no mistake. (A typical touch, that – conscien-
tious Pauline.) The meeting duly took place – but a car full
of police was waiting also.

I learnt rather more from Burnley, once I was transferred
from Marcus's Alfa to the solicitor's BMW. Burnley was an
elderly man, whose silver-haired, family-lawyer airs and florid
complexion were contradicted by a high-pitched, slightly ef-
feminate voice. Maybe he was not really as shocked by this
case as his tone made him seem to be, but the impression
was of appalled distaste. I could only hope that the police felt
more respect for him than I did.

I began to ask him what exactly Pauline had said to the

man in the pub with his hidden recorder. Marcus had not been able to tell me, but I assumed that Burnley, at least, would have now heard the tape or been allowed to read a transcript. I was, however, wrong: the law, as he explained to me with the air of a man accustomed to deal with his intellectual inferiors, does not work like that.

'But surely you will eventually be allowed to hear or read the evidence against my sister? How otherwise could you organise her defence?'

'Eventually, yes – at or subsequent to the committal proceedings . . .' He droned on for a bit about different types of committal to the Crown Court, while I sat thinking about barristers – QCs? – and wondering if Pauline would get legal aid. Of course, that would depend, ironically, on Toby's salary.

Having established his credentials as a stickler for protocol, to his own satisfaction if not mine, Burnley unbent sufficiently to tell me what the police superintendent had told him – that, according to the tape, Pauline had wanted the man she was trying to employ to make the killing look like a burglary that had been interrupted.

'My nephew and niece think that perhaps she didn't really mean him to kill Miss Davis, just to frighten her. What do you think?'

'I can't answer that.'

'Well, but you've talked to my sister – you're the only one who has. What does she say about it?'

'I'm not at liberty to discuss that, doctor. Mrs Baird is my client.'

Well, damn you, you old fool, I thought, perhaps unfairly. But I could not risk antagonising him at the moment: I had several other things to ask him. The phrase 'the man Mrs Baird was trying to employ' had reminded me of something else I had thought about on the plane and which was puzzling me.

'Surely no man, whether in good faith or as a part of a charade, would agree to murder a stranger, except for substantial payment?'

Mr Burnley moistened his lips and paused before answering.

'One would assume that to be so, yes.'

'Well, then? My sister has no money – that I know of. She and her husband have never been well off, and I know she did not inherit anything personally from our parents. What they left, which was not a great deal in the end, they left in trust for their grandchildren. But of course, you made her will, you must know for yourself about her financial circumstances.'

'Quite.' He hesitated so long that I thought he wasn't even going to answer. But finally he said:

'Since you are her brother, it is perhaps not improper to tell you that Mrs Baird does in fact appear to have some thousands of pounds at her disposal. I gather that she has, er, saved this not inconsiderable sum out of the housekeeping over the passage of years. Being a frugal, careful housewife, as I understand it.'

'Well, I'm damned.' There really seemed nothing else to say. I was extremely surprised at first, remembering all Pauline's talk, over the years, about being so hard up. But then, the more I thought about it, the less surprising it seemed.

'I have advised Mrs Baird,' said Burnley, 'that she should offer this amount as her own security for bail, but the police have indicated that other substantial security will probably be required.'

'Well, yes, that's why I am here. Or so I've gathered.'

We had a brief discussion about money, which is not a problem to me. I have no one but myself to consider these days. Christopher earns enough at present for his uncomplicated needs, and otherwise appears quite uninterested in the stuff. In any case, as I understand it, you do not go bail for someone if you expect them to vanish, and whatever I currently thought of Pauline I did not feel that she would do that. It was not that which made me hesitate.

'Are we,' I asked, 'hoping to get my sister released on bail tonight?'

'That is what I would hope, now that you have arrived. She could possibly be released into your charge tonight, if you undertake to produce her in the magistrates' court tomorrow. Though I must warn you that the police are entitled to keep her still if they choose, till her appearance in court. And of course there is no actual guarantee that the magistrates will then see fit to bail her at all, though in practice I am fairly confident that they will, in all the circumstances.'

He spoke soothingly, and I suddenly realised that of course he expected me to be distressed at the prospect of Pauline being further detained, even for one night. Perhaps his priggish refusal to discuss the case with me was partly embarrassment and a kind of squeamish solicitude for what he assumed I must be feeling. However, I had a different preoccupation. Through jet lag that was coming and going now like flu, I summoned reserves of bullying energy to say:

'I think I should make it clear now that though I am quite prepared in principle to put up bail money for Mrs Baird, I will not do so unless and until I have had the opportunity to talk to her first. In private, if you don't mind.'

'Oh, I'm afraid I can't guarantee that.'

'Well, if you don't, you've got no deal. Sorry, but that's the way it is.' I was infuriated by his tone, that of the professional impeder, and was on the point of adding: And in that case I've more or less been brought home under false pretences. I just stopped myself saying it. Till that moment, I had not fully admitted to myself how much my instant response to Marcus's cry for help had been influenced by my more primitive desire to ask Pauline some questions. Had the bail been the only issue on my mind, I might have pleaded important commitments in Asia and tried to satisfy the police with a telephone call and a faxed statement to show in court.

'You misunderstand, doctor,' said Burnley peevishly. 'Whether or not you may see your sister doesn't depend on me. It depends on the police. You may feel that you have a moral right to see her while she is in custody, but you have no legal right.'

'But I assume we can ask the police if I may?'

'I can, of course, put the request to them. Explain that, as her brother, you feel strongly on the matter – '

'It doesn't seem to me so much a matter of "feeling strongly" as of common sense,' I said. 'Naturally, if I'm to put up thousands of pounds of bail money for her, I want to be sure for myself that she understands the serious position she's in – and that she hasn't gone quite off her head.'

'Oh, I think you will have to trust me over that. I have emphasised to her myself the serious nature of the charge.'

'Wait a minute. It's not only that. At the moment, this situation seems to me to be completely fogged by things one is not allowed to know or not allowed to do – '

'The law, doctor – '

'OK. I know what you're going to say. That's how the law works.' I hesitated for a moment. My temper was short. I gathered my forces to demolish him.

'As you say, I'm a doctor, not a lawyer, and I can only act in the way I consider proper. I mean that I am accustomed not only to taking responsibility but also to relying on my own judgement, not on anyone else's. And I have to know the facts. So I am telling you now – and you are welcome to tell the police – that in my judgement it would be not only wrong but quite impracticable for me to put up bail for anyone without being given the opportunity to talk to them first. And what's more – ' The idea suddenly occurred to me as I was speaking so I went on, though he was opening and shutting his mouth, trying to speak – 'What's more, you can tell the police that if they insist on my bailing my sister sight unseen, so to speak, and then when I have talked to her in private I find that I am not satisfied . . . then I shall bring her back to the police station.'

He looked shocked. In retrospect, I am not really surprised.

'I doubt,' he said, 'whether the police will take kindly to having terms dictated to them.'

'Then I shall say all that to the magistrates tomorrow morning. They at least will have to hear me out if they're considering bail at all, won't they?' My mind, so sluggish and erratic from all those hours out of life in the air, seemed to be back in gear now. Scraps of legal wisdom picked up from reading or from friends had risen to the surface.

Burnley had sunk his chin into his neck and looked cross again.

'Well, I'll try. I'll do my best for my client, of course. But what you are suggesting is most irregular and, ah, not what I have been expecting – '

'If it has to come to a discussion in court,' I said, rudely but with sudden intuition, 'you'd better leave the magistrates to me.' I thought, but did not add: I'll quite likely know or be known to one of them anyway.

I don't normally rejoice at pulling rank in this way: it's too easy for doctors to do that. But in the present situation, with Burnley sitting beside me like an obese incarnation of a rule book, I felt a dull glow of satisfaction.

And, it turned out, everything occurred as I had foreseen. The police initially stalled – which mercifully allowed me to go home and collapse into bed. The following morning in court (a building ghostly-familiar to me from the occasional inquest), my request for a private interview with my sister was promptly granted.

I wondered, as I was led through the Victorian corridors of the adjoining police station, whether I was going to have to confront Pauline in an underground cell. There, presumably, she had spent the last two nights: I had not allowed myself fully to contemplate this fact till now. As I walked behind the duty sergeant I suddenly saw in my mind chipped, white-tiled walls like a municipal wash house, a bunk with one thin blanket, an unscreened, seatless lavatory, a door with a grille, a ceiling light burning inaccessibly. It waits for all of us, that cell, but how very few of that class to which I and Pauline both belong by birth ever see the inside of it?

Nor did I now. I was shown into a small, anonymous, windowless room with a table and four regulation-issue chairs, and there Pauline was already sitting. She had been in court, of course, when I had been called into the witness box to say my piece. But I had not looked at her, beyond a quick glance, and I did not get the impression she wanted to look at me either. Now we were face to face and, as promised, the sergeant left us alone, indeed locked in. He told us to phone through when we were done: the door clicked shut as he left.

We did not kiss. We never do. She seemed the same as always, in trousers and one of her heavy woollen cardigans. She looked white and lined, but she has looked like that, too, for years.

In my mind, ever since I was handed that piece of paper at the High Commission, I suppose I had been seeing the young Pauline of around 1950, high-coloured and sure of herself in a tennis dress. Now, faced at last with the Pauline of today, so dowdy, almost old, I was momentarily thrown. I just looked at her. It was she who eventually spoke.

'It's nice of you to come home.' Thin, neutral voice. Did I detect a touch of irony?

'It *is* quite nice of me, as it happens.' I was not going to let any gratitude or abasement from her, I thought, deflect me now from my purpose. But, evidently, I need not have worried, for her next words to me were:

'Still, you can afford it, can't you? Flying around the world, I mean.'

Well, well. You never know, unless it is revealed by chance after, perhaps, a lifetime of dissimulation, what someone else has most resented about you all along.

I had not yet decided how to respond to her remark, if at all, when she went on: 'I suppose you want to know why I've done what I've done before you graciously agree to use your wealth to bail me?'

I sat down carefully on one of the chairs, several feet away from her, and took my time about answering.

'No, Pauline,' I said at last. 'I'm not going to ask you anything about that, as it happens – not about Helena Davis, that is. Of course, if you want, you're welcome to tell me. No, not now!' Tense as a spring, she was already trying to speak again. 'Later, if you wish. But first I am going to ask you about something that happened longer ago – oh, much longer . . . Can't you guess what? I've just come back from the Far East remember.'

I would not say that that was when she began to look frightened, for fear had been perceptible on her like an emanation from the moment I was shown into the room. But she did, at that moment, look completely stricken. Her pale eyes fixed on me, then shifted quickly away.

'I haven't the faintest idea what you mean,' she said.

'Haven't you? What did you do with the baby Tessa had in the City in 1951?'

I suppose, if I had expected anything, it was that she would bluster: 'What on earth are you talking about, Stephen?' and that I should have to bully her into an admission, citing places and exact dates, telling her how the existence of Baht Way had come to light. But instead she said almost instantly, sharply:

'It's dead. It died soon after it was born. Just as well. Why do you come bothering me about that now? Oh, I suppose you suspect me of murder there, too. Or would it be called infanticide in that case?'

'Very ingenious, Pauline.' (In the present circumstances, her manic suggestion did at least seem that.) 'But you didn't kill

that baby, did you? For he isn't dead. He's alive and living
in the City and has children of his own back in the Great
Land . . .' I paused, to see how she was taking all this. 'But I
see I'm not really surprising you with this news?'

My own mind was ticking over quickly also. When she had
said 'It's dead' it occurred to me that she might really believe
this to be the case – that shortly after she had registered
the birth Tessa might have told her, for whatever reason,
that the boy had died. If so, this did not exonerate her from
the continuing pain she had inflicted on our parents by
keeping them in ignorance of Tessa's reappearance, but it
might rather mitigate the whole picture of her behaviour.
After all, as Julie Barron had said, an illegitimate child at that
time . . . Pauline may have felt overtaken by events.

But I could see, watching her face, that these excuses were
not going to be relevant. For Pauline was not surprised to be
told of Baht Way's continuing existence. She was not feigning
bewilderment, she did not even ask me how I knew that the
child had lived. Instead, she said in an absurdly high-handed
tone that, in the circumstances, seemed almost valiant:

'I don't see what on earth business it is of yours to ask me
questions about poor Tessa's baby.'

'Well, since you've apparently been keeping his existence
secret for forty years and Tessa is now dead, you seem exactly
the right person for me to ask.'

'Well, I'm not going to answer. Why should I? Tessa's dead,
as you say. Why don't you leave the poor thing alone?'

' "Why don't you leave the poor thing alone?" That, coming
from you, Pauline, is pretty rich. Why didn't you leave her
alone? You registered the birth for her. Your name is on the
entry. Just what exactly did you get up to after that?'

It was a shot in the dark, but Pauline must have thought I
knew more than I really did. She began to look scared then,
and did not reply.

'I'm waiting,' I said after a while, adding absurdly: 'I'm not
leaving this room till you've answered.' How readily, in a
situation of unprecedented drama, do the set phrases of
melodrama come to hand. But this was real, and I meant it.

'Well, I won't answer, that's all. It's none of your business.'

'In that case,' I said, having arrived at the point I had
envisaged ever since Marcus had phoned me and all those

unsleeping hours on the plane, 'I shall of course have to leave in the end. But it will be without you, Pauline, get this straight. I am not even going to consider putting up bail for you on the present business until you've told me exactly what happened on that other occasion when you tried to interfere with life and death to have things all your own way.'

She was beginning to disintegrate, I saw with nasty satisfaction. I too can be very unpleasant when I have set my mind on something; yes, it's true.

'Don't look at me like that, Stephen. You've no right. I really can't remember, it was so long ago, but I'm sure I was only trying to do my best – '

'Tell me. I just want to know.'

'No. You're only a man. You wouldn't understand.'

'Then I won't lift a finger to get you out of this place. And what effect do you think that will have in court? "After talking to her, her brother decided he could not stand bail for her." What will that look like – either here in the Magistrates' Court or at your trial? Your chances of avoiding a jail sentence in the end look pretty slim anyway: do you want them to go down to zero?' Aghast, perhaps by the way I was myself behaving as much as by the horror of my elder sister and everything she represented to me, which I found welling up in me after all these years, I shouted:

'Pauline, *wake up*! This is not a bloody contest in which you have to prove once again how superior you are. This is real. You know, Pauline, reality, that thing you cover over with the layers of posing and do-gooding and pushing other people around. All that claptrap about "helping people talk through their problems" – well, this is an urgent problem for you, *now*. Talk to me honestly about what happened with Tessa and that baby – everything, yes, everything that you know – and I'll help you with the present business all I can. But if you don't, I won't lift a finger for you. Now or later.'

How liberating anger is. How readily one gets drunk on one's own righteous cause. I think that even as I was shouting at her, there in that stuffy, soundproofed room where no doubt many people had been questioned and threatened, I was aware that my avenging wrath was not entirely to my credit. Evidently I, too, the esteemed, reliable old doctor, enjoy power over others. I have been luckier than Pauline in that my life has provided more acceptable and straightforward outlets for power than hers can have done. All right, I was 'justified': I was using back to her the very weapons of menace and manipulation that (I now guessed) she had used on Tessa, when the little sister was at her most vulnerable and wretched. But still, weapons are weapons. I now, in my turn, was using them against someone cornered.

There are other things we share, also. My upbringing, with its early happiness, then its descent into fear and misery and the long years of exile, may have left me wounded, if only with the classic wound once suffered by so many British children from expatriate families like ours. Once, in considerable distress and frustration, my wife Sarah said I was a damaged character. In time, mainly after her death, I have come dimly to perceive that she was right. But then, by the same token, is Pauline damaged too? It is possible that Pauline's headgirlish inability to treat other beings as equals, her self-aggrandising charades, are also the product of a childhood spent away from home? She too was cast into an uncaring place too young. Perhaps she found then that she could only cope by huddling herself in a carapace of pretences that, in time, grew and stuck to her skin till she no longer knew what she was. 'Being their natural selves' is a luxury unknown to those children who are pushed hither and thither at their parents' convenience. 'Pauline is such a competent person', our idle, soft, kindly but profoundly self-centred mother used to say, with a note of complacency which even before I was fully adult grated on my ear and sounded an obscure warning to me. Perhaps Pauline, this schemer, liar and prater of 'principles', who seemed to have lost touch with any sense of principle or even with what a principle might be, learnt to manage in childhood in the only way she could?

I did not want to see her like this. I could not afford, yet, to feel pity for her. I could not afford to remember the elder sister by my side on the boat that carried us away from the Bundar, dashing tears angrily from her own eyes, hiding her grief from me with a brisk show and only giving way to it at night when she thought I was asleep in my lower bunk. That sister was irrevocably lost to me, far more lost than my dead Sarah, or Tessa, or even Jill, who, in the end, did not want me enough. With a whole orchestra of emotions working within me, I found myself shouting:

'You're a destroyer, Pauline, that's what you are. Not a very successful one at the moment, which is why you find yourself here. You haven't got a properly functioning heart, and you emotionally mutilate other people – the Lay Balint of the Home Counties. Undermining people and gobbling them up has been your way of life for decades. And the people you can't treat in this way you resent and try to damage in other ways. Oh yes, you do! Remember the vendetta you ran against that Comprehensive School head who wouldn't agree with you that Plod is "really" bright? You got the poor sod sacked, didn't you? And remember the way you came telling tales to me about Sarah that you hoped would break our marriage? That was no different, in essence, from what you've tried to do with Helena Davis. It's just that real murder is against the law – did no one ever tell you that? Or did you think you were too special for that to matter?'

'I – I . . . Stephen. Please don't. I can explain.'

'No, Pauline. For once you can't explain. Don't even try. Instead, you are going to tell me right now, without any flannelling, just exactly what happened to that baby of Tessa's. How did you work it? Come on, I'm waiting.'

And so on and so forth, so that, in the end, even she saw that she had to tell me.

'. . . I was trying to do what seemed best. I really was. Oh, I can see you don't believe me. You just hate me, don't you? Everyone seems to, these days. Toby does. I'm not so stupid that I don't know that. Even Plod said . . . And of course that was before All This Business with the police happened . . . No, no, all right, I'm not going to talk about that now. Actually, I can't bear to . . . Where was I? Yes, Tessa –

'You see, she came back to the City . . . When? Oh, quite early on, I think. With that boyfriend of hers. As soon as there was a bit of a lull in the Troubles and they could get back again from the place upcountry where they'd hidden. There'd been some sort of incident. One of their team had been killed, I think, and the rest . . . Well, anyway, they had an awful time. But eventually Tessa and that boy got back to the City. Of course I didn't know for months – I really didn't, don't look at me like that, Stephen, I *am* trying to tell it just as it was . . . The pair of them disappeared into a slum called

Teyn Something. Teyn Bira, that was it. And she didn't
contact me at all.

'. . . Why? Well, because she was pregnant. And she considered herself in love with him, I suppose. You know how
immature she was . . . Well, yes, I agree, she was very young
and didn't know what to do. *Gosh*, I was furious with her
when I finally did run into her. But actually, to be fair, she
had no idea I was still in the City. Most of the Europeans
had got out. She told me she had gone looking once for
Mother and Father, but the bungalow was all shut up and so
she thought I had gone with them.

'. . . Where did I run into her? Oh, on Main Road, in that
sort of square, you know, where the other big road – yes,
Ferguson Road, that's right – ran down towards the market
quarter and then on to the railway station and Teyn Bira.
Well, I imagine it still does . . . No? Well, I don't suppose I'll
ever go back there to see. But I remember absolutely clearly,
as if it was only last year, catching sight of her from the far
side of the square and belting after her all among the carts
and the cycle rickshaws. There were hardly any cars on the
streets then, of course. Only the army had petrol.

'I finally caught up with her near the station. Awfully
pregnant. Such a shock. I was horrified. She was quite near
her time. And she looked so much older and, well, almost
dirty. Peaky, you know. And her hair all stringy. Of course
she'd gone short of food as well as everything else. I really
couldn't imagine what she'd been through . . .' She cried a
little, as if the appalled incomprehension was something, not
of forty years ago, but of the present moment.

'. . . No, no, that boyfriend was dead by then. Killed. No,
I don't know how. She wouldn't say. I was frightfully sorry
for *her* of course, but I have to admit I wasn't totally sorry
he was dead, because I realised at once that in the long run
this might simplify things. I suppose you think that was awful
of me? Well, perhaps it was. But none of us ever liked him
much, did we? And look at how he'd led her astray and ruined
her life.

'. . . But you *did* meet him, Stephen. At least once, I know,
I remember it. He came to the house, and Father was pretty
short with him. That young journalist or whatever he was. A
sort of professional troublemaker, we thought. Father used to

call him That Bloody Hack. Remember?

'His name was Wayland Clark, I think. Yes, that was it. We always used to think it such a pretentious first name for a very ordinary English boy from a northern town. Well, I suppose we were all fearful snobs in those days, weren't we? I know that was his name because Tessa told me he was the one who – oh, and because of something that happened quite a few years later which helped to fix it in my mind . . . Well, I don't suppose it matters now one way or another, but I might as well tell you, if I've got to tell you everything. It was some time after Father died; Mother got this letter addressed to Father and naturally opened it. It was a sort of round-robin that was being sent to all the members of the Old Citizens' Society – you know, they used to meet once a year in London at the Oriental Club for a nostalgic gossip. I expect they still do, the ones that are left.

'The letter was from Wayland Clark's family. They were trying to find people who might remember him, and who might be able to tell them just how he died. All those years after the Troubles were over. It seemed a bit morbid and pointless to me, though of course I felt sorry for them. I'd always wondered if he'd actually deserted Tessa and she hadn't wanted to tell me. But it looks as if he did die, just as she said.

'. . . Well, Mother showed the letter to me. Naturally she knew nothing at all about what happened between him and Tessa and didn't seem to suspect anything, but she asked me whether she should answer the letter. I don't know what she thought she'd find to say if she did. You know how hopeless she was at deciding anything for herself once Father had gone. So I just said: "Give it to me. I vaguely remember the boy – I'll write a little note to his parents. Don't mention it to Tessa." I said, "If he's dead, she might not want to be reminded of him, as he was a friend." And Mother said: "No, no, of course I won't" – you remember we never did mention anything about the City or the Great Land to Tessa once she'd come home . . . No, *I* never did. Of course not.

'I put the letter in the bin. What else could I have done with it? In all the circumstances.

'. . . I *am* coming to the point, Stephen. Don't glare at me like that, I'm doing my best, I really am.

'Anyway, when I ran into her like that in the street, Tessa wouldn't tell me where she was living. Of course that was because – well, by that time there was this other man looking after her. I met him. A local.' Pauline's voice sank lower. I could tell that, after a lifetime's earnest theoretical condemnation of 'racism', the thought of Tessa in such a situation still shocked her.

'Baht Something,' I said. 'He was called Baht Something?'

'Yes. That was his name. I'd forgotten it. Baht Tye, I think it was.' Pauline did not ask how I knew. She remained silent a moment, her face crumpled in thought, remembering.

'Go on, Pauline. Go on.'

'He – Baht Tye – hardly spoke any English. Just a few words he'd picked up and a few more Tessa taught him. God knows how they managed to communicate. I suppose she'd learnt enough City-lingo after all that had happened to her. He was a migrant worker from upcountry. And not even particularly young – years older than Tessa; well, I don't know: all those people look the same age, don't they? He was working as a cook in a cheap restaurant where she had gone to look for work, washing up or something. He'd taken pity on her, I suppose. Maybe she didn't look pregnant at first. Or maybe she told him and that made him even more sorry for her. I imagine he was rather a simple person himself, not even a city type, and didn't realise that a European girl like her would have a family somewhere, another life . . . She even hinted to me they'd gone through some sort of marriage ceremony together. Just in a local temple, of course, not official . . . Oh, it was all impossible.

'Tessa asked me not to tell them at home till the baby was actually born. Well, that seemed reasonable, as she reckoned it was practically due. And it must have been even more due than she thought, because when I turned up three days later outside that greasy little restaurant where she'd agreed to meet me – I'd said I'd get some money for her – only Whatshisname, Baht Tye, was there. In his cook's overall. He told me that when she was in labour he'd taken her to St Saviour's Hospital in Teyn Bira because a friend told him he should, but he didn't know yet if the baby was born. He seemed worried but a bit, you know, scared of presenting himself there again in person. I think the nurses there may have made him feel he was out of place. Where he came from, I shouldn't think anyone had ever seen the inside of a hospital.

'So I went along myself and there she was. She'd had the baby. A boy. The babies were all yelling together in the nursery – hospitals kept them apart from the mothers in those days, if you remember – and Tessa was lying in bed all weepy. I mean, she hadn't really had the time or the chance to get keen on the baby yet, and she just wanted to get out of that place. The Sister in charge could see something wasn't right – no father in evidence and so on – and was treating Tessa like a bar girl.

'Well, I dealt with the Sister. She wasn't really a bad sort of woman, and she quite saw my point when I said that by far the best thing would be for Tessa to give up the baby for adoption and forget all about it. Oh, don't look at me like that, Stephen. That was a perfectly respectable thing at the time. Perhaps you've forgotten, but it was. It's only in the last twenty years people have got so sentimental about these things.

'. . . No, I didn't say what I thought to Tessa, it wouldn't have been any use. I knew she wouldn't see it like that. You know how self-willed she was.

'The Sister said that, what with the Troubles and the City virtually under siege at times, there were unwanted babies all over the place and their church orphanage was bursting at the seams. I could see she was afraid I was going to ask her to take on Tessa's baby too. So I said not to worry, I'd try to fix something up. And naturally she was relieved, and left it to me. I also told her I'd register the birth.

'. . . Well, since I'm having to be honest with you, I didn't really mean to when I said it. But the Sister had said that the consular official used to call sometimes at the hospital, and I was just a bit afraid she'd check up that I *had* registered it, meaning to be helpful. And then if I hadn't, there might have been a schemozzle at the High Commission, with Father and Mother in England getting to hear. I thought it was much the best thing that *I* should tell the High Commission Tessa was found and had a baby, and, yes, everything was being looked after, thank you – and that would be that.' She stopped talking for a bit.

'And that,' I said at last, 'apparently was that. Till just

recently . . . But I still don't understand exactly how.'

'Oh, it wasn't very difficult.' But she looked away from me.

'The truth, Pauline. I want the truth.'

'You forget. The world was quite different in those days. Girls Tessa's age weren't so conscious of their rights. They didn't have any rights. Nor did people like that pathetic local man. In any case, as I said, the whole thing was so impossible . . . Well, I just did what seemed best to me for all concerned – for Tessa herself, for Whatshisname, Baht Tye, who needed to go back to his own kind. I did what I thought was right, Stephen. So don't try to tell me otherwise.'

'I won't try to tell you anything, Pauline.' (She had begun to cry again.) 'But you haven't yet told me – *what exactly did you do*? How did you fix it up?'

'I don't know what you mean.'

'Yes you do. How did you persuade Tessa to give up that child? It was Wayland Clark's child, and if she was in love with him and he was killed . . .'

'I told her,' said Pauline, in a choked voice, 'that the baby had died.'

'What? You couldn't have. Even you couldn't have done that.'

My comment was in human terms, but she took it as a purely practical one.

'Oh yes, I did,' she said, with a dim triumph, wiping her eyes. 'Like I said, it wasn't even very difficult. I thought it all out before I came back again to the hospital. First I had an interview with the Sister and told her that I – well, I said "the family" – had found someone to take the baby on, and that I could take it away with me that very day. (It was on bottles, luckily, I'd made sure of that.) I asked the Sister not to talk about the whole thing to Tessa because Tessa was upset – just to tell the nurses not to mention the baby to her at all. And she said that wouldn't be a problem because Tessa was due anyway to be moved to their convalescent block further out in the suburbs. That was how they did things in those days. It was called "lying-in".'

'Yes, I remember lying-in. Well, go on.'

'So the Sister was just glad that I'd taken the problem off her hands. By that time I'd paid for Tessa's confinement and everything of course, and as a lot of the patients never paid anything, everyone was grateful to me. Then I went back to the ward and told Tessa – well, that the poor little baby had suddenly died.' Her voice trembled faintly on the phrase, as it must have done with conscious artistry forty years ago – or as if this were indeed, at some level, a real death she was reporting.

'Of course Tessa was completely ignorant about babies,' she went on after a while. 'Well, I was then, too. I think I said he'd had "a sudden convulsion" and that new babies sometimes did. I knew it wouldn't occur to her to think that he'd been OK when he'd had his morning bottle, or to ask to see the doctor or anyone.

'. . . Upset? Well, of course. It was a shock, naturally. She seemed almost struck dumb for a bit, which was so unlike her. When she did say something it was about how disappointed Baht Tye would be – how he'd been looking forward to her bringing the baby home to him. Oh yes, Stephen, she really did seem to have had the impossible idea that she and Baht Tye and this baby from someone else were going to set up house together in some ghastly little room in Teyn Bira. Go public, so to speak. Tell Mother and Father and everyone. I mean – I ask you! Do you see why I had to put a stop to it?

'Anyway, I told her not to brood – that it was probably all for the best and so on, and that she should go off to the convalescent home right away and get up her strength. I helped her pack her bag and went over there with her, in a cycle-rickshaw, so none of the hospital nurses had a chance to say anything stupid to her. I said that quite soon, as soon as I could wangle passages, she and I could both go back to England and put the whole thing behind us, that no one in England need ever know and that she and I need never talk of it again. When I left her at the convalescent home she actually seemed quite grateful to me, Stephen. You may not understand that, but she was.

'. . . And then? Well, I went back to the hospital. The sister had already told the nun in charge of the babies' nursery that I was going to take the baby away with me. It was just handed to me, in hospital clothes, swaddled in a sheet in the way they did there – and that was that.

'I took it straight round to Baht Tye's restaurant.

'. . . No, that wasn't so very difficult, either. I tell you, he was a humble sort of person. He believed what he was told – once he'd managed to understand what I was saying.

'I told him that *Tessa* was dead. Well, what else could I do? I knew that otherwise he'd come looking for her and make a nuisance of himself. It was much the simplest solution. He didn't even seem terribly surprised. I expect women often died after childbirth in the world he came from. I said I'd been with her just before she'd died, and that she'd wanted him to have the child, so here it was. He didn't seem to take it in at first – well, his English was very bad, and he was upset, I suppose. But then, when I kept telling him "Tessa said you keep baby", he seemed almost pleased. Pathetic, really, when it wasn't even his child. I mean, you could see it was entirely western. Obviously it was that Wayland boy's.' She added:

'I gave him some money. Quite a bit, actually, because I was rather sorry for him. And of course I'd had to tell him there was no possibility of him coming to her funeral or anything like that – that it just "wasn't our custom". I gave him a photo of her, as far as I remember – the one I'd had earlier, to show to people when I was looking for her; it was still in my handbag. I thought afterwards that it might have been a bit unwise of me, but anyway, as I say, I was sorry for the poor little man.

'Well, he took the baby. He said he'd call it by the name he knew she'd wanted. And he said he'd give up his job and leave the City and take it back to his village. I expect he found some woman to look after it there. These people had huge extended families.

'I know what you're thinking. *How could I?* Well, to be honest, once I had babies of my own, I wondered that myself. But at the time . . . It was for Tessa I did it, for her sake, so that she could make a fresh start. A new life. It was much the best thing for her that the baby should disappear and that she shouldn't even have to make a painful decision about that. And if, as you seem to think now, that baby did survive and grow up, doesn't that seem to show I did right?

'I acted for the best – please try to understand that, Stephen, even if you think that what I did was wrong. And I was all ready to bring Tessa home with me, as a lovely surprise for Mother and Father, but she just disappeared

again. From the convalescent place. Simply vanished without
a word to me. I looked everywhere for her. I told them that
at home, that part was true. But she just wasn't anywhere. I
was as surprised and relieved as any of you when she turned
up again the next year.

'Sometimes I feel as if I've spent my whole life trying to do
things for other people, and nobody understands . . .'

She does not give up, Pauline. You have to grant her that. I
had thought, earlier, that in forcing this confession out of her
I had broken through her carapace and found something
vulnerable and alterable beneath. But no, the mask of self-
esteem has stuck to her flesh and become part of it. Were I
or anyone else really to succeed in pulling it away, then what
would be uncovered would not be tender skin but a flayed
and bleeding death's-head, eyes staring from their raw sockets
at a life too real to be borne.

It seemed to me now that both the long-ago Tessa business
and the present attempt at murder were acted-out fantasies
just like Pauline's other games: Happy Families, indefatigable
good works for the community, Christianity, counselling.
Pauline the problem-solver and purveyor of insight. Pauline
the child-abolisher and murderer, trotting about arbitrarily
pronouncing this or that other person dead, as in a competitive game. Some of the playlets in which she was both director
and star were ostensibly realistic and some were preposterous.
One, a monstrous one, had succeeded by a fluke for forty
years; another, still more monstrous, had by another fluke
been instantly exposed – but did she really understand in any
of them what she was doing? I felt now that I would never
know.

I did not want to hear what elaborate, passionate and
circumstantial excuses she would mount for her attempt to
abolish Helena Davis. If, indeed, that was what it had been.
I did not even ask.

I told her I was ready to bail her, for whatever good that
would do for the present. She nodded, for the moment spent,
wordless. I picked up the phone to call the sergeant.

As it happened, there was a further complication in the bail
business which I had not foreseen. That booby Burnley had

not made it clear to me that I might also be asked to have Pauline living for the time being under my roof. Perhaps he had taken it for granted that I would agree. However, when asked about this in court, I made it clear that an urgent professional matter required me to return to east Asia almost immediately.

'I see no point in my sister living in my house when I'm not there. She would surely be better off in her own home?' I was about to add 'and that's much farther from Poole than my house is, so she won't be tempted so easily to try on anything else', but realised in time that this might sound frivolous and would further embellish the story for the two young men scribbling on the press bench. The local papers would be brighter than usual this week – and that, I realised with foreboding, would be just the start of it. *Vicar's Wife in Revenge Murder Bid . . . The Vicar, the Wife and the Mistress . . .*

A whispered conference among the three members of the Bench. A further question to Burnley. They seemed to think that Pauline should not be left on her own. It is true that Pauline does not like being on her own, but that is a rather different matter.

Burnley announced that Mrs Baird's husband and elder daughter had now arrived. (I had not known this.) Perhaps if the Bench would be so good as to stand the case out again for a few more minutes?

The Bench, continuing their amiability, agreed.

In the hall outside, Toby clasped my hand in both of his.

'Awfully good of you to come back, Stephen. Marcus has been telling me. Really, terribly good – '

'Well, I do what I can.' It seemed a fair assessment and I did not want to sound too enthusiastic. From what Toby said next, fervently backed up by Vanessa (who had evidently made her peace with him again), he appeared to think that getting Pauline out on bail was 'half the battle'. It was not for me to tell him that the battle between Pauline and the Criminal Justice Act had hardly begun. I was rather surprised that he took it this way. I should have thought he might, for Helena Davis's sake, be only too glad to have Pauline kept in custody.

I said to Vanessa that I was glad to see her, and that I was sorry but that she and Marcus and the others were going to have to work out a chaperonage system for their mother without my help. I went out of the building to stretch my legs and breathe a little. I needed to, after the time with Pauline in that sealed room. I felt weak, really, almost vague. Drained. The weather had cleared: a mild, uncertain, late-summery day. It would indeed be unpleasant, I thought, to be locked up for any length of time. Oh, Pauline! What a mess she'd made of everything.

Presently Marcus came out to join me.

'I think we've got it sorted out,' he said. 'Dad's going to offer to come home for a bit.'

'Good heavens! Well – I mean, of course, that's fine, if he will. I'm very surprised, though.'

'Old Burnley's pleased. He says it will impress the court more than anything else. When it comes to the actual trial, that is.'

'Yes, I suppose it would. You mean, it makes whatever your mother's been doing look less serious? If your father's prepared to, uh, condone it.'

'Something like that,' said Marcus. We exchanged weary smiles.

By and by he added, with what might have been irony but also embarrassment: 'Don't forget, Dad's a great one for Christian forgiveness.'

'Well, I know. It's his job, I do realise. But honestly, Marcus, surely even your father can't hand out forgiveness just like that? I know he wasn't the direct victim of the plan, but he was the next person, so to speak.'

'Oh, he knows that. In fact, I think that's what shocked him into coming here today. He told me it made him realise what he had really done. You shouldn't underestimate Dad, you know,' said Toby's son to me, with veiled reproach and, I thought, some dignity.

I answered submissively that I did not underestimate Toby. But I added that I could not quite see how this triangle of murderous wife and threatened lover was going to be settled with Toby dashing between them trying to administer emotional support on both sides.

'Oh, I'm not sure he will be. Dashing, I mean.' With a return to his more usual irreverent air, Marcus added: 'Between you and me, I rather think Helena Davis has gone off him since she's heard about Mum's doings.'

'You mean, she wants to stay clear of people who mean trouble? Not worth the risk of being killed and so forth?'

'Well, that's what I think. From something Dad let slip last night on the phone to me. He was pretty upset about it. Well, he's upset about the whole business, not surprisingly . . . but that's rather what I gathered, yes. That Ms Davis had chucked him out.'

'Well, well.'

'I've just looked into his car and it's full of stuff – clothes and books and things, all over the back seat.' Marcus caught my eye. We both wanted to laugh, and neither of us liked to.

'I must say, I hope so,' said Marcus robustly. 'Dad introduced me to her at one point, and I thought she was rather a cow. Not a bit good for him. Look, there's Vanessa on the steps. She wants us. I suppose we've got to go back into court again.'

As I followed him to the building, I said:

'So your mother may actually have got her way after all.'

If he heard me, he pretended he had not.

PART VI

So, once again, the magic carpet descends over the City. Over the glittering, deceptive towers, into the mouth of the sleeping volcano.

In England, it seemed many weeks since I had landed here like this. But now, doing it all again – the same plane hovering in the blue air over the brown river, waiting to slide between the same tall blocks, then, down below, the same taxi there to take me to the same hotel – I realise that it is barely two weeks since I lived this exact sequence of time before. Life is repeating itself, as in my deepest night dreams, all the same, the same – and then not the same, not quite. Some modification, some new factor.

And so it was. This time, when I arrived at the hotel, where my suitcase was waiting for me in the check room like a stored existence, and the desk clerks acknowledged me with a temperate welcome, I braced myself to cope again with the cycle of hope and disappointment. But this time a letter was placed in my hands. Christopher. At last.

I delayed opening it till I was upstairs. (The same blandly lavish room, only with the picture hanging opposite the twin beds arbitrarily altered from a sunset to flowers, and the view from the room shifted slightly with a similar arbitrariness.) The envelope was stamped as having been posted in the City, with those multicoloured stamps which have become one of the standard exports. But as soon as I had it open and saw the bulky, close-written pages torn from one of Christopher's usual notebooks, I realised that this was actually a communication from the Great Land.

'*Dearest Dad,*

'*If my plans work out, this letter should reach you before I do. I'm very sorry you have been left for so long without news, but once I was on this side of the border the complexities of travel and sheer distance took over and I realised that I had underestimated the time it would take me to go and return – even if finding the person we want had been straightforward, which it turned out not to be. Then, when once I knew I was on his trail, I could not bear to give up. Well, you know me and that beckoning horizon. Forgive me.*

'*And, in the end, I haven't yet found the actual person. But I found his father. Stepfather, I should say. But the old man speaks so much as if my double were his born son that it seems appropriate to call him the father.*

'*He had a shock when at last I appeared in his village – after a false trail to another one elsewhere of the same name, damn it. The real village is right in the mountains, really the end of the world. The end of the road, the end of everywhere. And beautiful, one of the most beautiful landscapes I've ever seen. But God, remote. No wonder our boy grew up here without ever seeing a film or being able to recognise his own looks as Western. 'Western', here, isn't even a concept, it's barely a word. Just a vague, Platonic notion of some Other Place.*

'*Anyway, one of the villagers found me where I'd got off the weekly bus, bumbling round the goat pens at the foot of the final uphill drag where wheeled traffic can't go, and took me to see the father. The old boy thought for a moment I was his son. "You're back again soon," he said, or words to that effect. (My command of the local language has come on a lot in the last ten days. It's had to.) And then he said, looking just puzzled rather than absolutely flabbergasted; "But you've grown a lot – how come?" Of course he's pretty blind these days. But it seems that I and the son really do look alike – everyone in the village noticed it, and was intrigued though not amazed (that's the way these people are). But apparently I am much taller. Such is the difference, I suppose, between a western diet in childhood and the gritty cereals and interminable dried goat cheese that people subsist on up here.*

'*At first it was almost as if the old man were ready to accept me as a version of his son, a sort of ham-handed imitation, as it were, in which he must place faith rather than judgement. For the first time I understood how it is that impostors and pretenders succeed so well, sometimes without even trying. Perkin Warbeck and Lambert Simnel, I mean, and the various Anastasias. But once I had got him to understand who I really was and he got used to the idea, he was reasonably on the spot. He even began to produce a little halting English out of God knows what dusty recess of his memory, which made our communication a bit easier, if not much. In other ways, he was very vague and shaky, and recovering this lost language seemed to affect him with emotion. (It did me too, to watch him do it.) He actually remembered Tessa's proper name, which he said he hadn't been able to call to mind for years, because he'd called her by a "little" name.*

'To sum it up: it does all seem to be true, what you and I surmised. He even had a photo of Tessa, aged about seventeen, laughing. He said that "someone" — I couldn't quite gather who, a nursing sister, I think — had given it to him. Well, I dare say we'll never get all the details quite straight, but, surprisingly, I recognised it at once. I don't mean just Tessa, but the actual photo. It was a small copy of the one that used to stand on Granny's dressing table, along with Toby and Pauline at their wedding and that one of you looking brylcreemed and fierce taken on the day you qualified as a doctor. I can't tell you what a strange sensation it was, squatting on my heels outside his little shack with the sun going down in glory on the mountain and most of the village lined up watching our epic encounter from a discreet distance, holding that crumpled, faded photo of a pretty, lipsticked English girl in my hands — like holding some physical piece of the past. A fossilised leaf. A flint tool.

'Of course I told him that I recognised her and that other people would as well — in other words, that this was the missing piece of evidence that our boy had been looking for. I was just about to ask why the photo hadn't been carried off to the City at the beginning of the quest, as would have been only logical.

'But he forestalled me. He took the picture back from me for a moment and was crying a little. He said, in English:

' "My son not see this. Never see."

'I felt awful having to question closely this old, frail person, who'd taken on such an odd burden so long ago and had to make his own decisions about it. But I did finally manage to establish, in our joint, halting mix of languages, that the old man has always — yes, always, even now — kept the photo hidden from his son, just because he did realise that it might be a vital piece of evidence, and that through it he might lose his son to another life.

'He also said something like: "The woman told me she was dead. I

thought it wasn't true. But she say it, so I don't say anything. And then, later, I know it isn't true. When my boy grew up, and asked, I did not like to lie. So I say: Maybe, now, I don't know. And he asked me to tell him if she was still alive now.

'So I told him – that Tessa is dead now, but lived on for very many years.

'I don't know how I expected him to take this information and I don't think he quite knew himself what he felt. I got the impression I was not telling him anything he had not guessed already. He looked somewhat triumphant for a moment, his old mouth tightening under his drooping moustache like a toothless tiger; he almost grinned. But then he seemed to collapse and went all sad again. I rather think he may have been imagining her then for the first time as a woman well on in her life, and found this more painful than the distant memory of a lost girl.

'And then, when I tried to give the photo back to him, he said in effect: "You keep it. It's yours now."

'Well, Dad, I thanked him humbly and said how honoured I felt. And I thanked him, too, for everything that he had done, all those years, to bring up his – our – boy. On your behalf and Pauline's too, I thanked him. I hope that was right?

'I had to ask him, though, whether he wasn't afraid I would now tell the son about the picture when I do meet up with him. He just said something like "It doesn't matter now, I don't expect to see my son again."

'I asked him to explain because I wasn't sure if I was missing something else here. But he just went on repeating, touching his chest, "Old – very old." He also said "I told him when he comes here again, I – " and made that gesture which means vanished, gone, all over. Perhaps he really knows what he was talking about. I believe people sometimes do. You will be able to tell me, knowing more about death than I do.

'All this time he had not allowed anyone to stand near enough to us to listen to our conversation. You could see that, decrepit as he was, his authority in the village was still respected. But a youngish woman kept appearing, about six yards away, and looking anxious and getting waved away again. Finally she got more insistent, and the old man turned round to her with a what-is-it-now-woman? expression. She came up then, not looking at me, and started on at him in an undertone. It sounded like sort of standard well-intentioned female stuff from any culture, on the lines of "You're overtiring yourself, Grandad; now what did the doctor say? It's time you had your sleep/your pills/your soothing*

*pipe. You shouldn't encourage strangers — I expect you've been boring
the young man with your stories anyway . . ." So I took my cue and
said I would leave him now.*

'*The woman was the daughter-in-law, of course, our boy's wife and
mother of his rather fine-looking half-and-half children, who were said
to be too shy to talk to me. Once she'd got me away from the old boy,
she fussed submissively around me in true oriental wife style, arranging
me a place to sleep and serving me that awful tea they have up there
with curd floating in it, and cooking me a meal. But I could tell that
underneath these attentions, and the bowing and the lowered eyes, she
did not like me one bit. I don't blame her, actually. When you think
you've married a man whose looks make him unique, a one-off, and then
you are suddenly presented with a sort of badly faked double, too big
and clumsy, ten years younger, and an alien from outer space as soon
as he opens his mouth, this person must seem absolutely sinister. Also
I have an idea she wasn't quite sure how far her obligations to me might
extend. At one moment, I had the sudden feeling that she was wondering
if she ought to offer to sleep with me, too. She decided against that, I
was on the whole relieved to find.*

'*And I was sinister in any case in coming from that Other Place
which had swallowed her husband, and from which he sends money but
seldom appears. I seemed to know things about her husband that she
didn't, things that, in the village, have always been politely ignored. She
obviously thought I might be Bad News all round. I felt guilty at
upsetting her so. Particularly when, from her point of view, my journey
all the way to the village was quite unnecessary — though for my part
I shall always be so glad I went there. The point was, as I eventually
established but should have said at the beginning of the letter, our boy
was indeed on a brief visit to the village about a week before me, but
has now left again to return to the City. Evidently we have been following
each other around in an elaborate circle.*

'*She was most relieved to see the back of me the following morning,
and pressed on me all sorts of goodies for my journey of the stuffed-
miniature-pancake variety which I hardly liked to take: these people are
really poor. The old boy I did see again for a few minutes, but after
all that remembering he seemed to have retreated into age. I think he
was quite glad to see me go too.*

'*The slight anxiety which I think both you and I had initially — that
these people might hope for all sorts of material things from us and
might, in justice, make a moral claim if not a legal one — seems to have
been right off course. I think you can set your mind at rest about that.*

'So now I'm on my way back too. I'm finishing writing this at what passes for a bus station in these regions. There is one hand-pump for diesel, and thin cows are wandering about attempting to graze on a flowering creeper I don't recognise that has draped itself on everything. Cows, pump and flowers are all whitened with the choking dust of a neighbouring cement works. This letter is going to be taken for me by someone I've met who's likely to be in the City before I can realistically be, which is why I hope you will get it soon. My route up here was inconspicuous and circuitous, and so must my return be. If all goes well – I mean quietly – I hope to be confronting the last hurdle at Jedu Sumna by the 14th or 15th at the latest. Bear with me. I will appear.

'All love, Dad, as ever, C.

'PS I was just about to add a few lines saying "if you don't get this letter" when I realised the futility of such a remark. I think my brain must be addling up here at this altitude!'

I turned back to the beginning and read the letter through again, several times.

There was so much there. Technically, I now knew more about Baht Way's origins than Christopher did, but what had been told to me as a piece of dead history, in Pauline's grudging, unresonant voice, now in Christopher's letter became life itself, continuing reality. Yet what a veil of anonymity my careful son had spread over the whole matter. I had been momentarily baffled by this, even asking myself testily what he was trying to keep from me now – when it came to me that of course it was not I who was supposed to be kept in ignorance of precise detail but any less friendly reader into whose hands such a letter might fall. I still had no idea what his route across the Great Land might be; he had mentioned neither the name of the village in the mountains nor its region. Nor had he used one single proper name by which a thread could be damagingly traced back to its source: just 'the person we want', 'our boy', 'the old man', 'the quest'.

The one piece of firm evidence was the date on top. Over a week old, I now saw.

In my absorption in the letter's content I had been reading it as if its information were up to date. But of course it had been written during my first days in the City, before I had met Julie Barron at the High Commission party, before my sudden recall to England, and had taken its own time and mine to reach me. The 14th, the earliest day on which Christopher hoped to be 'confronting the last hurdle at Jedu Sumna' (the military frontier post, that must mean) was now the day after tomorrow.

Time was playing tricks in other ways also. The evening arrived much too soon, as it does when you have flown eastwards round the globe. I fell asleep, but my body must have thought it had merely been required to take a late-afternoon nap, for after a couple of hours I was wide awake again. Yet for all this acceleration and skipping of hours, perceived time had stretched itself out: I felt here as if my conversation with Pauline had taken place not days but weeks ago.

And even within the separate world and time scheme of the United Kingdom, where Pauline and Toby confronted each other over the fiasco of their marriage and Pauline's attempted plot, matters seemed to have moved with unnatural speed. 'Confront' was already not quite the word. As Marcus had indicated to me outside the magistrates' court, Toby seemed to have returned home. In the hours after Pauline had been bailed, her release was treated by both of them as if it were a first step on the road to vindication and acquittal, rather than the temporary stay of impending justice which is all it represented. 'We're going to see this through together' was the phrase that now fell repeatedly from Toby's lips, while Pauline, clinging to his hand, contented herself and everyone else by reiterating how wonderful Toby was being, how brave and mature. Irrational, despised, cowardly Toby suffering from white-bread allergy had evidently been expunged from the record by instant mutual consent, bundled right off stage along with the Other Woman. Even as Tessa's baby had once been. Just another error that did not fit the family image.

I could see that this was probably a way for Pauline and Toby to cope, in all circumstances. It was, and is, not for me to tell them that the law is unlikely in the end to take such a benign, amnesiac view of Pauline's attempt at murder, or that the judge will not be deterred from passing sentence for a crime against a third party by the information that 'our relationship is now stronger than ever'.

Knowing that they will need all the help they can get and more, if Pauline is not to end up with a lengthy prison sentence, I urged them to enlist the help of a local psychiatrist whom I know and have only ever half respected. Over the years I have seen a number of manipulative patients take this well-intentioned man for a ride. Let him do his best to persuade the courts that my sister should be pitied as a temporarily sick woman now restored to penitent normality, rather than the long-term abnormal menace I now believe her to be. There is, thank God, nothing more I can do or might be expected to do.

On the plane coming eastwards again, I felt an odd lightness. It seemed as if I had shed some obscure burden of much longer duration than my recent concern about Pauline's role with Baht Way. Perhaps an alliance that I was forced to enter when I was young and vulnerable has now been discharged: a cycle has run its course.

At times, my lightness is pierced by a faint pang in the guise of a visual image: a dazzling garden wall with toys lined up on top, canna lilies below, a shadowed, creeper-hung lawn under the patter of sprinklers; two small girls in the white dresses of subtropical childhood and the hair slides of the 1930s – the elder sister with whom, in my weakness, I had to ally myself, the little one whose love and need I betrayed without even realising I was doing so.

I now surmise that some terrible female struggle was going on there already, in that garden, years before it erupted into an adult contest, while I, the small male, played oblivious.

But the pang retreats again: it is obsolete. Gone, over, extinct, as that garden itself has gone. Three days ago, in a windowless room in a Dorset police station, I avenged Tessa, and Pauline's real punishment will not be dealt by me but by the machinery of the state. So, I am free at last. Empty in a way. Oddly happy.

And soon, surely – Christopher.

In the night I dozed and woke, dozed and woke, abandoning all attempt to gauge the notional time. When it was already bright light beyond the venetian window blinds, I fell into another sleep, and did not finally get up till halfway through the morning.

One of the desk clerks accosted me on my way through the marble hall to the coffee shop.

'A lady asked for you, sir. But she didn't want us to disturb

you. She will be back again at approximately twelve noon,
she said to tell you.'

'A young English lady?', thinking with pleasure that it would
be Julie Barron.

'No, sir. Not a young lady. A local person, sir. She didn't
leave her name.'

'I see.' In fact I was mystified. 'Local' is the approved City
word for indigenous.

I went into the coffee shop and ordered an elaborate
American pancake because it sounded good. When it came,
I was not sure I really wanted it. Just then, I was called to
the phone.

Mike Isaacs.

'I got your note,' he said, 'I'm glad you're back so soon.'

'I was determined to get back here.' I was going to say
'before Christopher does', but Mike cut in:

'Look – Baht Way has disappeared.'

'Since when? He apparently visited his home village not all
that long ago. Well, you knew he'd gone there, of course, it
was you who told me. But I've had corroborative news of
that.' I told him about Christopher's letter.

'I know all that,' said Mike disconcertingly. 'But Baht Way
should have reappeared here in the City before now. He
hasn't contacted me, he's not at his address in Teyn Bira and
no one there has any news of him.'

I made concerned noises and then waited. There was
nothing I could do to find Baht Way. What did Mike want
of me? Just to express his anxiety, perhaps.

'I'm afraid,' said Mike, 'that this time he may have been
caught trying to slip back across the frontier.'

'Oh, dear.'

'*Confronting the last hurdle at Jedu Sumna*' – those were the
words Christopher used in his letter. Christopher. Now Baht
Way. Damn it, I thought, with childish annoyance at my own
impotence, I can't worry about both of them at the same
time.

By and by Mike rang off, telling me he would 'keep me
informed'. I told him that I now expected Christopher tomorrow or the next day. I did not say, though I rather wanted
to, that Mike's information about Baht Way on the same route
had raised new and more specific anxieties in me.

... But Christopher is western. He will have his passport with him. They wouldn't have any reason to ...

Don't think about it just now.

I abandoned my partly eaten pancake and went out into the seething, disciplined streets. The streams of neat, stylishly dressed, dark-haired people. The long lines of City-green Mercedes taxis, the spotless air-conditioned orange buses with their pneumatic doors, the chauffeur-driven business cars mostly of foreign make, the shoals of Italianate motor scooters especially favoured by Levantines. People don't run private cars in the City, much; since the Great Land has been cut off behind the frontier, there has been nowhere to go in them.

I thought of the colonial tourers, the dilapidated cabs and horse-drawn buggies and cycle-rickshaws of my youth, which had made this stretch of road chaotic with their constant horns and cries. I remembered the people who had lived with their few possessions under the arcades of the ochre-roofed houses that were now gone also. And I remembered Pauline speaking of the carts and rickshaws through which she had dodged to catch Tessa when she had glimpsed her on the other side.

I now knew from Pauline something Mike Isaacs did not know – that Baht Way's father had been the young British reporter, dead before his son's birth. Not a missing, just possibly recoverable father after all. I decided that there was no need for me to tell Mike that this bit of mystery was solved and void: I did not think he would want to hear it.

Suppose Pauline had not gone down the street that day, or had simply not turned her head in that direction. How different life would have been. For Tessa herself, and Baht Way of course. But perhaps for others also.

If, by another of those freak chances, I were now to spot an unmistakable Baht Way wandering in the crowd and accost him, perhaps that encounter too would have momentous and far-reaching effects? Or perhaps it would in fact, make little difference to what that enigmatic and elusive person eventually decided to do, or not to do.

Would Christopher or I ever meet him face to face? Maybe, after all, we would not. But he knew we had come looking for him. That was what mattered.

Unless of course Mike Isaacs's fears were justified and Baht Way was even now dead in a rocky ravine of the Great Land.

Or chained in a police post near some provincial highway. Or already on his way to a prison camp so remote that he would never, ever return, a place without even a name that would enable the world to speak of its existence: a place where he would pay for a brief taste of freedom with a lifetime of non-existence.

I began to hope very much that it might be of Baht Way that my unknown morning caller wished to speak. She might even have some news.

Baht Way. Christopher's double. My shadow son.

I was back at the hotel soon after twelve. This time I was handed a small envelope. Inside was what I believe is known in the stationery business as a notelet. The front flap showed two fluffy kittens far removed from the skinny white cats of the East, frolicking improbably against a green field and a thatched cottage drawn by someone who had never seen the real thing. Inside, the old-fashioned copybook handwriting said:

'*Dear Dr Mason, I should be so grateful if you were able to spare time to have a cup of tea with me, either today or any day this week. I am at home every afternoon these days, and would so much enjoy a talk with you for old times' sake. Thanking you in advance for your time and trouble, as I am sure you are a busy man. Yours in hope, an old family friend, Myrtle Brown. PS My little home is quite close to your hotel. Turn left at the corner of Mye Longit Boulevard (Victoria Road, it used to be) and up past Citicorp and the new Mitsubishi building.*'

'You won't remember me, I expect,' she said. I sensed that, while she knew that this was so, if I confirmed it she might take offence all the same. Or just be wordlessly, politely hurt. She gazed at me, and her black eyes, with their telltale pleat at the corner, were opaque but held a suspicion of pain – or maybe it was the lipsticked mouth, with its tiny lines round the edges, that seemed vulnerable, or just the whole pudgy, neat face under its helmet of dark hair (dyed?) above the tidy pink blouse, cardigan and string of pearls. Like her exact ethnic origins, her age was difficult to determine, but I sensed that, while not looking old by any of the usual measures, she was certainly in her sixties, perhaps even her seventies. Her voice, with very little of the City accent, was that of a young

girl, breathy, overcontrolled. 'Convent-educated', as the advertisements for good-class local office staff used to say in my
youth. Office staff – of course!

After a few seconds I was able to say:

'Wait a minute. Didn't you work for that outfit – I forget
the name, but my sister Teresa, who is now dead, worked
there? To do with refugees – '

And her wordless pleasure, her unspoken relief.

'Such a fine man, your father! Of course I worked for his
company, you see, before the war' (I'd forgotten or never
known that) 'and by the time he came back I was already
working for the Displaced Persons' Advisory Bureau.' (So
that's why Tessa was sent there. Myrtle Brown was supposed
to keep her out of trouble.) 'Otherwise, I'd have gone back
to the Company. Mind you, the DPAB was ever so interesting,
very worthwhile, and they said they couldn't spare me from
there. Me having the local lingo and knowing my way around,
in a manner of speaking. But I was always a bit sorry I didn't
go back to the Company. I was ever so fond of them all –
your father particularly, but his second-in-command too – yes,
Mr Daintry, that's right, fancy hearing that name after all
these years! And of course I knew the families and everything.
I and the other confidential staff used to get invited to your
father's house for lovely occasions, Christmas Day and so
forth; I'll always remember those times. One big happy family.
Why, I even remember you, doctor, as a wee boy in white
ducks!'

So, in her seventies. This picture of paternalistic Company
warmth and intimacy did not quite square with my own
vaguer but pervasive memories of the class and race consciousness in which my early childhood had been passed. An image
came to me of my mother, applying powder before her looking
glass with a big swansdown puff, talking disparagingly of 'the
Company bash' at which she and my father 'had to put in
an appearance'. But since they were no longer alive to put
Myrtle Brown in her place, I certainly wasn't going to say
anything that might dim her glowing recollection. I said how
happy my father would have been to know that he and the
Company were still so fondly remembered.

'But Miss Brown – '

' "Myrtle", please!'

'But Myrtle, if you had gone back to the Company after the war it would only have been for a few years, wouldn't it? The whole operation was wound up once the Troubles really got underway. My parents had to leave in a hurry, for the second time. Well, of course you must know about that.'

Myrtle Brown indicated that, yes, it was All That she wanted to talk to me about – she was coming to that in a minute . . . 'But I have sometimes regretted, all the same, that I wasn't with the Company still when it happened. Quite a lot of its staff, particularly people in my position, were sent back to the UK then, you see, and most of them took the chance to settle there. Later, of course, it wasn't so easy. Just one of those opportunities I sometimes feel a wee bit sorry to have missed.' She added shyly, but with an air of bravado: 'I've never actually been in the UK, you see, not personally, though of course I've relatives there. I've a cousin living in Ruislip. We still exchange cards every Christmas. I'm told Ruislip is a very pleasant, good-class place, convenient for running up to town?'

I agreed helplessly that this was a fair description. The room we sat in was tiny, with a kitchen in a cupboard off it and a divan bed in another alcove: a bedsitter rather than a proper flat, a version, no doubt, of the 'luxurious rabbit hutch' Julie Barron had said she lived in. The window was tight shut against the street noise, the air conditioning hummed and every foot of space seemed to be occupied by some talisman of that other life which Myrtle Brown had never visited in the flesh, though dwelling in it in spirit. On the walls lilac-pattern paper formed a background for more pictures like those on her stationery – more kittens, rabbits, cows in a damp meadow. Men on horseback pursued a fox across a Scottish-looking moorland, others in a beamed tavern toasted each other in punch. A restrained English sun set into the sea off what I recognised, with a sudden surprise, as an idealised version of Poole harbour; snow lay on bare beech woods above a village of Chiltern cottages. On several small tables were disposed cloths with the sort of pallid embroidery that was taught to English schoolgirls of my youth, a shell-and-coloured-sand lighthouse marked *A Present from the Isle of Wight*, a china mug bearing the arms of an Oxford college, a doll dressed as a Beefeater, and a tray of primrose-patterned teacups, the milk jug covered with a beaded net. Myrtle saw my eyes dwell on this vision from my childhood.

'You'll have some tea, won't you? And I've made some scones. I expect you miss afternoon tea while you're here? Even the big hotels don't seem to serve a proper tea these days – it's because Americans and Australians don't want it, they say. Such a pity. Of course there's no one left here from the old days now. No one like your parents. Lots of international business people. But that isn't the same.'

I wanted very much to ask her why she had summoned me. I had a sinking suspicion that I now knew, and wished, if so, that we could get it over. I was also aware, however, that Myrtle Brown was herself wary and feeling her way. She asked me if I hadn't been surprised to get her note. 'I said to myself; He will be surprised.' She told me that she had learnt of my presence in the City from someone who had met me at the High Commission party. 'She and I are both members of the Animal Rescue League, you see. She helped out at a bazaar in aid of the League at the church I go to, St Saviour's – you know it? Of course it isn't what it was, though we have some very regular attenders at morning service...' She rattled on about the church, which I had seen standing like a relic in Teyn Bira. It became clear that I was not to be allowed to get down to essentials till I had dutifully drunk my tea and eaten fresh scones and slightly stale Marie biscuits.

At last the moment came.

'Of course I remember your sister Tessa well. Dead, now, you say? Tch. She was a lot younger than me. We worked together – you know, at the Bureau. Such a pretty, sweet girl.'

'I'm glad to hear you say so.' I meant it.

'Of course she was awfully naughty sometimes – you know, impulsive. Like a character in one of those girls' stories I used to enjoy when I was young – *The Madcap of the Chalet School*, that sort of thing. Oh, you'll laugh at me, doctor – I'm laughing at myself! – but I did enjoy those books when I was a kiddie; we had them in the library at St Saviour's High School. Anyway, your sister really reminded me of my favourite characters. She was such a nice person. You couldn't help loving her.

'And of course I wasn't the only one. Yes, I'm thinking of poor Wayland. Wayland Clark, the boy from the *Gazetteer*. He did have it bad for Tessa. Well, I say "poor" because of what happened to him afterwards, but when I knew him and Tessa together of course he was as jolly as anything. Very much Mr Get-Up-and-Go – all sorts of ambitions, he had. And a clever boy, too. Of course he wasn't quite what you would call a gentleman, if you know what I mean – not a gentleman to your parents' way of thinking. I'm not surprised they weren't too keen on him. But he was a really nice, sincere boy. Believe me, doctor, he was.

'Well, at first I was rather disapproving, too. When I noticed how much time Tessa and Wayland were spending together, I mean. The difference in background, and both being so young . . . But when I saw how sweet they were together, and how fond they were of each other, I didn't have the heart to tell them to stay apart.'

'As I remember my sister, I don't suppose it would have made any difference if you had.'

'No?' She seized on this eagerly. 'No, that's what I've often tried to tell myself. Afterwards, you know, when it had all become so tragic . . .' Her voice trailed off, her face set. Her old, black eyes looked as if they were contemplating something she would not allow to appear in her expression.

I said carefully (for I had a feeling she might cry, even now, after all this time): 'What did happen, exactly? To Wayland Clark. I – I know about Tessa and the baby, I should explain.'

If Myrtle Brown was disappointed that she was not going to be called upon to make a total revelation, she honourably did not show it. She merely looked thoughtful for a moment, as if my way of expressing the matter was being slotted into place in her mind.

'I said to myself you probably did. I expect Tessa told you? She was always very fond of you. Her big brother.'

'Er, no, it was Pauline who did, actually. My other sister.'

But it became apparent that Myrtle hardly remembered Pauline or did not choose to, and did not realise she had stayed on in the City with the British army. (Perhaps Pauline had been offhand with her at an earlier stage in their acquaintance.) I was relieved: I had been cringing at the thought of hearing of Pauline's role in the baby business all over again from a third party. As it was, I managed to leave the whole matter of Pauline's knowledge in decent obscurity and move on: Myrtle evidently had other things to impart.

'Wayland was one of the party going up in the jeep to the Great Land. That's why Tessa was so keen to go too. I begged her not to, that morning at the Bureau – told her about the news that was coming in, and how it wasn't safe and so on. But she just wouldn't listen.

'Well, they went, with two other volunteers from the Bureau – Mr and Mrs Pawley. I'm not sure if you ever met them? They'd both been teachers before, and she grew up here like me, actually. The four of them, and the driver. Wayland was very involved in getting people from the Great Land who were at risk into the City, though none of us quite realised that. I don't know how much Tessa herself realised at that stage . . . We *were* supposed to be an official organisation. Well, Mr Pawley was in charge, and he was such an experienced man, and as Beryl Pawley was going too it didn't seem exactly wrong to let your sister go, so I just hoped for the best.

'. . . Yes, they were stopped by the Lay Balint, of course. And they were ordered out of the jeep and it was set on fire. And dreadful things . . . I never did hear all the details. I suppose I didn't really want to ask. Mr and Mrs Pawley and the driver were killed, and I was dreadfully sorry – particularly about the poor driver, because he was only doing his job and was a very decent sort of man with a wife and several kiddies, and I believe he was treated rather horribly . . . Of course I was sorry for the Pawleys too, but at least it was Mr Pawley's own responsibility – he would go, he told me it would be all right – and he got shot at an early stage. Or so I understand. And I never cared much for Beryl Pawley, if the truth be told, though, poor woman, I shouldn't speak of her like that. She did give herself airs, rather, being married to a real Britisher . . .

'She fell over a cliff, or so I heard. Running away. I do hope she fell and wasn't thrown. I just can't say.

'Anyway, Wayland and your sister managed to escape and hide. Somehow. I don't know how. Of course it's very wild country in those parts – or so I'm told. I don't know. I hardly went up into the Great Land much, even in the days when it was all one country. I've always been a City girl.

'And at last, after all sorts of adventures, more dead than alive, they managed to make their way back to the City. Oh, weeks later. I can tell you, I cried with relief when I opened my door one morning early – we lived in a bungalow in those days – and there were Tessa and Wayland on the doorstep like two stray kittens. I wanted them to stay with me; I wanted to keep them safe. I remember making them breakfast. But of course they went off again soon, to a room Wayland had, down near the port, I believe it was. Well, it was far too late for me to object to that on moral grounds, you understand, doctor. They'd been together for weeks and weeks already.

'Afterwards, I was rather hurt they didn't keep in touch more. I would have done anything I could for them – money, or anything – but they didn't seem to want . . . Well, of course they were very much in love and just wanted to be together, and I realised afterwards that Wayland was so busy running the escape route for refugees that he wouldn't want anyone like me to know too much about it. I'm afraid that's probably why they didn't contact the High Commission or anyone else either. And that, of course, is why Wayland went back to the Great Land.

'Yes. He was caught and killed. No, I don't know the exact circumstances. I don't think Tessa knew. I hope not. I heard the news from another source, someone who'd been shown his body. Mutilated, I rather think. Of course one doesn't know at what point . . . But dreadful. That poor boy! And so terrible for your sister.

'I knew she was expecting because she'd already told me. She was really pleased about it – and I'm afraid I showed I was very shocked. I've always blamed myself for that. It must seem very stupid to you, doctor – it seems very stupid to me now, when I think what young people are like today. But I'd been nicely brought up and had always kept myself very respectable. That mattered a lot to people in my position. I'm sure you understand.

'I'm afraid it was probably because I let her see I was shocked that Tessa kept away from me after that. When I heard about poor Wayland being killed I went to look for her in one or two places because I was worried about her, but she'd just disappeared. I didn't find her again till much later, when the baby had been born, and then it was only by chance. The Sister in charge of the maternity ward at St Saviour's Hospital was a friend of my aunt, and I went there one day with Auntie to see her. They were tut-tutting about all the illegitimate babies they had, and it just came up in passing that this British girl called Mason had had a baby in the hospital and that it had gone for adoption. I remember my auntie saying as we were coming away again: "Wasn't it a Mr Mason you used to work for?" But I just said: "Oh, Mason's a very common name, Auntie." Well, I didn't think it was any of her business, you see.

'I was rather surprised, though. About the adoption, I mean. Because Tessa had been so thrilled at the idea of Wayland's baby. I thought that, if she'd let it go for adoption, she must be in a state, and that I ought to try to see her. I even wondered if perhaps it was my responsibility – that I'd been so discouraging about the baby, you see . . . So off I went the next day to see if she was still at the convalescent home. She was, though she was almost ready to leave.

'Well, I don't know if you already know, doctor, what I found there? . . . Yes, that some wicked person had made her believe the baby was dead. At least, *I* think that was a wicked thing to do.

'. . . No, I never did discover who it was. I don't think Tessa wanted to say. I blame that hospital Sister myself. Some of these nuns, if you'll forgive my saying so, were not as Christian as they ought to have been.

'Naturally I had assumed that Tessa knew the baby was alive and had been sent away, and then, when I realised she didn't, it was too late to go back on it. I couldn't unsay what I had said. Oh, it was awful – she cried and screamed so, I didn't know *what* to do for the best . . .

'I invited her to come home with me. I said that Mother and Auntie would understand – thinking that I'd make sure they did – and that we'd discuss the whole thing and what was to be done. But she wouldn't. She said she had to go and look for the baby, and that she thought she knew where to find it. Something about someone who worked in a restaurant in Teyn Bira. I don't know. She just wouldn't let me come with her. She wouldn't let me help her in any way. She was like some little wild animal. She'd been through so much by then, of course. It was dreadful to see.

'So she disappeared. Again. I wondered so much where she'd gone. I wondered about the baby, too. I'd been very fond of Wayland Clark.

'Years later, someone who'd worked for the Company in the old days showed me a copy of the *Old Citizens' Newsletter* which had a report of your elder sister's wedding in it. There was a photo, with your parents and the three of you there clearly; you in one of those smart tail coats like your father, and Tessa in jeans, it looked quite a contrast! I said to myself, That's the modern style. Tessa was described as "Miss". So I suppose that she never found the baby after all? It was a relief to know she got back home safe and was with you all again, but – poor girl. Poor baby.

'. . . You think she went up in to the Great Land to look for it? What a strange idea! In that case, you must know something I don't. But the Great Land is enormous. And so wild. Barbaric. Even if she had a name of a place it would have been so far . . . That poor girl on her own! Well, I don't know, I'm sure. Perhaps we'll never know, now?

'But what's worried me for years, doctor, is *did I do wrong?* To tell her, I mean, that her baby was still alive? Of course I did it without meaning to. But I've often wondered over the years, was it right that she should know? I'm inclined to think that it was, because I've always been a rather truthful person myself – I was brought up that way. But if she was getting used to the idea that it was dead, and then I caused her further suffering to no purpose . . . sent her on a wild-goose chase, even . . . Oh, it's hard sometimes to know what to do for the best, isn't it?'

'It is,' I said. 'It is.'

There was a last silence between us. For the first time I was aware of an old-fashioned clock on a high shelf ticking slowly, a tick that belonged on a mantelpiece in another place and time. From down below in the excluded street came the slow, muffled whine of a police car. Myrtle had got out a handkerchief with daisies on it and was quietly wiping her eyes.

'I think,' I said at last, 'that Tessa may have found her baby in the Great Land, or established that he was there. It is possible.'

'But in that case why didn't she take him back?'

'I don't know. But she may have had her reasons.' I remembered Christopher's letter, quoting Baht Tye: '*The*

*woman told me she was dead. I thought it wasn't true . . . And then,
later, I know it isn't true.'* Maybe there had, after all, been some
further communication, even a meeting between them.

I could not explain all that to Myrtle. She had never known
of Baht Tye's existence. Better leave her with a clear, straight
image of the young English lovers, uncorrupted by change.

'As you say,' I said, 'we'll probably never know now. But
I'm sure it was a good thing that you told her he was alive.'

'Really?'

'Yes, really,' I said firmly, sounding more certain than I
sometimes feel. 'It's always better to know things.'

It was time for me to go. I felt it, but did not know, now,
quite how to leave gracefully. I started an inconclusive conversation about the frontier with the Great Land and when
it had finally become official. Myrtle was vague about this;
she said she hadn't been over there for many years.

'I don't suppose I ever will again. There's nothing to go
for.'

'Is it as hard to hop across the causeway unofficially at Jedu
Sumna as some people say?' I asked. I had been formulating
a plan. She looked surprised.

'Oh, not for you, no. If you're here as a tourist you can go
to the legation in the morning and queue up and get a pass
to go over for the afternoon, I believe. But the pass only lasts
till sunset and it's only for a mile or so beyond the causeway.'

'I didn't realise one could do that.'

'Well, as I say, that's for you. They say the Great Land
legation allows it so as to get hard currency. Each pass costs
something like fifty City dollars, scandalous really. It's harder
for us – City locals, I mean. And people like me who stayed
on here. And domiciled foreigners too, I believe. The Great
Land authorities don't like giving us passes even for a few
hours. They think that way their people will form links with
us or something. So stupid. As if most of us City types would
be interested in links with them! Years ago I cared about the
refugees, yes, but that was different, things were different then.
I mean, today it's another world beyond the causeway. No
contact any more. Nothing.'

When I left Myrtle Brown's flat, the brief, gaudy sunset of

the City was painting itself again behind the blocks, above
the unseen river. Soon the unresting night would come too,
and I thought I might stroll in it. I might eat noodles in a
brilliantly lit arcade where a fountain plays blue-green-gold,
blue-green-gold; I might have a beer afterwards in one of the
few remaining small streets I had discovered at the far end
of the Bundar, where the light bulbs are dimly orange and
the bar girls look hopeful when you enter. I might – but part
of my mind remained, ruefully, with Myrtle Brown. She was
no inhabitant of the City's night. She would close her blind
against the flickering neon glow, and tune in briefly to the
BBC World Service and then to one of the English TV soap
operas or serials that were available on the City network and
were (she had told me) her staple entertainment. So, she
would knit her next cardigan, while the lovable *bon mots* of a
mythical working class on the other side of the world
nourished her solitude. She, far more than the Citicorp Bank
or the Mitsubishi building, was the legacy left by the City
founders, by my own people. She, and Baht Way, who might
be wandering now in this same lighted City, and whose adult
existence I had not even mentioned to her because I had not
known how to or whether I had any right to.

What I had said to Myrtle was, after all, true: it was
impossible now to discover the result of Tessa's search.
Whether she simply wandered the roads and mountain paths
of the Great Land, in her grubby local frock, a prey to random
strangers, without ever finding again her child or her faithful
friend – or whether she had actually found them in the village
but made her own decision to leave again, abandoning them
for another way of life – was not now recoverable. As
alternative truths, each offered a different version of pain. I
felt I could see why Baht Tye had never wished to claim either
one or the other as fact.

For me, of course, there was no conflict. I wanted very
much to believe that Tessa had found them, and had stayed
in the village, however briefly. Not only would this mean that
Pauline's dishonest plot had failed in practical terms, it would
also shift the pattern in a more general way: Tessa had
escaped and made her own choice in life, after all. Messy and
unfortunate though much of Tessa's life had been, at least, in
that case, it was her own.

*

The following morning I made some phone calls to my long-suffering colleagues in Singapore. Then, instructed now by my conversation with Myrtle, I went to the Great Land legation. It proved to be an unpleasant, low-key cement building in Soviet-brutalist style at the wrong end of the Bundar, left over from some fleeting and long-repudiated period of entente with Russia. This enclave of the People's Socialist Republic of Mayer Dhar was guarded by young men with ill-fitting grey uniforms and sub-machine-guns, who looked facially just like a million others within the City but of course were not, and were not apparently allowed to speak to anyone in any language.

There, I stood in a queue for two hours between an Australian travel courier and a Dutch engineer on holiday from Borneo, while touts passed discreetly up and down the line organising us 'for a consideration' into nominal groups: evidently this was the system that the City, with its usual freelance acumen, had devised to satisfy tourists and circumvent the regulation that only group travel was permitted to the Great Land. Finally, by this means, I obtained my afternoon's one-mile pass for the other side of the frontier.

It was the 14th, and I had discovered that the daily train, passing on its long trajectory down the inhospitable coast of the Great Land, would stop soon after four in the afternoon at the station on the far side of the Jedu Sumna causeway. I had no means of knowing if Christopher would in fact arrive this day, or if he would come by train at all, but since this was the most usual means of transport for licensed travellers coming and going from the upcountry regions, the probability seemed quite high. I was hoping to greet him on the station platform. It was as simple as that.

Getting through the police posts at each end of the causeway presented no particular problem: it merely took a long time. I had, for administrative purposes, been arbitrarily allocated to a 'group' mainly consisting of elderly Australian ex-servicemen in the charge of my travel-agent acquaintance from the morning's queue. That was all right. In my bush shirt I could look like an old Australian.

I reached the little station, a colonial relic in fretted wood, pretty but falling to bits; the sort of thing that, on the City side of the causeway, has long since been swept away. In a nostalgic landscape of water towers, coal bunkers and derelict warehouses, the only set of rails that seemed to be in use gleamed brilliantly in the heat. Battered and locked doors on the platform said in English 'Station Master', 'Second-Class Waiting Room' and 'Ladies Only'. Other apparently exhortatory notices plastered at random over windows and walls were in a script I could not read – the pre-modern alphabet to which the Great Land reverted after its secession. I waited some time before a man in the grey uniform of the military guard passed by and told me in a cleft-palate accent; 'Train is late.'

'Late?'

'Is most often late.'

'How late?'

'One hour.'

I suspected from his detached, pitying manner that 'one hour' was a rhetorical answer and that it might be considerably more. I decided to wander out of the station for a bit.

Scruffy, Julie Barron had said, but pretty. 'Poor-looking . . . a lot of ruins even after all these years . . . a lot of flowers.' I saw what she meant. The wide road from the City which swept on to the causeway degenerated abruptly, on this side, into a two-lane strip of bumpy tarmac off which dirt paths led between the gaping shells of one-time stone houses. But the shells were inhabited; matting and sheet-iron roofs had replaced the original tiles, their forecourts were full of jerry cans, washing and battered plastic chairs. Outside, children and stray dogs poked around in the dust among coconut husks and piles of empty bottles. There was a stench of fish oil, salt swamp and drains, but over all were spread, like a glowing but ineffective benison, luxuriant swags and swathes of creeper, innocently flowering.

As soon as I had gone a hundred yards up the road from the police post and the station, children surrounded me, nagging brightly but mechanically for 'pennies' or 'pens'. Their feet were bare, their clothes ragged, their black eyes fixed on me like those of small feral cats. I strode on, ignoring them, for if I began to hand out cents I feared I might start a riot, and they fell back again and returned to their game in the dirt, philosophical, indifferent. I reminded myself that you cannot judge a whole civilisation by its frontier slums.

By and by the populated ruins and the stray children petered out. I found myself on the edge of paddy fields – and, more startlingly, in the suddenly recognised territory of my early childhood. Hereabouts, we had come for trips on Sundays. Here and there the same straw-hatted man or woman waded bare-legged in the water beneath the virulent greenness, here slaty buffaloes with birds perched on their backs wallowed in deeper slime along the shore of the great brown river. Along the road ahead of me, two white oxen slowly pulled a solitary wooden cart, desultorily prodded by the carter. A few antique bicycles clicked by; their riders stared at me. The road began to climb, and once it reached higher ground the Indian corn of my youth made a miniature forest for hide-and-seek. I found I even knew that there were battered shrines, hidden from the road, among that corn. I had forgotten them for decades, and had not recalled them when Mike Isaacs had told me they were a favourite spot for spirit weddings. But now I knew: I and my sisters had called them 'the dolls' houses', from their design and from the broken clay figures we had found scattered near them.

And here, magically, just where I had known it would be, was a field path to the left slanting up the hill between the spikes of corn: if I followed it, I would soon come to the first dolls' house, the one with a tiled roof still balanced on carved wooden pillars.

In my childhood, the grass was kept short in a wide circle in front of each shrine. Here City parties, mainly European, used to come with wicker baskets and thermos flasks and even wind-up gramophones. (Did the local peasant corn growers mind their shrines being used as picnic sites? I don't remember the matter ever being raised. It occurred now to my adult self that in fact these shrines were ancient burial chambers: we had been picnicking and playing popular songs in someone else's graveyard.) As I came near the first remembered dolls' house I saw that the green apron had disappeared; corn grew right up to the ring of worn stone incense burners. Behind the altar, trees growing in the ditch there trailed branches right over such broken tiles as were left in the roof. The whole place was rotting, wood and stone and fired clay slowly crumbling back into the earth from which they had risen. Yet it was not disused. As I came up to the stone slab I saw, as I had by St Saviour's Church in Teyn Bira, the pecked remains of a loaf of country-style bread, a bottle of some rancid-looking liquid, a burst melon mobbed by flies: not food for dolls or the leftovers from other picnics, as I and my sisters had innocently supposed, but provisions for a dead bride and groom to take on their mighty journey.

I looked around on the ground for the remains of manikins. Tessa had liked to collect them and wrap them in mango leaves so that they resembled swaddled babies, tied with twists of grass. But I saw nothing but a broken mess of clay and the ashes of fires. The noise of flies was loud in my ears, and they were beginning to leave the suppurating melon to investigate the sweat on my face. Suddenly the whole place seemed not nostalgic, but claustrophobic and a little sinister. I decided to make my way back to the open air.

Even as I turned to go, I think I was half aware I was not alone – that there were suppressed movements coming from the tree-clogged pit behind the shrine which was always said to be the 'secret way in' to some hidden core of the place. It now seems to me I had even heard a murmur, the clink of a bottle, the click of dice.

I had gone only about twenty yards back down the path through the maize when they caught up with me. There were three of them, local and quite young, and one arrived on either side of me while the third one slid ahead, barring my way at a little distance and watching me to see what I would do.

My mind had been on the weddings and on the shrines' possible history as tombs; my first thought was that I had disturbed some private ritual and must quickly apologise and withdraw. But even as I sought appropriate words it dawned on me that the men's aggressive manner was not indignant so much as furtive and tense.

'Change? Change money – City dollars?' The man on my left was speaking to me.

'US dollars?' That was the man on my right, more insistently. He laid a hand on my arm.

'No US dollars,' I said flatly, shrugging off his hand. 'No change.' I attempted to stride onwards, but they quickened their own steps and the man in front of me stood his ground.

I should have dodged and run at that moment. Stupidly, not wanting to believe what was happening to me, I hesitated and stopped. It was what they wanted. All three surrounded me now.

'Change! You change money – '

'City dollars – you give.'

The third man did not seem to speak even this much English, but began talking to me in his own pattering, throaty tongue. He put his face close to mine, dodged back, then came forward to touch my cheek, then jerked out of reach again. The other men laughed. Clearly fun was being made. Fresh sweat broke out on my face. I was conscious of the wallet hidden but readily accessible in the buttoned pocket of my bush shirt.

I had nothing, as it happened, in the hip pocket of my trousers, but when I felt a hand exploring in that direction I swung round automatically and swore at the boy to whom the hand belonged. Another mistake. They began to get angry, or pretended to.

'Dollars – you give us US dollars.'

'You American. You US spy – '

As if in imitation of the ringleader, the young man on my left gave me a glancing, mock-playful blow to the cheek. I swung round at him, fist raised, and he backed off, tittering, relapsing into his own language. The next instant I felt a blow to my head from the other side which, for a moment, knocked me off balance.

They closed in on me then, all three filling my ears with a suppressed, shrill muttering, like starlings mobbing a larger bird. Their soft, prodding hands were everywhere, not hitting me again for the moment but seeking out my wallet, which of course they soon found. One of them brandished it in the air with a puerile crow, opening his mouth wide so that I saw he had lost many of his teeth.

I have never been any good at the diplomatic, propitiatory gesture. Instead, I tried stupidly to grab my wallet back. They tossed it from one to another, taunting me, laughing and jostling me.

My instinct was to lunge at my nearest tormentor and hit him in the middle of his repellent Mongoloid face. I was much larger and heavier than he was, a different version of a human

being. But in the same moment I knew that I was probably
three times his age, that there were several of them and only
one of me – and that the theft of my money and credit cards
might not be the worst thing I had to fear. I had been slow
on the uptake, as an overprivileged western man used to
command and being obeyed is slow, his more primitive and
wary perceptions lulled into complacency. But suddenly, as
another sharp blow landed on the side of my neck, a real and
atavistic dread swept over me.

Tommy MacFarlane. My friend and fellow. Dead, long ago,
in this land.

You missed your fate once, by a lucky chance. This time
you're for it –

I'll get you, Mason, I'll get you . . .

The jeering faces of the lower school gang were round me,
the smell of their breath and bodies was in my nostrils like
the smell of my own fear. But this time round the circle of
time I was not a child among children.

You're going to die, Mason.

I stood back, breathing heavily, arms by my side. The chief
bully had his arms down now, too, one of them behind his
back. What did he have there? Had I seen, as they were
jostling me, a coil of rope? Visualising myself pinioned, I
quickly stuck my elbows out.

I was not supposed to be there. I had no reality in that
place. I had certainly come more than a mile from the
causeway, and any identifying papers I possessed were in my
wallet, which was now lost to me. It came to me, like a
physical rush of blood to the head, that here, among the
concealing corn, the sky might fall. I might in a few moments
be trussed, mutilated, killed and so disappear without trace.

No one in the City or in the rest of the world would have
any power to find me. The Australian group with whom I
had passed through the checkpoint were strangers to me: they
would not wonder where I was. The useless paperwork of
passes and permissions meant nothing: more likely it would
be my hotel who would, after a while, signal my nonappear-
ance. Then I would simply be a name – *'The British High
Commission have no information'* – a target for random speculation
(*'You American spy, you'*). A warning, an example, a statistic,
finally nothing. The fate which, for weeks, I had dreaded for

my son, dreaded so much that I had not even formulated it fully to myself, was now, it seemed, going to be my own. It was not, after all, Christopher but me that the Great Land had all this time been waiting to reclaim.

'*Oh, the horror of it*,' wrote Great-Aunt Alice long ago, struggling to cope with something she sensed but could not even name. Later she learnt to ignore it, and so did her descendants, but of course it was always there. My parents and I just escaped it, cravenly averting our eyes, leaving Tessa to encounter it for us. And now it had got me, and it was my own fault; I should have known. Indeed it seemed to me in those endless seconds that I had known, for years and years, that everything was very gradually but inexorably leading to this point. 'You know more about death than I do,' Christopher wrote in his last letter. The path did not, after all, lead to the open sea, but inland, towards the inaccessible mountains, into the maize, to a green, secret, foetid place of obsolete rituals that had degenerated into random viciousness and buzzing flies. Flies on spoiled fruit and on the ruined body of a man, on the congealing wounds, on his half-shut eyes. Quite soon, in this humid heat, corruption would set in, rendering all unrecognisable: a melon, a man's battered head –

In a sudden inspiration born of pure terror, I plunged my hands into my trouser pockets and scattered everything on the ground: pen, handkerchief, a pocket knife Jill once gave me, all my loose change. I added my watch. I was under no illusion now that simple theft was the heart of this confrontation – the rope was being swung tauntingly in front of me, another of the men had got out a knife, a third flourished a heavy stick – yet my gesture worked. My tormentors were momentarily distracted – for just long enough for me to dodge, rugger-move, out of their square and run down the path.

One of them recovered almost at once and raced ahead of me between the tall stalks. I managed to trip him up and aimed another wild kick as I passed, which must have connected with his groin for he doubled up with a shout. By some benign mercy which I did not deserve, he was not the one with the knife. That one came up behind me, and I felt a sharp pain in my shoulder. I bolted ahead but they were quicker than I was and were almost on top of me.

You're going to die, Mason —

And yet, I became aware that they had suddenly fallen back.
A moment afterwards I saw what they must have seen. On
the path ahead, near the bottom where it joined the road, a
woman in a white dress stood, staring up at us.

As I came thudding down, she opened her mouth and
shouted something loudly at the men behind me in their own
language, repeating it several times.

I skidded to a stop near her and dared to look round. I
found my heart banging in my chest and sweat running into
my eyes. The three men were retreating rapidly into the maize
from which they had come. A moment later they simply were
not there. Gone, like a bad dream.

'Your shoulder's bleeding,' said Julie Barron in a shocked
voice.

She was applying pressure and a handkerchief to my shoulder.
'He was aiming at the carotid artery. You were too tall for
him.'

We were sitting on a broken wall halfway between the
maize-covered hill and the causeway. I had maniacally insisted
that we leave the place at once; Julie had been insisting with
equal firmness that I should sit down and let her investigate
the knife cut. Hurrying down the road, clutching each other
by the hand, we had both been shaking; now, as she examined
my shoulder, her lips pressed together, her hands felt firmer.

'It's only a flesh wound.' She drew a deep sigh. 'Does it
hurt?'

'Yes — now you mention it, I think it does. But not horribly.
I mean, I'm perfectly all right. Let's go on.'

She said, in the choking voice of someone almost at the
point of letting go:

'I was following you on the road for ages. But I kept well
behind because I thought you might not want me there. I
noticed you first on the station.'

'You were there? I never saw you.'

'I was there. I know it sounds rather silly, but I'd come
over to meet the afternoon train. I — I'd had a little note from
Kit, saying the 14th or the 15th. And it's the 14th today.'

'You too,' I said. We stared at each other in joint commiser-
ation. I thought distractedly how pale she looked, her curly

hair damp and straggly on her forehead, and that earlier that afternoon she had had a sticky drink which had childishly stained the corners of her mouth. 'You've got your uniform on,' I said.

'Yes. I came straight from the hospital. One of our registrars lent me a Red Cross pass that he had, so I just hoped that the guards wouldn't look at me too hard if I was in uniform, and they didn't. The whole thing's a farce anyway. The guards put on a show of making things difficult, but really they like people coming over so that they can make them change money and get a rake-off.'

'I've noticed.'

She said quietly, but with emphasis: 'Thank God you're all right. Things – awful things – have been known to happen near the shrines. You'd have been all right if you'd stuck to the road. I knew that, I should have warned you.'

'I should have had the sense to think of it myself. Thank God you turned up.' I wanted to say 'You saved my life' for it seemed to me true, and yet to voice it seemed in itself too terrifying an admission.

Instead, I asked: 'What did you shout at them to make them back off?'

'Oh, that – I just said: "The military guard are on their way. Run quick!" '

'Not true?'

'No, of course not. But, you know, there's something odd about attacks in the Great Land. And even in the City itself. It's as if, once something is triggered, the people don't quite know what they're doing. We see the results of it sometimes at the hospital – violent assaults and so forth. Really, *horrors*. As if there was some sort of manic feeling that then evaporates again and the people themselves seem surprised. They even make daft excuses for it that obviously aren't true. Something hysterical there . . . Let me look at that cut again now we've sat here for a few minutes.'

We had both been speaking in small, light voices, almost hushed, feigning a controlled articulateness neither of us felt. As we sat, I had become conscious that my heart continued to beat at twice its normal speed. Perspiration, cold now in spite of the hot sun, crept between my shoulder blades near the hot ache of my cut. My head ached too where I had been hit. My hands twitched a little; I clasped them together to still them. How intricate the human metabolism is. How fragile this life of its own, this insistent pump in my chest.

Presently we made our way back along the road to the military post and the causeway, and I suppose my adrenalin level began to fall again; I felt faint and sickish. Once we stopped for me to put my head between my knees. How odd, I thought muzzily, I've heard patients talk about this feeling and never understood before how specific it is.

At the military post I sat on the ground in a small patch of shade and shut my eyes while Julie argued with the guards. Listening to the voices coming from a distance, I could tell it was not so much that the guards disbelieved that she had an injured man on her hands, it was rather that they saw it was true and were made afraid by it. They did not want to get involved. By and by, with much theatrical stamping of papers, in an atmosphere of haste and resentment, we were hustled through, back to the world and the City. Before, I had thought of the City as flawed, strident reality, but now it seemed to me, as it must to the clandestine refugees, an infinitely desirable haven.

'We'll get a taxi,' said Julie. In its reassuring, air-conditioned interior I revived.

'I'll pay for this.' But as soon as I reached for my wallet I realised I had nothing. No money. No cards.

'It won't be much,' she said quickly. 'I told him to go to my place; it's not far. I don't have to go back on duty today. But about your credit cards: you must report them at once. We can do it on my phone.'

'But they're over on the other side. Surely they aren't usable there? They'll just have been thrown away.'

'Don't you believe it,' she said. 'The Great Land may seem the far side of the moon but things – people – go back and forth. Between that place and the City there are all sorts of links: cults, drugs, spies, refugees . . . By tomorrow, your cards could be somewhere like Teyn Bira.'

How does she know, this young vulnerable girl? Oh, let it go, she's probably right. This is age, when your children's generation are more worldly-wise than you are. Give up, let go, breathe gently. You are alive. Always knew you were a lucky fellow, in spite of everything.

By and by, I was stretched out in her small, high, light room. There was ice, and hot sweet tea. She carefully removed my shirt, and I saw for the first time with mild surprise and professional interest how much blood had soaked out of me.

'No wonder I felt a bit odd a while ago.'

'How do you feel now?'

'Better.'

'Lie still . . . yes, like that, on your side. Tch, it's still bleeding a little.'

I thought of asking her to fetch two mirrors so that I could look at it myself. Then I decided not to.

'If it's a simple knife cut it'll be all right, though,' I said.

'It's quite long, about seven centimetres – it gaped as you shifted around. I'm wondering if it's going to need stitches.'

'I don't feel like stitches.'

'Don't be tiresome.' Nurse's voice, speaking above me.

'I'm not. I'll be all right. I always heal up well, even at my age. Vulgarly healthy.'

'Mm. Are your tetanus jabs up to date, at least?'

'Yes, they are.' Truculent schoolboy. So there.

'They need to be, here in the East.'

She went, then was back again. Lying on my side away from her, I heard the sound of paper being torn, Elastoplast unrolled, scissors. I felt the wad pressed to my back. I lay quiet in my unaccustomed role, surrendering to her attentions. A foot or two from my eyes was a row of paperbacks on a shelf: a nursing dictionary, a fat novel that has become a celebrated film, some travel books, including Christopher's study of the Portuguese settlements, an obscure novel he very much likes and must have given to her. Nothing else particularly literary.

'It'd be neater stitched. Like this, you'll have a noticeable scar.'

'So? It'll be something to show my grandchildren.' At which, to my surprise and consternation, I began to cry.

After that, the sequence breaks up in my mind. Most of it, I think, I remember very clearly. But maybe not in the right order or not as Julie would tell it.

I know that Julie sat beside me on the bed and stroked my

head. And that when, eventually, I took one of her hands and brought it to my lips in helpless gratitude for her gentleness, I was stupidly surprised to find her fingers wet with my own tears.

She did not tell me 'It's just shock' or 'just a natural reaction'. She did not attempt to protect herself against my grief. When at last I said: 'It's Christopher, really,' she just said:

'I know, I know.'

I had in any case no words to convey coherently the terrible new desolation I was feeling. Loss of blood no doubt opens a temporary gateway to the demons of fear, loneliness, self-pity, weakness – ultimately to defeat and death itself – but demons are not created from nowhere by a transitory meta-bolic change. They are there already. They had been there in my case for years, since Sarah, since Jill – battened down, waiting their chance, in the vulnerable grey dawn hours, in the dislocation of jet lag, and now, after my frightening, humiliating encounter near the shrines, among the corn.

These demons, like incorporeal versions of the young men who had found me, came crowding round the bed on which I lay: presentiments of age, ebbing strength – extinction. And, most specifically, the sense that Christopher, my one inex-pressibly dear lien on life, the one immortal part of my own substance, was slipping further and further from me in his obscure quest for something else, beyond any horizon I could hope to cross.

I was no longer so afraid for his physical safety as I had been all these weeks. The insight that had struck me as the blows of my attackers had struck, had remained. It was as if, by the bungled assault I had suffered, like a rehearsal for death itself, I had drawn that danger on to me and absorbed it.

But even if he were to fulfil all our hopes and return tomorrow, with his pack on his back and his reassuring smile, it would be one of those returns that only presage a further departure, all the future departures, leaving no permanence, no stake in the time to come. And no right, even, to complain. A son gone out into the world is, traditionally, a success story, no cause for lamentation.

My own forebears had done just that. Yes, but they had

taken wives, begotten children to send back to the grandparents at home. Strong ties bound them helplessly, as they
bound me, to the world that had raised them. Whereas
Christopher – Christopher –

Once or twice, recently, it has even seemed to me that it
is Christopher, not his shadow twin Baht Way, that is the
changeling.

I heard myself say with something like a groan:

'He will escape me – go away.'

'I know. I do know.'

'It's nothing to do with loving or not loving . . . He just has
other things on his mind.'

'I feel exactly the same thing about him.'

'I – I found a long letter from him when I arrived back in
the City. All about visiting Baht Way's village and meeting
his stepfather. But I still don't have any real idea what he's
after.' I distracted myself by telling her the contents of the
letter, not really thinking what I was doing.

'It sounds a lovely letter,' she said wistfully when I had
done. 'I only had this little note – about his being back,
perhaps, today or tomorrow.' She fetched it. It was as she
said, a couple of brief sentences, a mere recapitulation of the
last lines of his longer letter to me, but ending: *'All other news,
sweetheart, when we meet. K. XXX'*

I was touched that she should show me this communication,
with its crosses and its one word of too light endearment, but
as I thanked her and handed the paper back I felt a momentary low triumph that she rated no more than this while I
had a whole account signed *'All love, Dad, as ever.'* Then,
instantly ashamed of myself – what morbidly possessive elder
was I turning into? – I picked up her hand again and kissed
it.

'I did so hope,' she said, 'he would be on this afternoon's
train. I expect you did, too? When I saw you on the station
I knew at once that you must have had the same idea as me.
That's why I kept out of your way, in case you wanted to be
the first person to greet him. I hadn't realised till I saw you
that you were already back again from England.'

It occurred to me only then that Christopher might have
been on the delayed train after all, the train that in the end
neither of us had managed to meet. I suggested this possibility.

'Oh, lie still! You'll start bleeding again. No, he wasn't. The train came in just after you'd gone, and I saw everyone who came off it. The man who told you it wouldn't be in for an hour was wrong; they usually are.'

'Are we crazy, Julie?'

'No. I don't think so. I was disappointed, of course. But I'll meet tomorrow's train too. Provided I can get across the causeway two days running. The guards sometimes make difficulties about that.'

'Will you be able to take time off work again?'

'Yes. I didn't tell you, but after I got Kit's note I arranged things so that I could take some leave that's owing to me. I don't have to be back at the hospital till Sunday.'

After a pause, I said: 'You must be hoping very much that he'll come – that you won't have wasted these days off.'

I saw the pair in my mind, clear and small as in a long shot on film, going off together arm in arm talking excitedly: lovers with two days all their own, a secret space in time. Time for so little and everything. Even a spirit wedding.

'Yes,' she said at once, 'but now I know you're here too – '

'Oh, well, I wouldn't want to hang round your necks. We could all have dinner together perhaps, but then – or perhaps just a drink,' I amended maniacally.

'You don't understand,' she said. 'If you're here he'll want to go back with you to your hotel. He would probably want to go looking for you anyway, even if you didn't appear at Jedu Sumna. Oh, he'll be glad to see me. But I do know that I'm not really that important to him. Not like you. Or – like other things are. Not people at all.'

'My dear girl . . . I'm sure Christopher's really fond of you.' I added, meaning well but probably sounding fatuous: 'How could he not be?'

She said, in the tone of someone who has learnt in childhood to face an emotional lack which will not be filled:

'Oh yes, he's fond of me. He likes me. We have good times together. All that. But. He somehow isn't . . . quite as most people are. I mean – don't worry, I'm not under any illusion that he might marry me.'

At this, one of my deeper unvoiced fears rose like a bubble and burst on the surface of my mind. I heard myself ask:

'I've sometimes wondered, is my son gay?' I faltered on the

last word (which in any case is not the idiom of my generation) because even as I said it, I knew it was not what I meant. Of course I know Christopher sleeps with women. But that is not the same as having the emotional taste for being a husband, a father.

Before I could explain, Julie said with a nervous laugh: 'Oh, heavens, no, not gay! He can be as loving as any other man, in that way. No, no, it's Mike Isaacs who's gay.'

'Ah. That didn't occur to me. But now you mention it . . . yes.'

Julie said: 'So you see, he and I are both – well, both in love with the same person.'

'Christopher?'

'Mm.'

'Yes. That hadn't struck me but, yes, I see what you mean. He has a rather intense manner when he talks about Christopher. But then so he does when he speaks of Baht Way.'

'Well, they apparently look so alike!' said Julie. We both laughed, glad of the release.

'Mike rang me yesterday. He's in a lather about Baht Way being missing now too,' I said.

'I know. He rang me as well. The trouble is, I never know how seriously to take Mike's fusses because I never know how much else he knows that he's not telling you. He has – oh, all sorts of irons in the fire.'

'Colin Darcy at the High Commission hinted that Mike is some sort of spy.'

'Mike himself says he's a foreign correspondent, freelancing for several American papers.'

'Well, he would say that, I dare say. I don't know. He seems to me a bit of a fantasist, so maybe he isn't really doing all that much here beyond filing the odd story that any local journalist might get hold of.'

'He likes to feel he's important,' said Julie, not sneering, merely stating the fact. 'But then perhaps he is?'

'Yes. The two things don't exclude each other. Mike really may be some sort of undercover agent. In which case he's probably a double agent because that kind of personality usually is. A chronic outsider. An outsider's outsider. So corrupted that in a sense he's incorruptible. No one is his master.'

'Mm . . .' She looked unhappy with my baseless worldly wisdom. 'Of course he's never said anything about that to me.'

'Of course not.'

When she had digested this, she said anxiously: 'If you're right – if – what might this mean for Christopher? And for Baht Way?'

'That's just what I've been wondering. Oh God, Julie, *I* don't know. I feel I don't know anything by now. I'm probably imagining things. So much has been happening. I feel I'm surrounded by people with different dramas going on in their lives, and inside their heads, that I don't properly understand. Pauline and Toby. Mike. Christopher. Another woman whom I met yesterday. Those boys near the shrines, too.'

But I thought, even as I said it, that Julie and I seemed to have found some temporary shared space in this tiny, anonymous flat, where the light was now declining from one minute to the next as the City sunset took over the blank sky beyond the window above the unseen waterway to the sea.

She said, lightly but with some sign of strain: 'It's funny you should say that about Mike. Because I used to wonder at first if *Kit* was in Intelligence of some kind, and that was why there was something going on there in his mind I didn't understand. Eventually, when he actually said something to me about being "a sort of spy" I nearly fell through the floor. But then I realised he didn't mean it literally at all.'

'He meant that a writer is a kind of spy – a permanent outsider,' I said. 'Didn't he? He said something like that once to me.'

'Yes. He tried to explain to me. He said that it's not that writers don't experience things like other people, but they're always experiencing them in another way as well. "Like having a ghostly twin" is the way he put it. And then he went on to say that, to simplify things for themselves as well as everyone else, most of the time a writer pretends that the twin isn't there. You don't exactly mean to fool people, he said, but you end up doing it all the same. Writers are two-faced, he said. Even when they're trying really hard to tell the truth.'

' "Ghostly twin",' I said, "shadow twin" – yes, I suppose I see what he means. The one who stands alongside the involved one and watches and records . . . A bit like the doctor attending to himself or to someone very dear to him. Split reactions.'

'I suppose so,' she said doubtfully.

'But he uses the same phrase about Baht Way. You told me that when we were having dinner together in that restaurant by the river. It struck me very much. That meeting Baht Way might be like meeting himself in a distorting glass, you said. Or like himself in another life, if the chances had fallen differently.'

'You see,' said Julie carefully after a pause, 'he thinks that he himself has had the life that Baht Way ought to have had. That Baht Way had his identity – his birthright, it's called in the Bible, isn't it? – yes, his birthright, stolen from him.'

'Well, he has a point there. But he didn't steal Baht Way's birthright.'

'No-o. But he feels that his – your – family did, one way and another. I think he wants to give it back.'

'How? Change places?'

'Well, of course he couldn't really do that.'

'Of course not. That's just a fantasy. A classic storyteller's invention. Not real. Damn it, he's not *writing* Baht Way. What magic powers does he think he has?' I was grumpy with obscure frustration. I also thought, but did not say: he's always liked playing tricks with his own identity. 'Christopher' to me. 'Kit' to the girl he sleeps with. 'Chris' perhaps not only to Mike Isaacs but to whole other ranges of people whose importance in his life I do not even suspect. Separate worlds. Never committed to any one of them. Deep-down selfish. Damn him. Oh, damn him!

So it was that, little by little, as the light faded in the room, I found myself telling Julie more about Christopher's child-hood, telling her about his passion of never-to-be-repeated naked grief when I came to the school to tell him his mother was dead. And how I had failed him, and known I was failing him even at the time, in not bringing him home for the funeral. And my deep-seated fear that I had allowed some-thing to happen in him that has profoundly affected him, made him assume armour or several armours.

Julie listened as I talked but did not say much. How could she, when she herself had said a short while before 'he somehow isn't as most people are'? But when I faltered or

paused she would say quietly 'do go on', or ask me another
question to prompt me further.

So it was, I think, that I also found myself telling Julie how
I have continued to regret at moments through the years that
Christopher has no brother or sister. No doubt it was the
notion of Baht Way as Christopher's alter ego that led me to
this, rambling on about Sarah's reluctance to adopt, about my
own lack of imagination – 'We thought: "Better not". We
thought: "We're comfortable as we are" . . . I've always felt,
till just recently, that we were probably right. But now, when
I think how Baht Way's stepfather took on this alien child,
when he had no money, nothing – I find myself ashamed of
my own prudence and judgement.

'Oh, of course Baht Way was born years before Sarah and
I even met, and we didn't know of his existence, but that's
beside the point . . . Actually, if Christopher thinks, as you say,
that our family somehow deprived Baht Way of the identity
and life he should have had, then Christopher does have a
point – even more than he knows. I haven't yet had a chance
to tell him everything I've uncovered.'

'As Christopher isn't here, tell me now,' she said.

'It'll take a while. I've talked so much already. Aren't you
tired?'

'Not a bit. We'll stop, of course, if you are. But I do want
to hear anything you have to say. Just let me check that
bandage.'

She did so, and rearranged pillows behind my head. I
settled back again. Dark had come fully now in her small
room, but it was not the heavy, chilly stuff of English dark
but the mere shadowy veil that is cast over a great lighted
city with a tropical moon riding above it. I raised my arm to
try to read the time, but found my wrist bare.

'I'm sorry about your watch,' said Julie at my gesture of
irritation and loss.

'It doesn't matter. I mean, I really don't mind that much.'

Shock was evidently waning: my shoulder and head still
hurt but remotely, as if the hurt belonged to someone else.
Not knowing the time, or the location of the place we were
in, I felt on odd sense of lightness, a kind of freedom.

As I had warned, it took time to recount the Pauline
business. I also found myself tending to stray from the main

subject, wanting to say other and different things which had not occurred to me before. At one point I realised, when Julie gently recalled me to a practical detail of Pauline's schemes, that I had spent the last few minutes ruminating aloud on whether I have been locked in a cold war all these years with my elder sister because she reminds me of some part of myself which I do not like and have tried not to acknowledge.

And so, by degrees, I told this limpid girl, more than young enough to be my daughter, this female creature who belongs to my son, things that I have never told anyone else and probably never will.

She contributed her own preoccupations too, of course. At one moment she remarked that what she found particularly alarming about the Pauline saga was that it had come to light by pure chance. Had Baht Way's picture in a British newspaper not passed under Christopher's eye last December, we would none of us ever have known of him, let alone of Pauline's role in the affair.

'And,' I said, taking up her point, 'if Pauline had been less careless, Toby's Helena Davis might now be seriously dead.'

'Ye-es. That's a bit different, though. I wonder, perhaps, if in a way your sister Pauline wanted to be so careless – needed to be found out?'

'Mm. That'd be the classic view, wouldn't it? But I dunno . . .'

'What I'm trying to say about the Tessa's-baby business,' she persisted, fiddling with the edge of the pillow behind my head, 'is that perhaps in the long run it might have been better not to find out, all this long time after? I mean, finding out can change nothing.'

'No. I see what you mean.' The thought did not appeal to me. My whole life and career had been predicated on truth, of a sort. It is always better to know things, I had told Myrtle Brown, only yesterday and an enormous span of time ago, in another flat in this city. Is it really better?

The fact is, I have often speculated fugitively on this question, imaging an alternative loop of time in which I did not know certain things.

It was pure chance, I suppose, that made Pauline see Sarah long ago in Oxford on the arm of the man who was for many years her lover. Yes, it was the desire to cause trouble that

made Pauline impart the fact to me, but she did not invent
it. Pauline is not a fantasist, her evil does not take that form:
she needed the random coincidence of seeing Sarah in Oxford, accompanied, in order to poison my heart.

And how do I know that this man was in fact a part of
Sarah's life for many years? Might he not have been just a
brief, excusable lapse, a passing fancy, one of those things that
happen? (I am not immune myself. I understand such things.)

I know he was in her life for years, firstly, because long
ago, when Sarah and I were still hoping to have another child,
she got very distressed one night and then withdrawn, and
finally burst out that she could not help thinking that the
problem might have evolved between ourselves: some allergy,
some antibodies – 'either of us, with someone else, it might
work'.

There was quiet between us for a bit, and then I heard
myself say, in that deliberately cool, 'fair' doctor's voice that
I sometimes use:

'Well, you'd better pick someone suitable.'

And then she made an apparent joke of it, suggesting all
sorts of famous and gifted men, speculating flippantly on who
might be flattered and 'come across' and who would 'run a
mile', and presently I too joined in the game. But some
obscure message passed between us then; where would Sarah,
who admired brains, seek them, if not among her own most
distinguished academic contacts? Only, if she did, I did not
have to confront that fact at the time, since evidently it failed
to produce a child for her, whatever else it did.

And I also know that it went on for years because it was
long after the Pauline episode that Sarah died. Years which
were, in the main, so peaceful and cheerful that I successfully
lulled my fears and suspicions to rest, daring to assume that,
after a tricky phase, Sarah was again wholly mine. Till she
was killed in that senseless accident, driving alone – on a
Wednesday afternoon, why? She had mentioned no such plan
– on the road to Oxford.

And as I guessed then, with the sudden percipience of shock,
who the man in question might be, I took it upon myself –
in charity? In retribution? In sheer grief? – to ring him and
tell him what had happened, and from his appalled reaction
I knew my surmise was true. Or something was true. Lover

still, or only loved? 'Only'.

Yes, Julie was right. These things too it might have been better if I had never known. Even as Jill's fortunate husband never knew about me.

As I had told Julie so much, I told her all this as well.

She did not say anything for a while. Her head was bent, with her curly hair falling over her face, and I half sat up trying to look at her in the dimness, wondering if I had finally shocked her with this middle-aged saga of failed love, suppressed pain. I was most disconcerted to find that it was she who was now crying.

'Darling girl, what is it?'

'I – I feel so sorry. It – it's dreadful to love somebody who seems to love somebody else more.'

Stuck on the idea of Christopher and her, I obtusely tried to suggest that at least no other girl was a rival for Christopher's love.

'Christopher?' she said distractedly. 'But I didn't mean him . . . I was thinking about this man your wife seems to have loved. And about the husband of your friend Jill. Particularly about him, actually, because you know more about him and he sounds – well, the sort of person you would rather she hadn't loved.'

'You could say that. Yes.'

'And that made me think of my stepmother. And how I hate her.'

'Oh,' I said, too facilely, at ease now that I had spilled out in front of this defenceless girl the great messy bundle of my own irremediable griefs. 'From what you told me before of your family life, I think you can feel free to hate your stepmother.'

'But how can I when my father loves her?' she said, inexorably honest. 'Maybe he loves her even like I love Kit – or you do. Don't you see? That's what hurts so.' She cried some more then, and there was for her no comfort in it.

What could I do but take her in my arms? We had become so close in the last three hours that there was nowhere to go but closer. I pulled her down on the bed beside me. My shirt was already off, and her hair lay over my bare skin. Of course, little by little, I encouraged her to shed her own few clothes, for one wears few in that climate, and of course I wanted to lay my head between her breasts, and then of course I was not going to stop.

She was anxious at first about my wound – wanted me to stay lying flat – but it didn't make any difference, I was still quite able to love her, and by and by she forgot about my wound and everything else and seemed happy, as women are.

You must not think I fool myself, Julie. I know that I resemble Christopher. Not so much in face, but in general build and type. The distribution of our body hair is similar, a stippled crucifix, and so are other things, as I recall. Except that I, a product of my class and generation, am circumcised, whereas he, in accordance with the revisionist views of my medical training, is not. It does not, however, make any difference one way or another to a woman, or so I have come to believe.

No, I do not fool myself that it was entirely me you lay with on that narrow bed. But you were very sweet to me. In the early hours of the morning we both woke, jammed against one another. It was after that you said:

'This is just for me and you . . . It's lovely, I'm so glad. I won't ever tell anyone else. You won't either, will you?'

'Of course I won't,' I said.

Later, you managed to say:

'Please, when you remember this – if you ever do – don't think I was pretending to myself you were Kit. I'm not.'

I was touched and pleased, I suppose, that you had said that. Though the very fact that it had entered your mind to say it did seem to carry its own message.

You went on bravely: 'I know I would go to the end of the earth for him. But I also know it's no use my feeling like that about him, and I've seen so little of him really since I came back here that I've almost got accustomed to it . . . I mean, you mustn't think I spend my whole time wishing he was with me. It's not like that.'

'Good!' I said, making a joke of it, for what else could I do? 'Shall I tell you what I'd feel if you were wishing he was here just now? Offended.'

And you laughed, and did not ask any questions about the blind, black triumph over a rival that was, however, temporarily, occupying my heart.

*

When I woke again it was full morning, another relentlessly sunny City day. I found I had the bed to myself and stretched happily, a little sore and stiff about my head and shoulder, but well. Julie came to the kitchen door and stood looking at me; then she brought me some coffee and toast. She was wearing her yellow dress and looked very nice. Presently she helped me wash, and changed the dressing on my shoulder. We were both a little shy of one another.

'I've nothing to put on. I've just realised, my shirt's all bloody.'

'Not now, it isn't. I shoved it in to soak yesterday afternoon as soon as I'd taken it off you. Later, in the night, when I went to the bathroom, I saw it and washed it out and hung it up. I've ironed it dry this morning.'

'How organised you are. Thank you very much.'

She laughed, and said in the tone of the one who's decided to be the strong one again: 'I've been up for hours. I came and looked at you from time to time. You seemed to be having a lovely sleep. I was pleased for you.'

'I was. I feel good.' I held out my hand to her, but she turned away, saying: 'I'll fetch your shirt.'

By and by, as she was helping me on with it, she said: 'Something to tell you. Some news. While you were asleep I rang Mike Isaacs. He thinks he's located Baht Way again. Back in Ak Teem. He's going there himself this morning to find out and he wants me to come too. So I said – well, I said I'd phone you and see if you could come as well.'

'Oh, fine,' I said brightly. 'Great.'

'It's exciting, isn't it? You meeting him at last.' But something in my tone or expression must have alerted her, for she came round to face me, studied me anxiously, and said:

'So long as you feel up to it. Do you? Baht Way's been so elusive, I thought we ought to seize the opportunity while it's there. But if you're too tired . . .'

'It isn't exactly that.' When we were together in the dark, I could have said 'I wanted to spend the morning alone with you' but now I felt she did not want me to say such things. Once we left the flat and went to Mike, who had known her far longer than I had and must not guess that we were anything more than acquaintances, that would be the end of it, of us being together.

'Of course I want to come to Ak Teem with you,' I said. 'But first — there's something worrying me I have to ask you.'

Yes, it was a bid to restore intimacy between us, if only for a last quarter of an hour. But it was also true, there was an actual anxiety lurking and it took me several minutes to bring it out.

'Last night,' I said eventually, 'I asked you at one point if you were on the Pill. At least, I think I did. But perhaps I dreamed it?'

'You weren't dreaming,' she said. 'You did ask.' And turned away.

'Yes, I thought I did,' I persisted. 'I nearly forgot; I'm out of practice at my age. Or rather, I should say, at the age of most of the women with whom I'm likely to . . . these days. But I did remember and asked, and you said you weren't on the Pill but that it was all right, I shouldn't worry. So I didn't.'

She looked up then and smiled quickly, but said nothing.

'Julie, I'm sorry, but I've been thinking and I have to ask: you weren't using a cap either, why did you say it was all right?'

No answer.

'Did you,' I asked masochistically, 'imagine that a man so much older than you could not make you pregnant? Because, if so, that was a very risky thing to suppose, my dear.'

She was annoyed then. 'Of course not! I'm not so ignorant.'

I felt pleased at least to have a response. I nagged on: 'I know you're not ignorant. So why? Why did you say it was all right? I want to know.'

'Because it is. I'm not worried, you can see I'm not. So why should you be?'

A horribly complex situation presented itself to my imagination. Oh, surely not, I thought. This girl isn't a schemer, and in any case — what a scheme.

'Julie,' I said, 'just what are you up to?'

'Oh!' She covered her face with her hands, and for a moment I thought I'd made her cry again. But then she looked up pinkly and gave me a sort of smile.

'Well, if you must know,' she said.

'I must.'

'I didn't want to tell you. It didn't — doesn't — seem, well, tactful. Or not good taste or something. But, well, if you must know why I wasn't worried about you making me pregnant it's because I think I'm pregnant already.'

We didn't speak for a bit. I moved about the small room touching things.

Yes, I knew it was true. Had known it already in the night without voicing the thought to myself, not wanting to. Even when one's mind is switched off one's hands don't forget. And I have spent a lifetime in general practice.

'Is it Christopher's?' I said at last.

'Of course it is,' she said, taken aback. 'Whose on earth else? It's not Mike Isaacs's, that's for sure!'

'Of course. I'm sorry. I didn't mean it like that.'

She said, apologetically now: 'You'll think I let it happen on purpose. I didn't. Really. Kit doesn't know yet. Nobody does – except, now, you. It must have happened just before I left England, in June, but it didn't dawn on me for a bit; I was so busy here with the new job and everything. My cap let me down. When I looked at it carefully I found a split near the rim. So, you see, I'm not so organised as you thought.'

There were other things I would need to know, to ask, perhaps to offer. But – 'I'm glad you're not organised. I'm so glad,' I said.

Julie had arranged to meet Mike Isaacs on a corner by the City bus terminal: as far as I could judge, this concrete space occupied the site of one of the old dockyard basins. From there we walked self-consciously, three abreast, towards Ak Teem. It seemed to me I could smell the scent of her freshly showered morning self, beneath her clean yellow cotton dress. Her lips seemed very faintly swollen, and she licked them once or twice: probably she did not realise she was doing so.

I felt unnaturally clean too, a little tired and empty-headed as one does, but quite calm now. I don't imagine Mike noticed anything. Why should anything occur to him? He wasn't thinking about Julie or me or even about Christopher, this morning. He was jubilant because he had located Baht Way again.

As we made our way down a commercial street clogged with trucks being unloaded, we kept glimpsing the great dirty

building at which we were aiming, isolated at the far end in
an oddly diminished perspective. An expanse of waste land
intervened between it and the busy quarter we were leaving.
Mike told us the block itself had been scheduled for demolition
for several years. The municipality hated it and were embarrassed by it; in spite of vested interests and obstructive lawsuits
it would surely vanish soon from the face of the modern City.

'It's an absolute anomaly here today. A rabbit warren. No,
more like a great ant hill. No proper drainage, no services –
just a lot of water pipes tapped illegally off the mains and
pirated electricity lines. It's run by gangs; they keep a sort of
order, it's quite peaceful at the moment, but the police don't
dare go in there. Which is an irony, because the whole place
was the jail in British concession days.'

'The outer wall round the compound was pulled down,
though, wasn't it?' said Julie, doing her bit. 'I remember Chris
telling me that when we came here before. I'd always wondered why there was this peculiar empty space round it. It's
as if it isn't part of the present-day City at all.'

I wondered if I, alone among the three of us, had seen the
one-time wall and the block bare and official without the
tacked-on cages – balconies that now rose in ramshackle tiers
above us like the nests of messy birds on some great, sheer
cliff. But, if so, no memory of it returned to me. In childhood
I had hardly come down to this part of town.

Mike said: 'The wall was demolished by the Japanese when
they were here in the war. They used the rubble to fill in the
dock back there, and parked their transport on it. The jail
itself was their barracks. When the City was liberated the
building was left derelict. That's how refugees from upcountry
came to squat in it and they've been doing it ever since.
They've turned each of the old cells into living units, with
one or more families in each and little stores and workshops
and God knows what all over the place. Illegal liquor stills
and drug-trafficking and dealing in stolen goods of course, but
all sorts of more or less straight one-man businesses too. The
whole place is like an alternative township. They even have
their own temples and brothels in there and a school they
run themselves.'

'People in our hospital say there's a particular Ak Teem
accent you can recognise that's different from the regular City

one,' Julie remarked. 'My ear isn't good enough to distinguish it.'

But I was remembering now that Ak Teem means the Forbidden Place, and as we slowly crossed the empty space around it, it seemed to me that this was another version of going over the frontier. I remembered too that Christopher had said that the words Ak Teem, though used literally as something like 'Private – No admittance', are also one of the many phrases in their language for death, heaven or some more equivocal after life. I recalled what he had said about the refugees from the Great Land that he had met there – *'Their hearts weren't beating any more. They'd had their identity destroyed by what they had suffered.'*

I felt cold, then, under the brilliant sun, as if the building were casting some invisible shadow. Not Baht Way, I thought. Not my nephew. Please don't let Baht Way be like that. Christopher did say: 'I get the feeling that his heart is still beating.' In spite of everything.

Forbidden, by reputation, the place may be, but after a short parley with a man lounging in a filthy doorway, during which money changed hands, we were allowed in.

Dark. Amazingly dark. Almost the moment we were inside the narrow passage we were swallowed up in it. A murky, greenish dark, as if we had gone under the sea. The salt-swamp reek of the buried one-time City assaulted our nostrils. The flagstones beneath our feet were slimy with a wet mulch of dirt, and water dripped everywhere from blue plastic pipes that coiled above our heads. As we fumbled our way along there were head-turning whiffs of rotting fish too, from storage arches that gaped dimly on either side: fish, petrol, another sudden awful stench which I diagnosed as bone-boiling, and something else more pervasive that I knew like a memory from a forgotten life but could not place.

'Rat's piss,' said Mike, with the perverse pride people sometimes show in the slums of their chosen city. 'Since the port was containerised they've migrated here from the water-front. Big as cats, some of them.'

We saw a huge, bedraggled one a few minutes later, limping ahead of us and squeezing into a break in the wall. I glanced at Julie, but she simply made a disgusted face. By that time we had mounted a floor or two, going up by iron staircases

that stood where two passages intersected, and as we went up
each level the light grew fractionally clearer and the smells
specific rather than all-pervasive so that we walked through
them as if through rooms: palm oil, offal, curry, soy, human
urine, live goat, chicken droppings. But the whole thing was
overlaid now and vaguely sweetened by sticks of incense
smoking in front of many of the open doors with their obsolete
barred spyholes. Although it still felt to me as if I were walking
in some oppressive, airless underworld, perhaps in the secret
passages that are said to lie beneath the shrines in the Great
Land, people were living here and carrying on prosaic lives.
Roughly painted yellow and red hieroglyphics on the doors
gave their names or trades. Children played in the corridors
among the pecking chickens, skinny cats ducked and scam-
pered, a dog whined on a tight leash, women queued at water
taps over chipped, cracked sinks, pans sizzled on small, dan-
gerous-looking kerosene burners. Radios were burbling and
we caught glimpses through doorways, among hanging
clothes, of men lying on bed frames in singlets or playing
cards or dismantling pieces of old machinery.

'It was the seventh floor before,' said Julie. 'I remember
from coming here with Kit.'

'Yeah, that's what the guy downstairs said. The staircase at
the far end of the sixth. Then turn to the right.'

When we finally reached the seventh floor, via a flight of
steps sheltering a pile of papers and old rags which two
women were picking over, the general atmosphere was much
easier to breathe: we seemed to be making our way upwards
towards invisible sources of air and life itself. It was much
lighter too, but with an odd, dappled light as if it were
percolating through the leaves of a wood: after a few minutes
I realised that the corridor we had now reached was partly
open to the sky, covered only with wire netting, and that the
speckled effect was due to litter lying around on top of the
mesh.

Mike stopped to ask the way of an old man attending to
candle ends in front of a small shrine, but he seemed not to
know of Baht Way and looked at us with a narrow wariness
as if he had hardly seen people like us before.

'It's along here,' said Julie. 'It's coming back to me. Right,
like he said downstairs, then right again. Then I think it's one

of the doors on the left.'

It was. Sitting by the door in question was a young but toothless man who seemed to have lost his hair, too, reinforcing my obscure, squeamish dread of what I might learn here. He recognised Julie and broke into a gummy, nervous smile. He stood up and gestured to us to enter, and the moment which I had been anticipating for almost nine months, as one waits for nine months for another sort of momentous encounter, had finally arrived.

Like many other men in that vast repository of hidden lives, Baht Way was stretched out on a tin bedstead with his hands behind his head and a radio chuntering softly beside him. He sat up abruptly as we were ushered in and, for a moment, seemed tensed, wary. Then, recognising Mike, he smiled and got to his feet, naked to the waist, wearing country-style cotton drawers. He came forward, holding out both hands to us, palms up, in the local gesture that means 'welcome'.

I remember that when Christopher was born, between my hands, I felt as if I were seeing for the first time some famous monument already familiar to me in theory. Something of the same emotion was there as I shook hands at last with Tessa's son. And yet, and yet . . . Yes, of course there was a marked general likeness to Christopher, but I had been prepared for still more: this not very tall man, ten years older but with the muscles of a manual worker, was not Christopher, was not in fact as like him in the flesh as he had been in the photograph. It was, after all, more like meeting a stranger who looks familiar to you, even intimately so, because you knew each other when you were both ten years old. The link is real, but it has long been rendered obsolete by different experiences on both sides. What, after the first affectionate and reminiscent exchanges, will you even have to talk about?

But he had a nice face, this known stranger, diffident but with a lively intelligence shining out of it. I also noticed that, after his own first shock of surprise and embarrassed pleasure at meeting me, he was quite calm, even assured. He did not seem like the man on the run I had feared he would be in this place.

Using Mike as the interpreter (Julie was adamant that his grasp of Baht Way's language was better than hers), I began, self-consciously, to tell Baht Way some brief facts selected from the many I now knew. The central fact was simple: 'I'm sure that you are my nephew, the only child of my younger sister who is now dead.' Then I hesitated, repeated myself, feeling that there was so much more to tell but uncertain how to approach it. 'My own son, your cousin, has been looking for you,' I said. 'Recently he's even been to your village in the Great Land, but you had already left there again.'

When this was transmitted to Way he made a long answer, which turned out to be a circumstantial explanation of how and why he had visited his home village so briefly. Although the frontier crossing and the long journey was normally only worth making for a stay of several weeks, he had been afraid, he said, of losing his job if he was absent for long just now. It was a good job, on a section of recently reclaimed land to the north of the City, where buildings would be going up for several years. He sounded proud of this development, sketching tall blocks in the air with his hands as if he had been personally concerned in the design of them instead of simply trench-digging and pipe-laying.

He had gone to his village at this time, he said, only because he had received word that his old father was unwell and wanted to see him again before he died. (So much, I thought, for Christopher and Mike's theory that Way had made himself scarce in order to incite us to go in search of him.) He started to say something else, corrected himself, and then, at a word of reassurance from Mike, explained that he meant his 'mother's husband' but that he always thought of him as his father. 'Of course,' I said.

Now, he said, he felt glad he had made the effort, and at peace with himself (thus Mike translated his words) because he had heard only last night that his father had died at the beginning of the week. He had, he said, been lying there before we came, thinking about his father and remembering times when he was a child.

'Tell him,' I said to Mike, 'that my son has seen his father since he left.' I was eager to embark on an account, from Christopher's letter, of his momentous visit to Baht Tye, but Mike stopped me, saying: 'I think Way already knows that.' There came a further flood of clear, throaty explanation from Way. 'Yes, he does. He's glad they had the chance to meet before the old man went. He thinks it must have been destined.'

Evidently Julie had been right when she had told me that communications between the Great Land and the City were much more efficient than official channels would suggest.

'Please tell him,' I said to Mike, feeling a little helpless now, 'how much Christopher is looking forward to meeting him.'

When Mike had translated this, Way made no answer. He wandered over to the door, perhaps to look and see who might be outside but perhaps because he was thinking. Then he came back, looked into my face as he began to speak, and then shifted his gaze to Mike as if to make sure that each sentence seemed to be fully translated as he continued his speech. This was the gist of it:

'I have met you now, honoured uncle, and I am realising that that will do. At one time, for several years until a few months ago, I felt passionate about finding my real family. It was my great ambition. But then, when my dream came true and Mike said he had heard from you, I began to think more ... I thought: these people are not dream people, and they do not belong to me any more than I belong to them. They have their own lives to lead. They may not want me in their life and really I do not need them. Why, after all, would I want another family? I have all my own people, my father's family, all my stepbrothers and sisters, my wife and my own children. It's greedy, and against nature, to want more.'

So he said it. It seemed to me that anything I could offer in return would be inadequate, or simply out of date. But, after a pause, I tried because I felt I must.

'We might be able to do something for you all the same. For instance, help you get your wife and children to the City?'

He intimated with apparent conviction that they would in any case be able to come by and by – 'Now that my father is dead. And I have a proper work permit now, you see.' He added something else, and looked towards Mike again. Mike hestitated.

Julie said quietly: 'He says: "Thanks to Mike! He has arranged my permit for me." Oh, well done, Mike! You said you might be able to.'

'It turned out quite easy,' Mike muttered. But he looked absurdly pleased, this man to whom power and a feeling of knowledge were necessary for his fragile sense of self.

Julie asked Baht Way one or two halting questions, and then explained: 'He isn't an illegal immigrant in the City any more. He can still get into trouble going to and from the Great Land, but here he is safe. He's not hiding now here in Ak Teem – it's just that, for the moment, he has nowhere else to live, as he gave up his room in Teyn Bira. Anyway, he says, he has friends here.'

Friends. I could imagine that, like Christopher to whom he bore a ghostly (but only ghostly) resemblance, this Eastern peasant would readily attract friends. No, he did not really need us or want our help. At some level he had wanted, perhaps, the chance to reject us as he had once been rejected, and this he had now achieved. What I had at first taken for diffidence was, rather, oriental politeness and circumspection. More dignified and formidable than the poor coolie of my thoughtless imaginings, he was also in some indefinable way more alien.

I said to Mike: 'I'd thought of telling him who his real father was, now I've found out – yes, you wondered, didn't you? Well, I've got the answer for you. But now, I don't know. Could you find out tactfully if he would like to know or not?'

More interchanges between Mike and Baht Way. Mike was pushing the matter, I thought nervously; no doubt he was curious himself. But Way seemed resistant. It was Julie who gradually translated for me:

' "The one I look on as father is the old man who has just died in my village. No, I don't want another one. What duties would I be able to perform for him? . . . No, it doesn't matter my not being there for the funeral of my village father. He has his blood sons, my younger brothers to take care of that." '

She broke off. Way was asking something else, some direct request, looking at me.

'He wants to know his mother's proper name,' said Mike. 'He's never known even her first name, you see.'

I told him 'Teresa Mason', and wrote it down for him in capitals on a bit of paper. He screwed up his eyes over the impenetrable hieroglyphics, and apparently remarked that, now he was a Citizen, he was going to have to learn to read the roman alphabet and dreaded it. We all laughed self-consciously. He wrote the name alongside, phonetically, in his own careful script that is like cubist paper chains.

'I think he wants it,' said Mike softly, 'to hold a spirit wedding.' He asked Way another question, and said:

'Yes. Now he's got her name and knows for sure she is dead, and his father is dead too, he will be able to pay a local priest to conduct a wedding ritual. They found and loved each other in life but were never able to make a life together as they should have done, so he will see that they are united in death. He's been wanting to do this, and now he can.'

'Yes, I remember you telling me about spirit weddings.'

I remembered too that Mike, that unattached wanderer between various worlds, had seemed to find the whole idea very moving. So, as a matter of fact, did I. But I thought, though did not say, What about Baht Tye's other wife? It was Julie who said it.

'Oh,' said Mike easily, 'I don't think spirits are tied to one place, one version of being, at any one moment. They can share themselves around. Unlike most people on this earth, they're free to be attached to more than one person.'

'How convenient,' I said.

Baht Way must at some point have indicated to the hairless, toothless guardian of the door that he should fetch soft drinks for us, for he returned now with three Coca-Colas. We solemnly toasted one another, and Baht Way laughed loudly, tickled by this exotic ritual, showing gaps where he himself had lost a tooth or two.

Then, raising the glass of water which was all he had consented to drink, he said, enunciating carefully; 'Christopher!'

Further talk followed between him and Mike, while Julie and I sat on the bed frame and surveyed the collection of different objects – suitcases, bedrolls, two bicycles, cooking pots, bags of rice and lentils – crammed into this small space, and wondered how many people occupied it at night.

'Hey,' said Mike excitedly, breaking back into English, 'know what Way's just told me? He came back to the City three days ago via Jedu Sumna and he ran into trouble. He'd paid bribe money to join the crew of a fishing boat and pass through with them, but then he saw the boats ahead of them in the queue at the lock were all being called over, so that wouldn't do. He got the captain to leave him on the jetty and then walked up the road away from the police post and over to the railway station, and hung around for half a day till the train came. Among the people who got off was a little group of westerners. He followed them down to the post – he hoped, because of his appearance, to slip through with them, pretending he'd lost his passport.'

Picking up the international word 'passport', Way grinned and rolled his eyes heavenwards at this point, in a pantomime of despair.

'It was really difficult for him, though. He also had to pretend to be some funny sort of westerner who didn't speak a word of English. Of course he couldn't risk opening his mouth at all, or his local accent would have given him away at once. He also felt, when he was actually inside the police post, that the men on duty weren't in the mood to let anyone get away with anything that afternoon, and he had no idea what to do.'

'Come on, Mike, put us out of our suspense. What did he do?'

'He remembered Christopher's name,' said Mike simply.

'Christopher's?'

'Yes. And he managed to say it well enough to sound convincing. At any rate, the guys apparently decided that must be his name as he hoped they would.'

'Chris-toe-phur May-son,' said Way, nodding vigorously.

'So they let him through just like that?'

'Well, not immediately.' Mike turned back to Way, and after a further exchange explained: 'Way says they looked the name up in a great sheaf of forms they had, with visa photos attached, and came up with Christopher's from when he had passed into the Great Land a week or two earlier. And, of course, the photo looked like him enough to be Baht Way, if you didn't look too close. So, after that, they were satisfied he was just returning and let him across.'

'Good heavens.'

'But didn't they think it rather odd,' said Julie, 'that someone with an English name couldn't speak any English?'

'Oh, I guess men in frontier posts aren't paid to think. Way says there was some fuss, and questions at which he just looked stupid – but so what? They let him through in the end and here he is!'

'We should go soon,' I said quietly to Julie. I felt that Mike was becoming over-voluble and would stay for hours if we did not intervene.

But then I saw Baht Way was trying to say one thing more. He fixed me with his grey English eyes and said something very emphatic and rather solemn. Then, to my embarrassment, he came towards me, bent down, and touched my shoes.

'He says,' says Julie after a moment of silence, 'that being able to use Christopher's name got him out of a difficult situation and may even have saved his life. So, your family have helped him after all. He wants you to know that.'

At the end of the morning, the noise and brilliance of the City streets seemed reassuringly ordinary but a little claustrophobic – more so, in a way, than the dark corridors of Ak Teem. 'Everything is Possible' is the slogan on which the children of the City are reared. But once you are in this mercantile citadel, it constitutes the entire world: there is nowhere else you can go. I had had enough of the City now; I wanted to go home.

It occurred to me to wonder, as Julie and I walked down Main Road from the snack bar where we and Mike had had lunch, whether Baht Way will have lost as well as gained in coming to settle in this place. He seems committed to the City now; he has his official work permit which is his ticket to the notionally free world of capitalism. By and by, even if not just yet, he will manage to bring his wife and children here. Jobs will be found for the older ones, money will be carefully saved, and later the clan will move out of whatever one-room shelter he has set up for them and into one of the neat flats in some tower block near the airport. So, they will all make a new life for themselves; some English will be learnt and the children, at least, will acquire in addition that sharp, distinctive City-lingo. They will learn to feel irritated and then forbearing towards their parents' old-fashioned country speech. But will Way, with his intelligence and his yearnings, come to reflect, as he collects his old-age pension and his free false teeth, that he has left something incalculable and irreplaceable behind him? The Great Land has figured for me so long as a cipher for dread, a place of darkness. Only now, when I believe that I will never set foot in its hinterland, do I find myself thinking of its vast, remote loveliness – 'one of the most beautiful landscapes I've ever seen', wrote Christopher, who has seen many others. In its beauty, and also its impregnability, this vast, strange country in the end accepts no one who does not submit to its own awful historical imperatives.

Julie and I caught the bus that goes out to Jedu Sumna.

'I hope you don't mind me getting rid of Mike like that,' she said after a while.

'Actually, I thought *I'd* been rather overdefinite about how you and I had something unspecified to attend to. I was afraid you might be annoyed with me.'

We smiled at each other and I wanted to take her hand but did not, feeling close to her but locked, now, into several different constraints.

'I was just about to tell him your dressing needed doing,' she said. 'But then I realised that neither of us had mentioned that whole business to him. I suppose we didn't want to?'

'I imagine not. If so, we should have told him as soon as we met him, on the way to Ak Teem.' I found I was grateful that she hadn't told Mike I had been attacked. Better, I told myself, to avoid any account of yesterday that could lead, by degrees, to the inference that Julie and I had been together ever since. But the truth was, my feeling about yesterday's encounter went beyond such considerations. I felt disgust as at something indecent, a victim's reluctance to contemplate my own totally unheroic role. And something else beyond all this, a sense of degradation that I suspected of being atavistic, racial. Perhaps you never know, till you are confronted with such a crisis, the extent to which ancient prejudices laid down in childhood are still intact under the surface of egalitarian liberalism. I had seen this in Pauline. I did not like seeing it in myself too.

But Julie, of a different background and generation, need not know any of this.

'Poor Mike!' she said. 'But he always tends to make such a thing himself about how busy he is at important, slightly hush-hush things. When he said at lunch he ought to be going, it was easy to take him at his word, wasn't it?'

'Well, I noticed that neither you nor I mentioned either

that we were going to try to meet Christopher again this afternoon, so presumably neither of us really wanted him to come too.'

After a while she said:

'Always providing Christopher's there to be met.'

'If he is on the train today . . .'

'And if we can get over the causeway again.'

'Oh, Christ – of course I haven't got a permit for today. I'd forgotten that. Damn! You'll have to go over on your own, love.' I felt unreasonably dashed at this final, minor setback. She saw I did, and squeezed my hand of her own accord.

'They may not let me over either.'

In fact it turned out, when we got to the frontier post on the City side, that no one was being let through that afternoon, because those that the City police had allowed on to the causeway had simply been sent back by the guards at the other end.

'What does it mean?' I asked anxiously.

The police shrugged. It happened sometimes, they said. The Great Land authorities were unpredictable in that way. Some incident, some alert. It might only last for the afternoon, or for a week.

'But what about foreign nationals already in the Great Land and only wanting to come out? Will they be allowed to?' Julie wanted to know.

The police thought so, but were not sure. They did not seem very interested. Watching the vagaries of an alien regime through binoculars must become tedious.

Julie and I went to sit on a bench under a jacaranda tree.

'You know what's worrying me,' I said after a while.

'Baht Way,' she said. 'He used Christopher's identity to get across here.'

'Quite. So now, presumably, the guards won't have that visa form and photo on file any longer. So how will Christopher, if he does turn up, persuade them to let him through?'

'Don't you sort of feel, though,' she said pleadingly, 'that Christopher will manage?'

'I don't know. I'd like to think that. I don't know.'

A massive irony seemed about to be enacted. Christopher's name and picture had saved Baht Way from trouble, detention or worse. What if that deception should now, by a terrible logic, cost Christopher trouble, detention at any rate for some hours – or worse?

'Yes, I expect you're right; I expect he'll talk his way through it – get them to ring up the High Commission in the City,' I said, seeing Julie's anxious face. But I did not entirely feel it. The Great Land guards are rural peasants with machine-guns, a world apart from the City across the water and answerable to none of its hierarchies nor yet to international ones.

We sat on. 'Look!' said Julie suddenly and I jumped to attention, but she was simply indicating a trail of black smoke over in the bright sky on the far side of the river. The afternoon train was in again.

Hope and dread were in me, and mixed feelings now attached to both, and time seemed very short for something I had to ask her. Sitting next to her under the tree whose feathery leaves made patterns on her bare neck and arms, it had come to me in an access of intense feeling that this compact young body at my side carried my flesh within it, my grandchild, all that might one day (soon?) be left to me of Christopher, of Sarah too, of the sum of my life. I had to ask. I said:

'Julie, what are you planning to do about this baby?'

She was a very honest girl. She did not say 'I don't believe in abortion, you see,' or 'It's too late for an abortion now,' or 'I'll have to discuss it with Kit, I don't want him to feel tied down,' or any of the other circumlocutions by which people try to veil in decent-sounding rationality a physical imperative which belongs to another, older order of things. She just said: 'Whatever happens, I'll have it.'

She knows that Christopher is not to be tamed into domesticity in this way. She knows that he will do what he feels able readily to do and only that. He will be amiable but relentless, his eyes fixed on other horizons.

She could not know, dear girl, because at her age one cannot know, the immense gift that she had just given me. Only then, in joy and relief at the prospect of a new life coming along to repair my own battered one, did I realise how unhappy I had recently been. Pauline, oh Pauline. What had passed between my sister and myself had destroyed more than, at our ages, we could ever hope to recreate, and the fact that I had right on my side was no consolation at all. To be right is not necessarily to be lovable, or loving.

Yet now some long-term pattern beyond the sequences of logical cause and effect seemed to be working for me. It was as if the baby our family had rejected long ago was being given back, through Christopher, by Julie. In place of the despoiled, severed links with Tessa, with Pauline, a new, indissoluble, for-better-or-worse bond was being formed. With the child. With its mother.

I said to her:

'Whatever you need, count on me. Trust me. I will look after you to the very best of my ability.'

And her quick, rueful smile of gratitude.

I rested my head then on my sweaty arms. I was conscious of the vague, diffused hurt of the wound in my back, and of the accumulated stresses of the last two days – two weeks? Far longer? The words that had just passed between us had laid such an anxiety to rest that, for the moment, I asked for nothing more. I really do not think immediate expectation was near the surface of my mind when Julie, whose eyes had remained fixed on the shore of the Great Land, suddenly said again:

'Look!'

I looked. And at the far end of the causeway, first hidden by the shadow of the railings and then silhouetted, very small, against the bright sky, a man was walking across the river alone, a pack on his back, his head raised to view the City to which he was returning. He was black against the light: I could not see whether his expression was anxious or cheerful, whether he was travel-worn or judiciously clean – but I would have known his walk anywhere. He was striding towards us. In a few minutes, if we stood up, he would see us too.